FRED AND BREAKFAST

PHOEBE MACLEOD

First published in Great Britain in 2022 by Boldwood Books Ltd.

Copyright © Phoebe MacLeod, 2022

Cover Design by Head Design

Cover Photography: Shutterstock

A CIP catalogue record for this book is available from the British Library.

Paperback ISBN 978-1-80426-258-0

Large Print ISBN 978-1-80426-258-0

Hardback ISBN 978-1-80426-260-3

Ebook ISBN 978-1-80426-257-3

Kindle ISBN 978-1-80426-256-6

Audio CD ISBN 978-1-80426-265-8

MP3 CD ISBN 978-1-80426-264-1

Digital audio download ISBN 978-1-80426-262-7

Boldwood Books Ltd
23 Bowerdean Street
London SW6 3TN
www.boldwoodbooks.com

To my father, Andrew, who would have been mystified by the adventure

PROLOGUE

I can still remember every detail about the day of the accident with almost photographic clarity.

It was a grim winter Friday, almost ten years ago. The skies were dark and brooding and the classroom windows were all steamed up, although I could still see the sleet running down the outside of the glass. The heating was on full blast, and I was struggling to stay awake as Mr Harker tried to drum the intricacies of plant reproduction into us. I remember being startled by a sharp rap of someone knocking on the classroom door and Mr Harker opening it to admit the head teacher, a formidable woman called Mrs Philips. I felt the first twinges of unease when, after a brief whispered conversation, both of them looked directly at me, but it wasn't until Mrs Philips asked me to accompany her to her office and bring my stuff that the unease turned to full-on dread.

As I followed her along the corridors, I was desperately trying to work out what I'd done wrong. Actually, there were probably plenty of things I'd done that could lead to a summons to the head teacher's office, but I was trying to work out which one of them had been found out. On the rare occasions that I'd joined some of the other girls behind the science block for a cheeky cigarette, we'd always been careful to stuff our mouths with Polos and douse ourselves thoroughly with body spray to disguise the smell. Things were also getting pretty serious between me and my boyfriend, but we hadn't actually had sex and, even if we had, it wouldn't have been in school.

Eventually, we reached her office and she opened the door and stood aside to allow me to go in before her. There were three other people in there, two police officers and another woman, and I remember assuming that they were going to arrest me, although I couldn't think why. Yes, I'd been there when Lee Reynolds used a stolen marker pen to draw a cock and balls on the bus shelter, but strictly as an observer. Surely they didn't arrest you for that?

The female police officer suggested gently that I might like to sit, and it was at that moment that I noticed they were all looking pityingly at me, as if I were a sick dog that needed to be put down.

The actual words were a jumble, I think my mind just wasn't able to process them. I heard 'your mum and dad', 'fatal accident', 'so sorry' and 'died instantly'. My parents had been on their way to spend the weekend at a country park hotel and spa, a prize my mum had won in the school PTA silent auction in the summer. I found out later that the driver of an articulated lorry coming the other way had lost control on a slippery section of road, and his trailer had swung round like an enormous bat and smashed head-on into my parents' car. They hadn't stood a chance.

I didn't cry. I think I was so shocked that I just shut down. I remember the woman who wasn't a police officer explaining that she was a social worker and asking whether there was anyone she could call to come and get me. Thankfully, my grandparents were already on their way to keep an eye on us while Mum and Dad were away for the weekend, so a quick phone call diverted them to my school. The female police officer took me down to the canteen to get a cup of sweet tea and some chocolate to help with the shock, while the social worker and male police officer talked to my grandparents. I still didn't cry.

I remember feeling numb as I collected my coat and the remainder of my things from my locker, before following my grandparents out to their car. We drove in convoy with the police and social worker to my younger sister Katie's school, where the whole grisly performance was repeated. Still, I didn't cry, even though Katie was distraught. I held her while she wept and promised I wouldn't let anything happen to her.

We didn't talk about it when we got home. I don't think any of us knew what to say. Nan and Grandad busied themselves with practicalities, making sure that we were fed. None of us could comprehend the situation. I didn't even consider the pain they must have been feeling. After all, they'd just lost their daughter too.

We had eggy bread and baked beans for tea. Katie and I barely touched it, even though it was one of our favourites. It was only after I had changed into my favourite fleecy onesie, turned off the light and climbed into bed that the events of the day sunk in properly and the tears came. I sobbed and sobbed.

I was fourteen years old.

'Fancy a drink, Daisy? You're on holiday now, it would be rude not to.'

I'm so engrossed in my work that the voice takes me completely by surprise. I glance up to see my colleague Grace standing over me, with her handbag already slung over her shoulder. I cast my eyes around the office and discover that most of the desks are already empty.

'Is it five thirty already?' I glance at the clock in the corner of my screen. Where has the afternoon gone? 'Give me ten minutes to finish this, and I'll be with you.'

Grace settles herself at the empty desk next to mine while I focus on the spreadsheet in front of me. My job is not exactly glamorous; I'm an accounts technician at Holdsworth & Speke, a small firm of accountants based in London. Most of my work involves reconciling the books of our customers before they go to the chartered accountants, who check them, combine them with other information, and submit them to HMRC. I was lucky enough to secure an apprenticeship here six years ago, after my grandparents staged an 'intervention'. Having been considered a bright child who would go far, I flunked my GCSEs spectacularly, failing everything apart from Maths and English. I just lost interest in all of it, and my results reflected that. The school wrote to Nan and Grandad to explain that sixth form wasn't really an option for me, but there might be some college courses I could look at.

Two years later, after I'd been fired from a succession of low-paid jobs, we had an uncomfortable dinner where my grandparents pointed out that my current career trajectory, plus the fact that I smoked and drank my way through every pay packet, wasn't what my parents would have wanted for me. I wouldn't say that I pulled myself together overnight, but the concern on their faces was enough to make me realise that something had to change. I stopped smoking, regulated my drinking, and somehow managed to land the job here. I still wouldn't describe myself as particularly ambitious, but Mr Holdsworth, one of the founding partners, took me under his wing and, among other things, sponsored me through the Association of Accounting Technicians qualifications, so I feel a sense of loyalty to the place. The pay is pretty good, too.

In the end, it's nearly a quarter of an hour before I'm ready to send the accounts on to Rob, one of the chartered accountants. I attach them to an email, write a quick note explaining what I've done, and shut down my computer.

'I'm ready,' I tell Grace.

'About time! I'm dying of thirst here.' She sticks out her tongue. 'See? Parched.'

'Let's go and fix that then, you poor thing.'

I wave to Mr Holdsworth through the glass of his office as we turn to leave, but he beckons me to join him. We're pretty informal mostly, but the two founding partners are always addressed as Mr Holdsworth and Mr Speke. They are also the only two people in the company to have enclosed offices; everyone else is in the open-plan section. I stick my head around the door.

'Is everything okay, Mr Holdsworth?' I ask him.

'Absolutely. I just wanted to wish you a happy holiday. How long are you off for?'

'Two weeks.'

'Excellent. I hope you have a lovely time, and try not to think about work while you're away. We'll look forward to seeing you fully refreshed when you get back.'

'Thank you, Mr Holdsworth.'

It's a beautiful summer evening as we step out onto the pavement but, as I pause to tilt my head and drink in the sun, Grace grabs my arm.

'No time for that. Come on. We're so late, there probably won't be any outdoor tables left.'

Grace hustles me along the busy pavements towards our usual pub, the Lord Nelson. Like a lot of pubs in the area, it's ancient and very dark inside. However, there is a tiny beer garden at the back, and we hurry through the bar to see if we can secure a table. Luckily for us, there is one left, and we quickly grab it.

'Chardonnay?' I ask her, as I rummage in my bag for my purse. Our Friday routine is well-polished; I buy the first round, she buys the second, and then we head off towards our respective stations for the commute home.

'Make sure he fills it up properly. I'm sure he gave me a short measure last week.'

Grace says this every week. I think she really believes that she ends up with a smaller glass, whereas the truth is that she just drinks much faster than me.

'So, tell me about your holiday. Mallorca, isn't it? Sun, sea, sex, and sangria?' she asks, after I've returned with the glasses and she's had her first big swig.

'I don't think there will be any sex, I'm going with my sister!'

'Really? What about your boyfriend?'

'He can't afford it, plus he's not really that interested in going abroad. His parents have a static caravan near Whitstable, and that's his perfect holiday destination. Fish and chips, beer he knows he likes, and everyone speaks English. So, ever since Nan and Grandad decided I was finally responsible enough to look after Katie, I do a week somewhere sunny with her, and then a few days in the caravan with Paul.'

'He sounds quite the catch,' she observes drily.

'Don't be mean, he's okay. He just isn't very adventurous, you know?'

'Do you love him?'

'You're very quizzy tonight. What's got into you?'

'Oh, I don't know. I think I'm just having one of my "Is this all there is?" days. Don't you ever have those?'

'I can't say that I do, no.'

'Really? Don't you ever look at the chartered accountants and wonder what it is that they do that makes them so much better paid than us? I reckon I could do Rob's job standing on my head!'

'Nope.'

'So where do you see yourself in ten years' time? Surely you don't intend to be still working here, living with your grandparents and going on holiday with your sister? Don't you want to get married, start a family?'

Grace thinks that every woman's destiny is to get married and have babies. Her workspace is festooned with pictures of her husband and children, and she frequently tells me (in great detail) about their latest antics and achievements when we're getting coffee in the office kitchen, or over lunch. It gets a bit wearing at times, listening to her describing the kind of happy family life that was taken away from Katie and me, but I try not to resent her for it. I remind myself that she's not doing it to be unkind; it's just normal for her in a way that it can never be normal for me. She's been with the company for even longer than I have, and I suspect they'll have to drag her out when she reaches retirement age. However, now that her boys are at secondary school and more independent, she likes to pretend she's ambitious and on the lookout for her next opportunity.

Marriage and children don't sound like the sort of things that would happen to me, and I've told her this in the past. Thankfully, I think I've dodged the conversation about whether I love Paul, which is a new one. I'm fond of him, but I'm not in love with him. It's more of a 'friends with benefits' arrangement, if I'm honest. After Mum and Dad died, the court awarded custody of Katie and me to Nan and Grandad, and we moved from our parents' home in Essex to their home in Kent. I was enrolled in the local compre- hensive school, but most of the people in my year had already formed their friendship groups, so there wasn't really a place for the traumatised teenager who spent most of her break times sobbing loudly in the toilets. They weren't horrible to me or anything, they were just wary, I suppose. Anyway, I was sitting by myself having lunch one day when this slightly geeky-looking boy asked if he could join me. We struck up a friendship, one thing led to another over time, and here we still are. To be honest, our arrangement suits me quite well. I don't think I could deal with the emotions and risks associated with falling in love.

The truthful answer to Grace's question is that I have no idea where I see myself in ten years. I don't think about it. When you've had all your hopes and dreams ripped away from you by a totally senseless and random event, any kind of planning for the future seems pretty futile. I live firmly in the here and now. My life is okay at the moment, and that is enough for me.

Grace's glass is nearly empty already. I've barely touched mine.

'Don't wait for me,' I tell her, indicating her glass. 'I'm only having one tonight because I've got to drive.' A trip to the bar will hopefully deflect her from her current line of questioning. She looks at her glass in amazement, as if it's somehow managed to empty itself.

'Are you sure he filled it properly?' she asks. 'I've only had a couple of sips.'

I smile at her. Her idea of a sip is a generous mouthful. I sometimes wonder if she'd be better off drinking beer – at least you can get that by the pint. I did suggest it once, but she said it made her feel terribly bloated, and she has a morbid fear (which I share) of having to use the toilet on the train. So, we play out the same rigmarole every week; Grace expresses outrage at what she considers to be the tiny measures, and I feign sympathy. I sometimes wonder if she has a bit of a drink problem, because I know she has a couple of large glasses when she gets home every night, but she always turns up looking bright as a button each morning, so I reckon it's probably none of my business. Also, I'm very conscious that I'm not really in a position to judge her, given my history.

I was right. She's completely forgotten what she was quizzing me about when she comes back from the bar, and the rest of our conversation sticks to much safer topics, mainly work gossip. Grace is convinced that Mr Speke is having an affair with Rosemary, his PA. I think it's pretty unlikely – the only thing that I've ever seen him get excited about is numbers, and he barely seems to notice people, even her. I'm also fairly sure Rosemary is a lot younger than him, although Mr Speke is one of those people who is almost impossible to age. She's a model of cool efficiency, always immaculately turned out with her hair in a perfect braid, and not a crease on her clothes. The idea of them getting hot and sweaty together is laughable.

'I was watching them yesterday,' she tells me, conspiratorially. 'She was in his office, taking him through some paperwork he was supposed to be signing. She was leaning over him, and her breasts can't have been more than a couple of centimetres from his face. She's brazen, I'll give her that! If he'd turned, I reckon he'd have been buried in her cleavage.'

'Did he turn?'

'No. He probably saw me looking at him, didn't he? But if I hadn't been watching...'

'Do you ever think you might be reading more into this than there is?'

'No. They're up to no good. I'm sure of it.'

'Perhaps you should set up a hidden camera in his office, so you can watch without them knowing,' I suggest, jokingly.

'That's a great idea! Why didn't I think of that?'

'I was kidding! Apart from the fact that you'd be fired so fast your feet wouldn't touch the ground if you were caught, I'm pretty sure it's illegal.'

She sighs. 'I suppose you're right. Shame.'

While I'm waiting for the bus to take me to Charing Cross, I check my phone to make sure that the trains are all on time. If one is cancelled, the train afterwards is always completely rammed full, so I avoid that and aim for a later one once things have calmed down. Thankfully, the gods are on my side tonight, and I arrive at the station with ten minutes to spare before the train leaves. There are a few seats left, and I tuck myself into an aisle seat next to another woman. I can see a guy further down the carriage watching me as I sit down, probably hoping for a glimpse up my skirt, and I give him a defiant stare. At least he has the grace to blush slightly as he hurriedly diverts his eyes back to his laptop screen.

As the train pulls out of the station, I start making a mental list of the things I need to pack when I get home. I bought plenty of sunscreen earlier in the week, and Katie and I went shopping last weekend to treat ourselves to a holiday wardrobe refresh, so I've got two new swimsuits, as well as a selection of shorts and T-shirts. Most of it is in a pile in the corner of my bedroom, so all I need to do is stuff it into my case and ensure I've got our passports, travel insurance, and money.

After I've run through the list a couple of times in my head, I start to relax a little. I think I'm ready for this break.

2

There's more of a rush than usual as my fellow commuters and I disembark at Paddock Wood station. We have to climb a long staircase to the bridge over the tracks, and then back down the other side to reach the car park. This is normally a weary trudge but, because it's Friday, everyone is anxious to get home and begin their weekends. Some of them are so keen, they're bounding up the steps two at a time. I keep well to the side and grip the handrail firmly. The last thing I want to do is fall and break my leg just before I go on holiday. When I reach the safety of the ground, I leave my car in the car park and walk straight out of the station towards the Chinese takeaway in the town. As I walk through the door, the woman behind the counter smiles at me.

'Hello, Miss Daisy. Your order is all ready for you.'

This is part of my Friday routine. I call in our order from the train, so it's ready for me to collect when I arrive. I don't even need to list what I want; we have the same things every week, so I just ask for my usual. I hand over my card with a smile, enter my PIN, and watch as the transaction goes through.

'I hope you enjoy it,' she says as she hands me the bag. 'See you next week?'

'No. I'm on holiday for a couple of weeks, but I'll see you when I get back,' I promise her.

Normally, I pop into the off-licence a couple of doors down and pick up a bottle of wine, but as I'm not staying at Paul's tonight, I walk straight past. I'm outside his flat a few minutes later.

'Hiya,' he says, as he opens the door to let me in. 'I've got the plates warming in the oven. No wine tonight?'

'No, I'm not staying. I told you, remember?'

'Oh, yes, sorry. Early start.'

We unpack the takeaway bag and load up our plates. I've got sesame prawn toasts and chicken curry, while Paul has spring rolls and sweet and sour prawn balls. We divide the rice between us and sit down at his tiny, rickety table. As we eat, he fills me in on his week and I tell him about Grace's latest theories about Mr Speke and Rosemary. Unlike me, Paul stayed on at school to do his A levels, but his results were far from stellar and he's worked in a mobile phone shop in Tonbridge for the last six years. He was promoted to manager two years ago and took the opportunity to move out of his parents' house into his rented one-bed flat in Paddock Wood as a reward. It's a typical man cave; the main room contains a huge TV with surround sound, a PlayStation with a wide array of games, a squishy leather sofa, and the table at which we're currently sitting. There are a couple of cheap prints on the walls and a rug to hide the bit of floor where the carpet has worn through. The kitchen has definitely seen better days, but Paul's landlord is adamant that there's nothing wrong with it, even though a couple of the cupboard doors are missing and there's a special technique to opening and closing the cutlery drawer without it falling off its runners and emptying itself all over the floor.

After we've finished eating, I relax on the sofa while Paul washes up. I turn on the TV and start flicking through the channels, but nothing grabs me. Paul flops down next to me and puts his arm around me. Our sex life, like everything else, is utterly predictable. I reckon I could set a timer and he'd be totally consistent every week. One minute with his arm around my shoulders, then he'll move to gently stroking my arm for a couple of minutes, catching an occasional brush of the side of my boob as he does. If I don't move away (which I pretty much never do), the brushing of the side of my boob will get more frequent until he moves his hand completely and begins cupping and squeezing. Every move happens in exactly the same way every time, as if it's one of those incredibly complex recipes you see on *MasterChef* where you have to do everything exactly by the book or the whole thing is ruined. The only variety is whether we stay where we are or move into the bedroom. From his moves, it looks like tonight is going to be a sofa night. I've noticed recently that the only time he ever kisses me now is as part of the run-up to sex. We used to kiss all the time when we first got together, but I guess he doesn't see the point any more unless it's leading to something. It's a shame, really; I quite enjoy kissing him, even if the actual sex often leaves a bit to be desired on my side.

Afterwards, I pick up my clothes and wander into his bathroom to sort myself out and get dressed. It's much like the rest of the flat; the ancient bath is discoloured and several of the tiles are cracked. There's an electric shower over the bath, and the shower curtain is so thin it's practically see-through. Thankfully, as I'm not staying over tonight, I won't need to try to wash myself tomorrow morning in the pathetic dribble that the shower emits. I sit on the toilet, rinse my mouth out with a little of Paul's mouthwash, and climb into my clothes before checking the time. 9.30.

It's still light as I leave Paul's flat, which is a relief, as I don't really like wandering around the station car park in the dark. In winter, I'm always careful to park my car as close as I can to one of the overhead lights, so as to minimise the risk of someone being able to hide in the shadows and jump out at me. The car park is nearly empty at this time of night on a Friday, and I hurry over to my car, pressing the button to unlock the door at the last minute and throwing myself in. For someone who doesn't particularly like driving, I spend a fortune on cars. My dad was the opposite, and one of the findings from the inquest was that the battered old Toyota that he'd nursed to nearly a quarter of a million miles simply folded up like a pack of cards in the impact, giving them no protection at all. As a result, I buy a brand-new car every couple of years to make sure I've got all the latest safety features. According to Grant, the salesman I deal with each time, this one has so many airbags that it would basically transform into the automotive equivalent of a bouncy castle if I were unfortunate enough to hit anything. That doesn't stop my palms from sweating a bit whenever I encounter a large truck coming the other way, though.

I pull up on the drive of my grandparents' bungalow in Five Oak Green just before ten. They moved here in the eighties, and the decorative style hasn't been updated since. Think chintz, pastel colours, bathroom units in pink or avocado, and you're pretty much there. It was only a few years ago that their beloved waterbed sprung a leak and had to be replaced with something more conventional. At least they redecorated Katie's and my bedrooms when we moved in, and they made it clear that they were happy for us to update them as we wanted to over the last ten years. They did put their foot down when I decided I wanted to paint all of my walls black when I was seventeen, but apart from that, they've been pretty accommodating. My room is currently sporting a very neutral palette, with magnolia walls, biscuit carpet, and terracotta curtains. Katie says it's dull, and that I should have patterned curtains at least, but I find the blocks of colour restful. She's not exactly in a position to criticise, as her room has the same floral wallpaper and pink curtains that she chose when we first moved in.

They're all in the living room when I walk through the door, so I give Nan and Grandad a kiss each, and then settle on the sofa next to Katie.

'All set for tomorrow?' I ask her.

'Yup. I think I've packed for every possibility except snow. I was just going to pack shorts, T-shirts and swimming costumes, but Nan kept coming in and muttering darkly about "layers", so my case is probably twice as heavy as it needs to be!' she smiles.

'It's better to be prepared, that's all I said,' Nan admonishes her.

'Nan, you do know the forecast is wall-to-wall sunshine and temperatures in the high twenties for the whole of next week, don't you?'

'Yes, but the forecast can be wrong, can't it? Just look at poor old Michael Fish and the hurricane in 1987.'

'I think you'll find that the science of predicting the weather has improved a little since then, Nan. Come on,' I say to Katie, 'let's go and have a look at your case.'

If you didn't know us, you might struggle to figure out that Katie and I are sisters because we're so different. We both have dark brown hair and blue eyes, but that's pretty much where the resemblance stops. I'm quite curvy, with a round face, large breasts, and wide hips, whereas she is more androgynous and athletic-looking. She's also slightly taller than me and wears round, heavy-framed glasses that give her a scholarly air. I show my emotions easily, but she is quiet and reserved. After the initial shock, we reacted completely differently to the deaths of our parents. While I went off the rails, she buried herself in her schoolwork, so it was no surprise when she passed all her GCSEs with either As or A*s.

From the way things are heading, it looks like she'll repeat the trick for her A levels next year, which means she'll hopefully have her pick of universities. I'm trying not to think about that too much; I want the best for her, obviously, but I also know that I'll miss her terribly when she goes.

Katie opens up her suitcase and we go through it together, taking out the thick jumpers, long trousers and coat that Nan insisted she packed. When we're done, she has three bikinis, lots of T-shirts, a couple of pairs of shorts, and a light dress for the evenings, as well as underwear and a couple of pairs of pyjamas. I take the opportunity to shove some of the insect repellent and sunscreen I've bought into the space we've created in her case, before retreating to my room to finish off my own packing. I hear the sounds of Nan and Grandad locking up and getting ready for bed, so I stick my head out of the door to wish them goodnight. We'll be gone before they wake up, so they wish us a lovely holiday and exhort me to take care of Katie.

'Remember she's only seventeen, Daisy. I don't want her out at nightclubs, dancing with unsuitable boys,' Nan tells me, firmly.

'I think you're quite safe there, Nan,' I laugh. 'Apart from the fact that my clubbing days are many years behind me, I don't think nightclubs are really Katie's scene, do you?'

Katie's head pops out from her bedroom door. 'I heard that!'

'It's true though, isn't it?' I challenge her. 'I can no more imagine you dirty dancing than I can imagine Nan, here.'

'I don't know,' Nan muses, as she gives a little wiggle. 'There's still life in the old girl, you know.'

'Nonsense!' Grandad laughs. 'You'd probably put your hip out as soon as you got onto the dance floor, and we'd have to call an ambulance to take you to A&E.'

'Well, just be careful while you're away, that's all I'm saying. Have a lovely time, but don't overdo it.'

'We'll be fine, Nan. Stop worrying. See you when we get back.'

Nan and Grandad haven't been abroad since we moved in. To begin with, they had their hands full just coping with me and, as Nan explains regularly, 'You were difficult enough to handle on home territory, how on earth would we have managed in a foreign country where we had no means of tracking you down at all?' We are close now, but the first few years were very rocky, and there were plenty of stand-up rows that ended with me storming out of the house yelling, 'You're not my mother!'

I finish my packing, double-check that I've got all the documents we need, and then get ready for bed. As my head hits the pillow, I allow myself to look forward to the week ahead. Just a little bit.

3

I'm still fast asleep when the alarm goes off at 4.30 a.m., so I wake with a start, and it takes me a moment or two to orient myself. I drag myself out of bed and knock on Katie's door to check she's awake, before padding down the corridor to the bathroom. Nan and Grandad have an en suite bathroom off their bedroom, so Katie and I have this one to ourselves. As I wash the sleep away in the shower, I run through my checklist one more time to make sure there's nothing I've forgotten. As well as a morbid fear of needing to wee on the train, I'm terrified of being turned away at check-in or the hotel because of a missing piece of paper.

Half an hour later, our cases are loaded into the boot of my car and we've checked the documents several times. I close the door as quietly as I can behind us, and we set off for the airport. Grandad pointed out that it would have been considerably cheaper for us to go by taxi than pay for the parking, but I'm not wild about being driven on the motorway by a stranger in a car of unknown age that's probably done what Rob at work would refer to as 'starship mileage'. At least I'm in control if I'm driving. The traffic is very light at this time on a Saturday morning, and we're on the airport road less than an hour later.

'Read me the instructions for the car park again,' I tell Katie.

'It's easy. You just need to pull up to the barrier, and it will recognise your numberplate from the booking and print your ticket,' she replies.

'No, read me exactly what it says on the piece of paper. I want to be sure we haven't missed anything, like a button we have to press or something.'

She rolls her eyes but obliges. We manage to get into the car park with no issues, and drag our cases to the bus stop, where there is already a large group of people waiting.

'Wow, there are a lot more people here than I was expecting for this time in the morning,' Katie remarks.

'Mm. I expect it will be heaving in the terminal then. First week of the school holidays, so everyone's going away.'

Sure enough, the queues in the terminal building are massive, and it takes us a good hour to reach the self-check-in desks. Between us, we manage to work out how to print our boarding cards and baggage tags, before loading our bags onto the conveyor that will take them deep into the guts of the airport and, hopefully, onto our plane. Another long queue snakes its way through security, but we finally find ourselves in the departure lounge just over an hour before our flight is due to take off.

'Breakfast?' I suggest.

'Absolutely, I'm starving!'

We settle ourselves at a table in the terminal pub and order a couple of full English breakfasts. We probably won't eat again until this evening, so we've decided we need something substantial to keep us going. While we're waiting for our food to arrive, I glance around at our fellow travellers. There are lots of families with children, obviously filling themselves up before the journey like we are, but there are also a couple of groups of young men, already sinking pints despite the fact that it's not even eight o'clock in the morning.

'What do you reckon, stag parties?' I ask Katie, indicating the men.

She wrinkles her nose as the men in one group start whooping loudly, encouraging the guy that I guess is the bridegroom-to-be to down his pint in one. A few of the parents in the family groups make eye contact with each other and raise their eyebrows disapprovingly.

'I hope they're not on our plane,' she remarks.

'I doubt they're going to Mallorca. More likely to be Warsaw or Prague, I suspect. Somewhere not too far away where the beer is strong and relatively cheap.'

A last call announcement comes over the intercom for an easyJet flight to Warsaw and one of the men shouts, 'Fuck, that's our plane!' to his mates. I smile as they hastily grab their belongings and start running towards the gate.

'One group down. Just got to see where the others are going,' I observe.

Unfortunately for us, it turns out that the other group is going to Mallorca, and one of them is sitting next to me on the plane. I'm not a fan of beery breath at the best of times, but it's particularly hard to stomach first thing in the morning. I turn away from him to try to avoid getting a lungful.

'All right, ladies? Off on your holidays?'

I sigh. Ignoring him is obviously not going to be an option, so I steel myself for a trying couple of hours making small talk with my semi-plastered neighbour. I'm quickly proved wrong, though, as, apart from the occasional strong whiff of beer, he's actually good company. He introduces himself as Mike, the best man on the stag do. He points out the bridegroom, who is sitting a few rows in front, and the rest of the party, although it's not hard to work out who they are from the amount of noise they're making. I learn that the wedding is in two weeks, and they've rented a villa for a few days for the stag. They're planning to swim, drink, and generally take it easy. He asks about us and is genuinely surprised when I tell him that we're sisters. The two hours pass quite quickly and, before I know it, we're descending into Palma.

The immigration queue is not quite as long as the one we encountered at check-in, but it still takes us over half an hour to get through into the baggage hall. I locate the carousel and I'm relieved to see that our bags are patiently circling, waiting for us to pick them up. I always have a niggle of worry that they will have somehow found their way onto the wrong plane, are not going to arrive, and we'll be stuck in a foreign country with nothing but the clothes on our backs. As we come out into the arrivals hall, I see Mike and the rest of the stag party negotiating with a couple of taxi drivers, and I give him a farewell wave. Katie and I follow the majority of the other holidaymakers towards the transfer buses.

'That guy on the plane was totally flirting with you,' Katie remarks, after we've found our bus and clambered aboard.

'I don't think so,' I reply. 'He was wearing a wedding ring, for starters. I reckon he was just being friendly.'

'I'm not so sure. I think he was hoping for a bit of "what goes on tour stays on tour" action.'

'Yuck. Where on earth did you learn that phrase?'

'Where do you think?' Idiot rugby boys boasting at school. They like to hint that they've got up to all these amazing exploits, but I bet its nothing more than a couple of sneaky cans of lager and a bro-mantic snog in the hot tub.'

'Ouch!'

'Honestly, you should hear them. How some of them managed to get into sixth form is a total mystery to me.'

'So, nobody's caught your eye then?'

'No. It turns out boys are just as stupid and immature in the sixth form as they were in the lower school.'

Typically, our hotel is pretty much at the end of the bus route, but I don't mind too much, as it gives me a chance to check out where other people are staying. The first few hotels we stop at, fairly close to the airport, are pretty grotty, but the standard seems to improve the further we go. Katie and I are booked into the four-star Villa Blanca and, as the bus finally turns into the driveway of our hotel, I sigh with pleasure. It looks amazing. The gardens are well-tended, with green lawns and brightly coloured flowerbeds. We're checked in quickly and efficiently, and I gasp with delight as I swipe the key card and open the door of our room.

It's massive, with an enormous double bed against one wall, a separate seating area with table, sofa, and chairs, and sliding glass doors that lead out onto the balcony. The air conditioning is running, so it's pleasantly cool in here. I stick my head into the bathroom to discover a good-sized tub and a separate walk-in shower with one of those rainfall heads.

'I think we'll be able to put up with this for a week, don't you?' I call to Katie, who has stepped out onto the balcony.

'Come out here and check out the view!' she calls back.

I slide open the insect screen and step outside. It's beautifully warm out here, without being stifling, and there's a gentle breeze. The balcony looks out towards the hotel's private beach and the sea beyond. The hotel and beach are in a bay, so the water is calm and the sea is just lapping gently at the sand. Only around half of the sun loungers appear to be occupied, and there are a number of people swimming in the water. Further out into the bay, there are a few anchored boats bobbing lazily. It's perfect.

'Let's get our costumes on and hit the beach,' I suggest.

Katie doesn't need telling twice and, after slathering on some factor 50 sun cream, we pack a bag with our beach towels, more sunscreen, and books, and follow the signs. I kick off my shoes as soon as we get there and enjoy the sensation of the warm sand against my feet. We take up position on a couple of free sun loungers and I pull out my book. The rest of the afternoon passes very pleasantly; we read, swim in the sea, and chat about nothing in particular.

'What's the deal with Paul?' Katie asks, as we're making our way back up to our room to get changed for dinner. The hotel is all-inclusive, with a number of different dining options, but we've decided to pile our plates high at the main buffet tonight. Breakfast was a long time ago and we're both starving.

'What do you mean?' I reply.

'Do you think you'll get married?'

'I doubt it. I think we'll probably just carry on as we are until one of us finds someone we like better, and that will be it.'

'That sounds a bit depressing. Aren't you in love with him?'

'Do you know, you're the second person to ask me that in as many days. What is this, quiz Daisy about her boyfriend week?'

'Sorry, I wasn't trying to pry. I'm just interested.'

'Because?'

'Well, because you two have been together for ever. I heard Nan and Grandad talking about it the other day, speculating about whether you'd move out to live with him.'

'No. I don't think I could live with him. He's a good guy, but I don't really share any of his interests, and his flat is a bit of a shit-hole. Besides, I couldn't leave you behind!' I put my arm around her and give her a squeeze, and she rests her head on my shoulder.

'Looks like Nan and Grandad are going to have to put up with us for a few years longer then, doesn't it?' she replies.

The buffet is reasonably busy when we arrive, but we're still able to find a free table without too much difficulty. A waiter comes to take our drinks order, and then we set off to see what we can find to eat. My stomach rumbles in anticipation as I walk around the various stations, helping myself to paella and a selection of salads. Our drinks are waiting for us when we get back to the table, and we drink a toast to a happy holiday. The food is delicious, and we eat pretty much in silence.

'God, I feel fat!' I exclaim, popping open the button of my jeans to relieve the pressure as I slump down on the bed later that evening. 'I definitely ate too much.'

'It was the puddings, especially that chocolate one. I couldn't get enough of that,' Katie agrees.

'I don't know about you, but the travelling, and then all the sunshine this afternoon followed by that sumptuous dinner has really taken it out of me. I'm knackered. I think I'll have an early night.' I cover my mouth as I yawn widely.

'Yeah, I'm pretty tired as well. It's been nice, though. I'm looking forward to the rest of the week.'

'Me too,' I tell her. We get changed, brush our teeth, and climb into the bed. Normally, it takes me ages to get to sleep on the first night in a strange bed, but this one is so comfortable that I'm asleep before I know it.

4

'Excuse me. We're going to play beach volleyball. Would you like to join us?'

Katie and I lift our heads from our books. The boy in front of us is tall, very skinny and, if I've got his accent right, German. He looks around sixteen, but has one of those faces that make it difficult to tell. He's pointing behind him, where a group of teens and twenty-somethings have set up a net and are obviously getting ready to play.

'Thank you,' I say to him, 'but I'm going to say no. Enjoy your game, though.' Even if I wanted to play, which I don't, the reality is that I don't think my bikini top could take the strain of trying to contain my boobs if I were jumping and leaping about. I definitely don't want to end up giving a load of strangers an accidental eyeful. I also have no hand-to-eye coordination where ball sports are concerned, so I'd probably just annoy them with my lack of ability.

He nods and turns to Katie. I fully expect her to say no as well, but she surprises me.

'Yeah, why not?' she says. 'I need to do something to counteract all the food.'

'Excellent. My name is Mark, please come and meet the rest of the group.'

I watch in amazement as my shy, bookish sister follows him across the sand. She smiles and shakes hands with everyone as he introduces her to the other young men and women. I set my book down and continue watching as they organise themselves into two teams and begin the game. Katie is a little tentative to begin with, but I can see her confidence increasing as she gets the hang of it. They seem like a nice crowd, and they are very encouraging. By the end, she's leaping and hitting the ball as enthusiastically as the rest of them with her long, lithe limbs powering her across the sand. She looks alive in a way I don't think I've seen before. I can't help smiling as I look at her. I know I'm biased, but she's turning into a beautiful young woman. Mark certainly seems to appreciate her, as I catch him staring at her on more than one occasion.

'That was fun!' she pants, as she flops back down on the sun lounger when they have finished. They played five games in all and, if I've worked it out right, Katie was on the winning team for three of them. After each game there was a lot of clapping and hugging, and I couldn't help but notice the way that Mark made a beeline for Katie and enveloped her in his arms each time.

'Mark was certainly very attentive,' I tease her.

'Was he? I didn't really notice. They were all so nice. They're not even a group, did you know that? Mark and Johann are brothers, you can see that, but the rest are from all over the place. Apparently, the hotel staff usually try to set up some beach activities, but they don't need to with the volleyball, because it just happens organically. A slightly different group appears to play every morning. You should join us tomorrow.'

I look at her sceptically. 'Katie, it's all right for you, you've got an athletic figure. I'm not made for leaping about – not without an industrial-strength sports bra, anyway.'

She laughs. 'Fair enough. I can't believe how much I enjoyed that, though. Fancy a swim?'

I follow her down to the water, and I notice some of the other volleyball players are also cooling off in the sea. Some of them are just bobbing in the water, while others are exuberantly splashing each other. They wave enthusiastically at Katie as we walk into the waves and, although she's trying to hide it, I can tell she's enjoying her popularity.

* * *

The rest of the week follows a similar pattern. After breakfast, we go down to the beach and Katie joins in with the beach volleyball, while I lie on my sun lounger and watch. Then we swim, read, and wander up for lunch before making our way back down to the beach for the afternoon. As the days go by, our pallid skin begins to develop a golden glow. Mark continues to be very attentive towards Katie, but she doesn't seem to be picking up any of the signs at all.

'He definitely fancies you,' I tell her, after a few days have passed.

'I'm sure he doesn't. He's just affectionate with everyone, that's how he is. Anyway, even if he does, it's not going to go anywhere.'

'Why not? Don't you like him?'

'I do, but what would be the point? We're going home in a few days, and then what?'

'Then you write it off as a holiday romance, and you look back on it misty-eyed in future and wonder what became of the handsome German boy you kissed in Mallorca.'

'Or...'

'Or what?'

'Or I could not kiss him and save everyone a load of hassle.'

'Don't you want to kiss him?'

'Not really. I don't see what all the fuss is about, to be honest. I kissed Stuart Green once, just to see what it would be like, and that was enough for me.'

'You never said anything! When was this?'

'A couple of years ago.'

'Did you fancy him?'

'God, no! But I wanted to try it, so I invited him behind the gym building. It was horrible, all slobbery. I can't see how anyone could find having someone else's tongue in their mouth erotic.'

'Wait and see,' I tell her. 'I think you'll change your tune when the right guy comes along. Are you sure you don't want to find out whether that's Mark?'

'Quite sure. Is it time for lunch?'

In the end, she doesn't quite get her wish as, after the final game on our last morning, Mark envelops her in a massive hug and kisses her hard on the lips. I can see her eyes widen in surprise behind her sunglasses, but she doesn't push him away. He looks delighted when they break apart; he's obviously been building up the courage all week.

'I can clearly see how much he doesn't fancy you,' I laugh, as she re-joins me on the sun loungers.

'Oh, shut up. It was just a goodbye kiss. They probably kiss their friends on the lips all the time where he comes from.'

'Mm. Do you think they do it that hard, and for that long? What was that, a full five seconds? Hardly a peck.'

'I don't know! I wasn't counting.'

'You didn't seem to mind.'

'Oh, stop! I'll say it, okay? It was nice. There wasn't any horrible slobbery tongue in it. In fact, there wasn't any tongue in it at all. There, do you feel better?'

I've paid extra for a late checkout, so we're able to shower and wash the sand off before the bus collects us to take us back to the airport for our evening flight home. I've really enjoyed spending the week with my sister, and it's nice to see her glowing from the sun and looking so relaxed as the bus trundles around to collect everyone else. As the plane takes off, my thoughts turn to home and the week ahead. I know Paul loves the static caravan in Whitstable, and I do enjoy walking along the seafront to the harbour and on towards Tankerton, but the caravan itself is a bit tired and smells faintly of damp. It's the kind of smell that gets into the fabric of your clothes, and I have to wash everything several times with strong fabric conditioner to get rid of it when I come home. I'm trying to work out what is the shortest time I can spend down there without offending him. He always tries to get me to come down for the whole week, and I have to invent reasons why I can't. I reckon I can buy myself a couple of days for just getting straight after coming back from Mallorca, and then I'll need next weekend to get ready to go back to work, so I might see if I can sell Wednesday to Friday to him.

* * *

It's very late when we get back home, but Nan and Grandad are still up, waiting for us. As soon as they see the light from my headlights turning in to their small driveway, they fling open the front door and come out to greet us.

'Did you have a lovely time?' Nan asks, after she's hugged us both.

'We did, thanks. Turns out Katie's quite the beach volleyball player,' I tell her.

'Really?' Nan turns to Katie in surprise.

'We'll just grab our bags, and then we'll tell you all about it. Why don't you go in and put the kettle on?'

As we're getting our stuff out of the boot, Katie turns to me.

'Don't tell them about Mark kissing me, will you? We'll never hear the end of it if you do.'

'Don't worry,' I smile. 'As someone said to me a week or so ago, "What goes on tour stays on tour."'

It's after midnight by the time we've filled Nan and Grandad in on the sanitised version of our holiday, and I can feel my eyelids drooping. Katie is yawning too, so we make our excuses and head to bed.

'I almost forgot,' Grandad says, as I'm kissing him goodnight, 'there's some post for you. Looked important. I'll just go and grab it.'

'Leave it,' I tell him. 'I'll have a look at it in the morning. I'm sure it's nothing so urgent that it won't keep for another day.'

'Okay. It's on top of the microwave in the kitchen if you change your mind.'

As I'm brushing my teeth, I can't help wondering about the letter. I don't exactly get a lot of post; all the household bills go to Nan and Grandad, so my post is limited to bank statements and occasional letters to remind me that my car insurance is due for renewal. Although I'm dog-tired and just want to sleep, curiosity gets the better of me and I tiptoe into the kitchen to retrieve it. The envelope feels substantial, and I can tell that the stationery is expensive. As well as my address and the frank mark, the front bears a logo: 'Moorhouse & Edgerley, Solicitors.'

Despite my tiredness, my anxiety goes up several notches. Why on earth would a firm of solicitors be writing to me? Am I being sued? I try to think what grounds anyone would have for taking legal action against me. Did I mess up someone's accounts? But no, that wouldn't come back to me, would it? Everything I do is double-checked by one of the chartered accountants and, even if they got it wrong, surely any lawsuit would be against the company and not an individual. I grab a knife from the block and carefully slit open the envelope.

There's a single sheet inside and, like the envelope, it has the quality feel that you only get from expensive paper. I draw it out and unfold it. At the top is the same logo that I saw on the envelope, but the text takes me completely by surprise. I read:

Dear Ms Jones,

Please allow me to extend my condolences to you on the death of your great-uncle, Frederick Jones. I had the pleasure of meeting him and his wife, Nora, fifteen years ago, when they engaged our firm to draw up their last will and testament. We also had the immense privilege of being able to offer our services as executors of the will when the time came.

I am pleased to be able to inform you that this task is now complete, and probate on your great-uncle's estate has now been granted. The reason that I am writing to you is that there are some aspects of the will that may pertain to you, subject to confirmation.

I would be extremely grateful, therefore, if you could contact me on the number below, so that we can find a mutually agreeable time to discuss these matters.

Yours sincerely,

Jonathan Moorhouse

Whatever I was expecting, it certainly wasn't this. I wasn't even aware that Great-Uncle Fred had died. What does he mean by 'some aspects of the will'? I'm wide awake now and could really do with Nan and Grandad's advice. However, the sound of snoring from their bedroom indicates that I'm not going to get anything from them until tomorrow morning. There's a thin sliver of light under Katie's door, however, so I knock and open it.

'Everything okay?' she asks.

'Look at this.' I thrust the letter at her. 'What do you think?'

She reads in silence and then considers for a few moments before she speaks.

'I think it means that Great-Uncle Fred has left you something in his will. It might be a bit of cash if you're lucky, or some horrible piece of tat that had tremendous sentimental value to him if you're not. Whatever it is, it won't be anything big. We hardly knew them, did we?'

'You're right,' I tell her. 'I'll call the guy on Monday morning. Let's hope it's cash and not a hideous china cat or anything like that, though. Thanks for that. Goodnight.'

'Goodnight, Daisy.'

5

I show the letter to Grandad the next morning, but his opinion is much the same as Katie's. I can't understand why Great-Uncle Fred would have left me anything, though. As Katie said, we really hardly knew them. The last time I saw him would have been at Nora's funeral, nine years ago. Nan and I had a hell of a battle over that, because it was only a year after Mum and Dad had died, and there was no way I wanted to go to any more funerals. She'd stood her ground, pointing out that we were pretty much the only blood relatives they had, and someone needed to represent our side of the family. I remember there being quite a few people there, but Fred had only appeared at the last minute, and had disappeared again the moment the service was over, so we didn't get to speak to him. I'm not sure he even knew we were there, a point I made forcefully to Nan afterwards.

By the time Monday morning comes around, I'm bursting with curiosity, and I dial the number on the letter shortly after nine o'clock. The phone is answered by a woman that I guess must be the receptionist, although her cut-glass accent makes her sound more like royalty than secretarial staff. I explain the letter, and she offers to put me through. After a brief pause, during which I'm treated to some suitably tasteful orchestral hold music, a deep bass voice rumbles down the phone.

'Jonathan Moorhouse speaking. How can I be of assistance?'

'Ah, hello, Mr Moorhouse,' I start. 'My name is Daisy Jones. You wrote to me last week about my great-uncle, Frederick Jones?'

'Indeed I did!' he booms.

'Would you be able to tell me more? I didn't fully understand the letter, I'm afraid.'

'Certainly, although there are some things we need to do first, such as verify your identity. Would you be able to come to my office? We're based in Sevenoaks, which is not that far from you.'

'I normally work in London,' I tell him. 'But I'm on holiday at the moment. If you could see me this week, I'd be very grateful, as it saves me having to arrange more time off.'

'Let me have a look at my diary.' There's a brief pause during which I can hear him clicking his mouse.

'I actually have an appointment free at two o'clock this afternoon, if that suits you? Otherwise, I could see you on Thursday at eleven.'

'Two o'clock today is absolutely fine, thank you.'

'Splendid. Now, I'll need you to bring some identification with you. Your passport or driving licence would be ideal, as well as a copy of your birth certificate. Do you have those?'

'Yes. I'll bring them with me.'

'I'll see you at two o'clock then, Ms Jones. I look forward to meeting you.'

'Well?' Katie asks, as soon as I hang up.

'I'm still none the wiser,' I tell her. 'I've got to go to his office this afternoon, take ID with me, and then he'll tell me what it's all about, allegedly. Seems a lot of faff for a china cat.'

'It's probably standard procedure,' Grandad suggests, looking up from his morning paper. 'It could only be a paperweight, for all we know, but if they accidentally give it to the wrong person then I guess they could still be in a lot of trouble.'

'I just hope whatever it is isn't too big,' Nan chips in. 'Imagine if it turns out to be a life-sized elephant statue or something like that. Where on earth would we put it?'

'If it's a life-sized elephant statue, I'll take it straight to the tip, I promise you!' I tell her, and she laughs.

* * *

Sevenoaks is not a town I know at all, beyond it being one of the places where the train stops between Paddock Wood and London. I always feel a bit sorry for the people who get on at Sevenoaks in the morning, because it's the last stop before London Bridge, so there are never any seats left and they have to cram themselves into the doorways and down the aisles. I deal with the guilt of always getting a seat by reminding myself that their season tickets are probably a lot cheaper than mine. In the evenings, it's the other way around, as they're the first to pour off the coastbound train, and anyone who has been standing from London gratefully sinks into the vacated seats.

I manage to find a car park, but wince when I see how expensive it is. I have no idea how long this will take, but I reckon I ought to allow two hours. I check my purse, which only confirms what I already knew: I don't have anywhere near enough cash to pay for the parking. With a couple of muttered oaths, I set about downloading yet another parking app to my phone (why can't everyone use the same app? Would that be so difficult?) and registering myself on it. Finally, after around ten minutes of fiddling, I manage to pay the fee, but I'm now running short of time to get to the solicitors' office. I've already put their postcode into the navigation app, so I set off at as brisk a pace as I can manage without actually running.

It takes about ten minutes to reach the offices of Moorhouse & Edgerley, and I'm sweating profusely by the time I get there. The building itself is everything I have always imagined a solicitors' office to be; it's imposing, with a brass plaque to one side of the double height door that simply states 'Moorhouse & Edgerley, Solicitors'. I push open the inner door, and it's like I've stepped into a different world. Outside, the sun is blazing on a hot summer day, but it's cool and eerily quiet in here, with just the faintest whisper coming from the air conditioning system. My feet are sinking into the deep carpet, and I can just make out the aroma of freshly ground coffee. It oozes sophistication and class, and I feel totally out of place. Thankfully, I did at least make a bit of an effort, changing out of my jeans and T-shirt into one of my work suits. I'd love to remove my jacket and stand with my back to one of the air conditioning ducts, but this isn't the sort of place where you can do that.

Tentatively, I approach the reception desk. The lady sitting behind it raises her eyes and smiles. I can't tell if it's a genuine smile or the sort of smile she reserves to get rid of lunatics, but it's obvious that I'm not the normal sort of client they get in here.

'Can I help you?' I recognise the same cut-glass accent from before.

'Yes, I'm Daisy Jones, and I have an appointment with Mr Moorhouse at two o'clock. I'm a couple of minutes late, I'm afraid. I had a bit of trouble parking the car.'

'I'll let him know you're here, if you'd like to take a seat in the waiting area.' She points out an area with a couple of sofas, some chairs, and a table with magazines arranged on it. I perch on one of the chairs and look around, as I hear her murmuring that I've arrived into the phone. The magazines are very different from the gossip mags that I enjoy leafing through at the hairdressers; these are editions of *Country Life*, *Horse and Hound*, and a couple of others that I don't recognise. Copies of today's broadsheet papers are also carefully laid out.

'I'm very sorry.' The receptionist's voice takes me by surprise. The carpet in here is so thick I didn't hear her approach. 'Mr Moorhouse has asked me to inform you that he's also running a few minutes late. Would you like a cup of tea or coffee while you wait?'

'Actually, I'd love a glass of water, if that's not too much trouble.'

'Of course. Still or sparkling?'

'Sparkling, please.'

She pads off as silently as she arrived, and reappears a few moments later holding a crystal tumbler filled with water.

'I forgot to ask if you'd like ice and lemon, so I've added them anyway. Is that okay?'

'That's lovely, thank you.' I take an appreciative sip of the water, which is cool and refreshing, and smile at her. She nods and disappears back to her desk.

It really is unnervingly quiet in here. Although the telephone rings frequently, the sound is muted and the murmur of the receptionist's voice is so quiet that I can barely make out what she's saying, even though she's only a few feet away from me. I pick up one of the copies of *Country Life* and start leafing though. The first section is filled with enormous country houses and estates in Scotland for sale, and I have fun imagining myself living in each one and deciding what I'd change.

'Ms Jones, I'm so sorry for keeping you waiting!' I recognise Mr Moorhouse's deep bass voice and look up to see a portly, white-haired man in an ill-fitting, pinstriped suit. The suit itself was probably expensive, but his gut is straining over the top of the trousers and there's no way he'd be able to do up the jacket. I suspect he's grown a bit since he bought it. Too many corporate lunches, probably.

'Would you like to follow me?' he continues. 'Do bring your glass of water with you if you'd like to.'

I pick up my glass, and he leads me into a small meeting room, where a thick folder has already been placed on the table. There's a label on it which reads 'Frederick and Nora Jones'.

'Take a seat, Ms Jones, and make yourself comfortable.'

Like the reception area, this room is pleasantly cool, and I decide to risk removing my jacket. I hang it on the back of the chair, and sit leaning forwards to maximise the flow of air around my back and hopefully dry out my blouse a bit.

Mr Moorhouse mirrors my actions and hangs his jacket too. I wonder if this is something he does with all his clients, to make them feel at ease.

'Before we start, do you prefer Ms Jones or Daisy?'

'Daisy,' I reply. 'Ms Jones sounds like someone at least twenty years older than me.'

'Perfect,' he replies. 'Please call me Jonathan.' I notice that he has a kind, smiley face, and his double chins wobble when he talks, as if they're trying to show their agreement with whatever he's saying.

'So, first things first. Have you brought in the ID that I requested?'

I fish in my handbag and dig out my passport, driving licence, and birth certificate. He studies each one in turn, spending the most time on my birth certificate.

'It says here that your parents were called Roger and Linda?' he queries.

'That's right.' Something about the way he's asked makes me anxious. Maybe I'm not the Daisy Jones he's looking for after all, and this is about a completely different Frederick and Nora Jones. It would be a hell of a coincidence, though, wouldn't it?'

'Perfect. I'm just going to give these to my secretary to photocopy, if that's okay with you, and then I can tell you what this is all about.'

I nod my agreement, and he disappears with my documents. After a couple of minutes, he returns and hands them back to me.

'Right, Daisy. Everything is in order. I'm sorry to have had to be a little bit careful with what I've said to you up to now, but we needed to be sure you were the right person before we could go any further.'

He opens the folder in front of him.

'As I explained in my letter, your great-uncle, Frederick Jones, passed away just over six months ago. You probably know this. Did you go to the funeral?'

'I'm afraid I didn't know, and didn't go to his funeral. We weren't exactly close.'

'Not to worry, these things happen. Are you aware that he and Nora did not have any children?'

'I did know that, yes.'

'Normally, when someone makes a will, the primary beneficiaries are the children. Of course, as there were no children in this case, Frederick and Nora had to choose different beneficiaries. Nora was an only child, so there was no family on her side, but Frederick had a brother, your paternal grandfather.'

'He died before I was born. I never even met him,' I tell him.

'Indeed he did, and your father was his only child. So, Frederick and Nora named your father as the primary beneficiary in their will, as he was their closest living relative. However, we always advise people to assume the worst when making a will, so we included a clause for the unlikely event that your father should pre-decease Frederick. In light of subsequent events, this proved to be wise.'

At this point he pauses, and looks me in the eye. 'Please allow me to offer my condolences on the death of your parents. It must have been a terrible shock.'

I can tell he's being sincere, even though he's never met me and clearly never met my parents.

'Thank you,' I say, quietly.

'So, back to the will. We added a clause that said that, if your father were to pre-decease Frederick, any inheritance would pass to his offspring. If there were no surviving offspring, then the final option was to split it among a number of charities. Am I right in thinking you have a younger sister?'

'Katie, she's seventeen,' I tell him.

'Right, so what this means is that you and Katie are the primary beneficiaries in Frederick's will. His entire estate passes to the pair of you.'

6

'I'm sorry, can you explain what that means?' If I've understood him correctly, we've inherited everything that Great-Uncle Fred owned, but I need to hear him spell it out.

'What it means is that you and Katie are, as of now, wealthy young women. It appears that Frederick was a wily investor. As part of the probate process, we've liquidated his investments and, after duties, taxes and fees, you are going to receive...' he looks down at his notes, '...seven hundred and ninety-five thousand, eight hundred and four pounds and forty-six pence between you as a cash inheritance.'

I do the maths in my head. That's just shy of £400,000 each.

'Bloody hell!' I exclaim. 'I thought you were just going to give me a paperweight or something like that.'

He smiles at my outburst. 'Before you leave, I will need your bank account details to make the transfer. As Katie is under eighteen years of age, the stipulations of the will dictate that her share must be placed in trust until her eighteenth birthday. We can help you with that, if you like.'

'Yes, please.' I have no idea how much that will cost, but I'm sure we can afford it.

'It would be my pleasure. Are you happy for me to put you as the main trustee? You won't have to do anything; the role is essentially to hold the assets for the beneficiary, in this case Katie. You can't access the money but, when she turns eighteen, the funds will transfer to her.'

I think I must be in shock. How else can I be talking about such enormous sums of money so calmly, as if I do this every day? To be fair, these are sums I deal with regularly at work, but this isn't a client's money. It's ours.

'I will transfer your share into your nominated bank account within the next few days. If you don't have any immediate plans, such as a property purchase, I would recommend you seek financial advice. Would you permit me to give you the card of an independent financial adviser that we work with frequently? She will be able to give you some ideas about how you could potentially invest some of it, either to provide a bigger lump sum later in life, or an income if you prefer.'

'Thank you. I'd like that.' I have no idea what to do with such an enormous sum, so professional advice sounds like a very good plan. I was quite pleased with the £8,000 I've managed to build up in my savings account, but this is in a totally different league.

Jonathan pushes a piece of paper and a pen in my direction. 'If you could just fill in your bank details here, I'll arrange the transfer. What we do is transfer a pound initially and ask you to confirm receipt. That just makes sure that we've got the right details. We wouldn't want to send your inheritance to a complete stranger, would we?'

I fill in the details of my savings account, which seems more appropriate than my current account. Whatever happens, the money won't be staying there for long. I remember the news stories showing people queueing up in the vain hope of getting their savings back when Northern Rock collapsed. I'm not prepared to trust one bank with all of it; these eggs will be spread across multiple baskets.

I pass the form back to Jonathan, who casts his eye over it and replaces it in the file. He extracts another piece of paper and slides it over to me.

'This is a form authorising us to place your sister's share in trust, with you as the main trustee. I hope you don't mind the presumption, but I hoped that you would appoint us to handle this for you. If you could just sign in the places indicated.'

I look through the form, but it's all written in legalese and doesn't make a lot of sense to me. I'm sure it's all above board, though; a company like Moorhouse & Edgerley wouldn't get far if they weren't scrupulously above the law. I sign in the places indicated and pass the form back.

'Excellent. We'll put that in motion and confirm the details with you once it's set up. Just for our records, when does Katie turn eighteen?'

'The twenty forth of March next year.'

He makes a note on his pad.

'Right, that takes care of the cash assets. Now we move onto property, if you're ready.'

There's *more*? I'm speechless and just nod at him. I hope my mouth isn't hanging open.

'I don't know if you're aware, but Frederick owned the freehold of a café here in the town, near the station. The café has two residential flats above it, which he also owned. We've had all of it valued for probate. Valuing commercial property is a complex task, as there are a number of variables that have to be taken into account, but the café on its own was valued at three hundred thousand pounds.'

If my mouth wasn't open before, it is now.

'That doesn't mean you'd get three hundred thousand pounds if you sold it, but it's a pretty good indication of the sort of sum you should aim for. The café is currently trading; as the executor of your great-uncle's will, I have had to step in as temporary director, and we have appointed a firm of accountants to look after the books. I have to tell you that, from what I understand, it is not a viable venture in its current state. It's not my job to advise you what to do, but if you were to dispose of it, you could either retain the freehold and lease it to a third party, or sell it. Either approach would give you and Katie a significant further financial boost. If you sell it before Katie turns eighteen, then half of the proceeds would go into her trust fund. If you lease it, then that's income rather than capital, and Katie can benefit from her share straight away.'

'So, just to be clear, I can sell it, rent it out, or keep it?'

'Essentially, yes. I have last month's accounts here, which you're welcome to take with you. I would advise you to employ an accountant to explain them to you. I will arrange for you to be appointed as the sole director of the business, as that is a legal requirement to give you the power to make decisions. Once Katie comes of age, it is then up to you, if you haven't sold the business, whether you appoint her as joint director. I've also got the details of the accountants we're using; you can either continue with them or appoint another firm.'

I cast my eyes over the books. He's not lying. The café was barely breaking even before Fred died. With the cost of the accountants and the fees that Jonathan is charging to be the director, it's currently making a thumping loss. Even in my shocked state, I realise that it needs to be my top priority, otherwise it will eat through my £400,000 terrifyingly quickly. At least I shouldn't have to pay Jonathan's fee for too much longer.

'Are you okay? Do you need a break?' Jonathan asks me. 'There isn't too much more to go through, but I realise this has been a lot to take in.'

'You're telling me,' I murmur, before I have a chance to stop myself, and Jonathan laughs. 'I think I'm okay to carry on,' I continue.

'Excellent. So, the final major assets are the two flats. As I said, Frederick owned the freehold on both of them, along with the café. He and Nora lived in one, and they rented the other one out for a number of years. However, my current understanding is that the chef from the café is living in the other one, for a nominal rent of one hundred pounds per month. The freehold of the café is tied to the flats, so you can't sell one without the other, if that makes sense. However, you could sell the flats on a leasehold basis. Based on a new, ninety-nine-year lease, the flats have been valued at two hundred and fifty thousand pounds each. Again, if you went down this route, then Katie's half of the proceeds would need to go into trust until her eighteenth birthday. Another option is to let them. You'd have to consult an estate agent to get a precise monthly rental, but I'm confident you would be looking at a sum comfortably north of a thousand pounds per month for each flat. Once again, as this is income rather than capital, Katie could benefit from her share of the rent immediately. I have to warn you that the flats are in need of modernisation, so you'd probably have to spend some money to bring them up to scratch before you could rent them out.'

My mind is officially blown. I've been keeping up with the numbers in my head, and Katie and I are potentially sitting on a total inheritance so far of nearly £1.6 million.

'I have all the property title deeds on file,' Jonathan continues. 'Would you like to take them, or would you like me to hang on to them for now?'

'Please keep them. I need time to decide what I'm going to do. I also need to talk to Katie.'

'Of course.' He slides a bulky-looking envelope out of the file and passes it to me. 'These are the keys to the café and the flats. The chef has a set for the café and the flat that he's currently occupying. We didn't identify any other keyholders. Are you happy for me to go ahead and appoint you as the sole director of the business? You won't be able to do anything at all with it unless I do.'

'Yes, that's fine.'

He passes a sheaf of papers across to me, and it takes forever to go through and sign them all, particularly as I have to get him to explain several sections. By the time we're finished, I've signed forms relating to the directorship, the bank accounts, and the properties themselves.

'There are only two other items of value that we need to discuss. It appears that Frederick lived a fairly frugal life on the whole, especially after Nora died, but he did own one item of note.' He pulls another envelope out of the file and pushes it across the table. I open it and slide out a rather boring-looking wristwatch with a metal bracelet. It doesn't look valuable, and I raise my eyebrows questioningly.

'It's a Rolex Explorer,' Jonathan explains. 'The funeral directors passed it on to me with his personal effects. My expert advises me that these things are worth more if you have the original box and papers. I don't know whether they're in the flat somewhere, but the valuation of eight and a half thousand pounds is based on the watch alone. I would recommend insuring it, if you decide to keep it.'

Bloody hell, my watch cost me eighty quid, and I thought that was expensive. I pick up Fred's watch and I'm immediately surprised by how heavy it is. I slip it onto my wrist and I have to admit, although it's much larger than my current watch, it looks good. I close the clasp on the bracelet but, of course, it's way too big and slips off.

'There is a watchmaker on the high street who will size it to fit you, if you want. He will also be able to advise you on where to sell it, if you go down that route. The final thing is Frederick's car. It's nothing flashy, but it's less than a year old, so it still has significant value. It's a Nissan Micra, and it's parked in his dedicated spot behind the café. The chef has been looking after it, starting the engine every so often and keeping the tyres pumped up. It has a similar value to the watch, around eight and a half thousand pounds. The chef has the keys, and I'm sure he'll be delighted to hand over the responsibility of it. I have the documents here.' Another envelope crosses the desk. Jonathan beams at me. 'I think that's everything. There are items of furniture and so on in Frederick's flat, but they weren't deemed to have significant value. You can either keep them or get a house clearance company in to remove them for you. Do you have any further questions?'

'I don't think so. This has all been a bit of a shock.'

'I'm sure. If you do have any more questions at any point, feel free to give me a ring. In the meantime, I'll get the trust fund set up for Katie, arrange for the cash transfer into your account, and process the documents relating to the café.' He reaches into his jacket pocket and pulls out a card. 'This is the financial adviser I told you about. By no means feel compelled to use her, but she's done good work for a number of our clients who have found themselves in similar circumstances.'

'Thank you.' I take the card and slip it into one of the envelopes now in my possession. I carefully take everything and place it into my bag. Jonathan stands up, and I follow suit.

'If there's nothing else I can do for you, allow me to say what a pleasure it has been to meet you.' He holds out his hand and I shake it. I'm surprised by how soft it is. 'If there's anything else you need, at any point, I'd be delighted to help you. If I may give you one final piece of advice, once you've decided what to do with everything, you might want to think about making a will, if you haven't already.'

I feel dizzy as I step back out into the heat of the sun. It's still the same warm summer afternoon that it was an hour or so ago, but the meeting I've just had with Jonathan has changed everything for Katie and me. I reach for my phone to ring her, but realise that this is something I'll have to explain to her face to face. I also need time alone to digest it first, as I think I'm in shock.

7

My legs feel like jelly as I set off towards the car park, and I realise I'm in no fit state to drive. I need to calm down and regain at least some of my equilibrium before I get behind the wheel, otherwise I may end up having an accident. I decide to find somewhere where I can sit down and have a cup of coffee and a piece of cake. As I wander around the town, I encounter all the usual mainstream vendors, but they always seem a bit corporate and soulless to me. When I'm at work, I go to a lovely little coffee shop near the office, run by an Italian family, and I decide to see if I can find something similar here. After a brief search, I come across a place in a side street just down from Lloyds Bank. The sign above the door features a daisy made from coffee beans, which makes me smile. It looks inviting, and there are some free tables on the pavement outside. I order a latte and a slice of carrot cake and settle myself at one of them.

I tilt my face towards the sun, close my eyes, and try to make a list in my head. I need to talk to Katie, obviously, but there's no doubt that we need to do something about the café fairly urgently.

I open my eyes, reach into my bag, and pull out a pen. I don't have any paper in there, so I slip the Rolex out of its envelope so I can write on that. I find making lists helps me to get my thoughts in order, and I definitely need to bring some sort of order to the current chaos in my head. I take a sip of my coffee and write:

Café – what to do?

After that, my mind goes blank and, try as I might, I can't think of any logical sequence. The café has to go, obviously, but I have no idea how best to dispose of it. It sounds like it and the flats could provide Katie and me with quite a healthy income, but what if I can't find anyone who wants to rent them? If I sell them outright, that will net us a huge amount of money in the short term, but is that the most sensible option? I wonder if the financial adviser Jonathan recommended would have any opinions on this. It's too big a decision for me at the moment. I pick up the pen again and add another entry to the list:

ADVICE????

I take a big bite of the carrot cake, which is rich and moreish. Nan and I finally bonded in the kitchen, and I like to think of myself as quite an accomplished baker, but this tastes better than any carrot cake I've ever made. I suspect it's probably because my body is craving sugar to help it cope with the shock, and it seems to be working. As I eat and drink, I feel the strength beginning to come back into my legs. I glance down and notice the Rolex glinting in my bag. At least I can do something about that, I think. I finish the coffee and cake, add another exorbitantly expensive hour to the parking using the app, and set off in search of the watchmaker that Jonathan mentioned.

The shop, when I find it, is small and unassuming. A large selection of watches and other jewellery is displayed on cushions in the window, and I can see little price tags attached to everything with string, but they're all face down so I can't read them. There's an old-fashioned bell over the door that rings as I open it. It takes my eyes a moment to adjust to the comparative darkness inside but, when they do, I see a long glass counter cabinet with even more watches displayed inside. The labels on some of these ones are visible, and the prices are high enough to make me shake my head in disbelief. Who spends thousands of pounds on something which basically just tells the time?

'Good afternoon, how may I help you?' The man behind the counter is thin, with thick-lensed glasses that lend him a slightly owlish appearance. I reach into my bag and place the Rolex on the counter and, as I do, I notice that it's telling completely the wrong time and the second hand isn't moving.

'I've just inherited this,' I tell him, 'and I was told you might be able to help with sizing the bracelet so it will fit me. Also, I've just noticed that it's not running, so it probably needs a new battery.'

The man picks up the Rolex and studies it, almost reverentially. 'That is a lovely piece, miss. Your benefactor had great taste. I can certainly help you with both those things. Let's deal with the second one first. This is a mechanical watch, so it doesn't take a battery.'

He carefully unscrews the crown and starts to wind the watch. After a few winds, he checks and shows it to me. I can see the second hand is now gliding smoothly round the dial. He waits until it reaches the twelve o'clock position, then pulls out the crown and sets the time using a clock on the wall behind him as a guide.

'There you are. These are extremely accurate timepieces, so I've taken the trouble of setting it exactly for you. It's also waterproof, so you need to remember to screw the crown back into the case after setting the time or winding it.' He shows me how to do it.

'I didn't know anyone still had wind-up watches,' I tell him. 'Do I have to wind it every day?' I'm fast coming to the conclusion that this watch may be more hassle to live with than it's worth, and I'm tempted to ask if he'll buy it off me.

'There are lots of people still making mechanical watches, although Rolex is by far the best known. People love them because they're magnificent pieces of craftsmanship as well as handsome timepieces.' He strokes the case lovingly with his thumb as he speaks. 'It's almost like a living thing with a tiny mechanical heart. A quartz watch will tell you the time, sure, but a mechanical watch has soul in a way that a quartz never can.'

I raise my eyebrows and he obviously realises that nothing he's just said is making any sense to me, as he swiftly changes tack.

'To answer your question, it has an automatic winding mechanism based on the movement of your wrist so, as long as you're wearing it and moving about normally, it should keep itself fully wound. It will stop if you don't wear it for a few days, but then it only needs a quick wind and reset, like I've just done. Now, let's have a look at this bracelet.'

He places the watch on my wrist and fastens the clasp. After a bit of humming and hawing, he disappears into the back of the shop. While I'm waiting for him, I consider what I'm going to do with it. On one hand, it sounds like a liability, with its little beating heart and all the other nonsense he spouted, but on the other it obviously meant a lot to Great-Uncle Fred, and it's much less of a liability than the café, so maybe I ought to keep it as a token of gratitude to him.

'Here we are. Try this.' Once again, he places the watch carefully on my wrist and fastens the clasp. This time, it fits much better, and I move my wrist back and forth, trying to get used to the heft of it. He hands me a tiny envelope.

'What's this?' I ask.

'Those are the links I removed from the bracelet. You should keep them somewhere safe. Rolex bracelets are notoriously expensive, so having the spare links will be important if you ever want to sell it.'

'Thank you. What do I owe you?'

'Oh, nothing at all. It was a pleasure to be able to help. I hope you have many years of enjoyment from it. It truly is a lovely thing. One suggestion, if I may?'

'Go on.'

'I'm not sure how old it is, but it might be a good idea to consider getting it serviced, particularly if you're planning on submerging it in water at any point.'

'I'm sorry, did you say *service*?'

'Yes. There are lots of tiny moving parts in there, and they need to be kept lubricated and so on. The waterproof seals should also be checked and changed regularly.'

It's obvious where he's going with this. He's given me the freebie to instil a sense of obligation so he can sell me something bigger, such as this service.

'I see. Is that something you can do for me?'

'Goodness me, no. Quite apart from the fact that I'm not accredited by Rolex, I don't have the equipment to do the waterproof testing. However, any Rolex retailer should be able to help. Mappin & Webb at Bluewater is probably the closest one to here. It won't be cheap, probably six or seven hundred pounds, but it's worth it to have the peace of mind.'

Okay, so maybe I underestimated him. I'm back to thinking this thing is a liability, though. My car doesn't even cost that much to be serviced, and I'm sure it's much more complicated than a bloody wristwatch.

'I understand. Thank you.' I really don't understand, but he might start explaining if I let on, and I'm suddenly quite keen to be out of here. It's like I've stepped into some horological version of *Alice in Wonderland*, where all the watches have come to life and are making ever more ludicrous demands.

I'm very aware of the weight of the Rolex on my wrist as I walk back to the car, and I'm convinced people are noticing and staring at it. They aren't, of course, it's just that I feel incredibly self-conscious wandering around with several thousand pounds' worth of watch on my wrist. On the plus side, the cake and the distraction of the strange watch man has stopped me feeling wobbly, and I'm ready to drive home at last. As I start the car, a thought occurs to me. I rifle through the papers that Jonathan gave me and find the address of the café, which I punch into the satnav. I might as well check it out while I'm here.

Five minutes later, I find myself in front of a small parade of shops, and my fears about the café are confirmed. It's very run down, a fact emphasised by the swanky-looking art gallery next door. It's also closed; the sign in the door indicates that it's open from 7.30 a.m. to 3 p.m. every day except Sunday, when it's closed all day. It's probably for the best, I decide. This is Katie's problem just as much as it is mine, so we should probably check it out together.

* * *

Katie, Nan, and Grandad are all in the living room when I get back, studiously trying to pretend that they haven't been sitting there for ages, bursting with curiosity about what Fred could have left me. I decide, perhaps a little unkindly, to string them along a bit.

'Ah, there you are. You were gone a long time,' Nan observes as I walk in, and I can hear the false nonchalance in her voice. She'd make a terrible actor. 'Where's the elephant?'

'It wasn't an elephant,' I tell them all, 'it was a watch in the end.' I take off the Rolex and hand it to her.

'Goodness, that's heavy. What's it made of, lead?' Nan exclaims, as she passes it to Katie. 'You'll end up with one arm longer than the other, wearing that!'

Katie glances at it briefly before handing it on to Grandad, who studies it intently.

'It's a Rolex,' he observes, after reading the dial. 'That's got to be worth a few bob.'

'Eight and a half thousand pounds, according to the solicitor,' I tell them, with a smile. Nan's mouth drops open in surprise, and I can't help but laugh.

'Eight and a half grand?' she repeats. 'Think what you could do with a sum like that. I'd sell it, if I were you. I'm sure you could use the money.'

'I am thinking about it,' I reply, 'but I've got a few other things to deal with first. The watch is only one part of what Great-Uncle Fred left to Katie and me.'

Katie's head snaps up. I've got her attention now. Time for the big reveal.

'Sorry, did you just say he left me something as well?' she asks. She's trying to sound indifferent, but doing nearly as bad a job as Nan did earlier.

'Yup. Between us, Katie, we've inherited just under eight hundred thousand pounds in cash, two flats worth a quarter of a million quid each, and a café. He left everything to us.'

The stunned silence is so intense that, even though the room is fully carpeted, you could probably still hear a pin drop.

'Oh, I almost forgot,' I continue. 'There's a car as well. I'm going to put the kettle on. Anyone want a cup of tea?'

8

They're all still sitting there, motionless, when I come back with the tray of mugs. I've put some biscuits on a plate as well; I don't want to be responsible for Nan keeling over from the shock. No sooner have I passed round the mugs than the interrogation begins, and I end up giving them pretty much a blow-by-blow account of my meeting with Jonathan Moorhouse. Katie is a little disappointed that she won't be able to access her share of the cash inheritance straight away, but soon recovers.

'What are you going to do about the café then?' Grandad asks. We've all agreed that this has to be my top priority.

'I was trying to think a bit about that on the way home,' I tell them. 'It's got to go, there's no doubt about that, but it's not the kind of thing you can just stick on eBay and sell in a week. I could close it and stop the rot, but then it's an empty unit sitting there doing nothing, which seems a bit wasteful. Also, I wonder whether it will be more attractive to a buyer if it's open and trading, rather than boarded up.'

'That makes sense,' Katie agrees. 'So, we keep it open until we find a buyer. How do we stop it draining our resources in the meantime, though?'

'My resources,' I remind her. 'Yours are safely locked up.'

'Yes, but this is our café,' she counters. 'Even if I can't access the money yet, I will pay half of whatever costs we incur until it's sold as soon as I'm able.'

I smile at her. She's always been much more generous-natured than me, and this is typical of the kind of grand gesture she loves.

'Let me go through the books properly. I had a quick glance when Jonathan first gave them to me, but I need to understand the details before we can really make a plan. We definitely need to get rid of the accountants, though. They are costing us a fortune.'

'Can you do that?' Nan asks.

'I don't see why not. From what I can see, we're potentially paying thousands of pounds a month for them to do the book-keeping, and I'm more than capable of that. This isn't a complex business, from an accounting perspective, so I don't think it would take an awful lot of my time.'

'Do you know anything else about it?' Grandad asks. 'For example, how many people work there? It's not just about the numbers, Daisy. Your decisions could affect people's livelihoods, remember.'

I sigh. 'I know, and the last thing I want to do is take away anyone's job. We've got to try to be a bit ruthless, though, because otherwise we'll just end up propping it up until we run out of money, and then we're back where we started. That doesn't seem a good use of Fred's investment pot, does it? I think we should go and meet them, particularly the chef. If nothing else, it sounds like we need to thank him for keeping the place running and for looking after Fred's car. I also need to understand a bit more about the deal with the flat he's living in. He's paying peanuts for it.'

'We should go down there tomorrow!' Katie exclaims. 'We

could go undercover, find out what it's like. They won't know who we are, so they'll just think we're normal customers.'

'That's not a bad idea, actually,' I agree. 'I'm going to set up a proper meeting with them as well, though. I'll call them in the morning. I'll call the accountants too, and let them know that I'll be doing the books from now until we sell.'

With the beginnings of a plan in place, Nan declares that she needs something much more interesting than a cup of tea and biscuit to celebrate our windfall and sends Grandad out to the local shop to get a bottle of fizz. While he's gone, I take the opportunity to scrutinise the books some more. Thankfully, apart from Jonathan's bills and the accounting fees, the outgoings of the café appear to be fairly low. There are the usual business costs and utility bills, as well as staff wages and the cost of the food itself. Unfortunately, the income is also pitifully low. It may have been breaking even when Fred was alive, but it definitely wasn't thriving.

I'm surprised to see how little the chef is paid. A bit of internet searching reveals that his salary is around half what he should expect to be earning, which confirms my suspicion that the flat is probably part of his package. That would explain the peppercorn rent. Apart from the fact that the café isn't making any money, there's nothing in the accounts that concerns me. I reckon I could keep on top of them fairly easily.

Grandad has gone the extra mile and reappears not only with a chilled bottle of Prosecco, but fish and chips from the local chippy for all of us as well. We settle ourselves at the table to enjoy our feast, and Grandad proposes a toast to Fred, which we join in with enthusiastically. By the time we've finished eating, Nan has polished off two glasses of Prosecco and is decidedly tipsy, so we're treated to one of her gushing monologues.

'I always hoped things would work out okay for you two!' she slurs, waving her glass animatedly. 'You've got so much going for you, and now you have the means to make your dreams come true. You can put the past behind you and focus on the future. I'm so happy and proud of you both.'

Katie and I roll our eyes at each other and smile. We both know we can never put the past behind us. No amount of money can get back what we've lost. It's nice to see Nan happy, though, even if Grandad is gently trying to persuade her to put her glass down before she spills the contents everywhere.

* * *

After a sleepless night, I'm up early, and I decide to strike while the iron is hot. I rifle through the documents and call the telephone number for the café. It's eight o'clock in the morning, so they ought to be there if the opening hours on the door are to be believed.

'Hello?' It's a female voice, and it sounds vaguely annoyed.

'Hello. Is that Nora's Diner?' I ask, worried that I've called the wrong number. Isn't it usual for businesses to announce their name when they answer the phone?

'Yes. Can I help you?' She's definitely irritated, and doesn't sound like she wants to help at all.

'My name is Daisy Jones,' I continue, trying to sound as deferential as I can so as not to wind her up any more. Maybe she's having a stressful morning. 'I wondered if it would be possible to speak to the chef?'

'He's working, and he doesn't take personal calls on this line,' she tells me abruptly, and I realise she's about to put the phone down on me.

'This isn't a personal call,' I explain, quickly. 'My sister and I are the new owners of the café, and I'd like to find a suitable time to meet with him to go through a few things.'

'I see. I will have to check whether he can talk to you. It's a busy time for us, you know,' she says, reproachfully. I can tell she's put her hand over the mouthpiece, because the background sounds suddenly become muted. Unfortunately for her, not muted enough that I can't hear the scorn in her voice as she explains who is on the phone.

'Hello, Matt Stevens speaking. How may I help?' This voice, although laced with caution, thankfully sounds much friendlier, and I prepare to relaunch my charm offensive.

'Hi, Matt, my name is Daisy, and my sister and I have just found out that we're the new owners of the café. I was wondering if we could find a time to come down and meet you, to find out a bit more about it and maybe talk through some options for the future.'

'When did you have in mind?' he asks.

'This week, if possible.'

'How about today, at three fifteen? We close at three, so there won't be any customers to worry about.'

'That would be fine,' I tell him. 'We will look forward to meeting you later.'

As I wander into the kitchen to make myself a cup of coffee and a piece of toast, I reflect on the call. Matt, the chef, sounds as if he might be okay, but the woman? I don't know who she is, but I've taken a definite dislike to her. The hands on the clock seem to take an age to crawl round to nine o'clock, when I can make my next call.

'Good morning, Horncastle Accountants,' another cut-glass voice on the phone. No wonder all these people are so expensive.

'Hello. My name is Daisy Jones and I'd like to speak with someone about Nora's Diner, in Sevenoaks?'

'May I ask the nature of your enquiry? As I'm sure you understand, most of the information we hold about our clients is highly confidential.' Unlike the receptionist at Moorhouse & Edgerley, who turned out to be lovely, this woman is evidently trying to patronise me from here to next week. What is wrong with everyone this morning? I'm not in the mood to play games with any more snotty people on the phone today, and decide to go for the jugular.

'Certainly.' I put on my sweetest voice. 'I have been informed by Jonathan Moorhouse, of Moorhouse & Edgerley solicitors, that your firm is currently contracted to do the accounting for the café. As the new owner of the business, I'm ringing to terminate that contract.'

There's a brief pause, but I have to admire her nerve when she comes back because she sounds completely unruffled.

'I see. Let me put you through to Mr Carter, one of our directors, who can advise you on the next steps.'

There's a long pause, and the hold music loops a couple of times before a male voice comes on the line.

'Ms Jones, Alan Carter here. I understand you wish to terminate our services with regards to Nora's Diner, in Sevenoaks?'

'That's correct,' I tell him.

'I see. Unfortunately,' and I hear a smug, patronising tone creep into his voice as well, 'it's not something we can simply do over the phone. We would need you to come to our offices and provide evidence that you're legally entitled to act on behalf of Nora's Diner before we could consider releasing the books. May I ask why you no longer wish to use our services?'

'It's simple,' I tell him. 'The café can't afford you.'

Like the receptionist, the bluntness of my response doesn't seem to bother him at all. He sounds just as smug as he continues.

'I understand. That is an unfortunate situation. However, I would caution you against making a false economy in this case. When you consider the range of services that we offer and the levels of expertise that we have in our team, our fees are actually extremely reasonable. You might be able to find companies prepared to keep the accounts for a lower upfront fee than us, but it will probably end up costing you more in the long run, because they won't be able to optimise your tax position in the way that we can. Why don't we discuss it some more when you come in? I could see you tomorrow afternoon, at half past two, if that suits?'

Who does he think he is? I doubt very much that his firm could 'optimise my tax position' on a business that's barely breaking even. I bite my tongue as I agree the appointment time and we end the call. It will give me immense pleasure to pull the rug from under him.

'Morning.' Katie wanders into the kitchen in search of coffee and breakfast. She's obviously just woken up, because her hair is a mess and her eyes are bleary behind her smudged glasses. 'Who was that on the phone? You had your "I'm smiling while I plot to kill you" voice on.'

In spite of my irritation, I can't help but laugh.

'I've been making some calls to set up appointments,' I tell her. 'First, I had some woman at the café oozing pissed-offness at me because I dared to disturb her by making her answer the phone, and I've just finished talking to one of the most patronising accountants I think I've ever come across.'

'Did you tell them what you do for a living?'

'No, I thought I'd keep that as a little surprise for them when I go in.'

'Nice. So, what's the plan?'

'We're due at the café at three fifteen to meet Matt, the chef. He sounded all right, actually. I thought we could get there a bit earlier, maybe have a bit of lunch?'

'I'm definitely up for that.'

'I also thought that we should take the train over there. I'll ask Grandad if he'd mind giving us a lift to Paddock Wood.'

'Why?'

'Because then we can pick Fred's car up while we're there. I'm sure Matt will be delighted to see the back of it, and it'll be easier for us to decide what to do with it once we get it back here. I'm sure Grandad will have all sorts of ideas.'

'I thought you weren't keen on cars you don't know?'

'I'm not, but this one is apparently less than a year old, and the more stuff I can get done before I go back to work, the better.'

A thought comes to me, and I reach for the telephone again.

'Who are you ringing now?'

'Jonathan Moorhouse. He's still technically the director until the paperwork goes through, so I need to make sure I have everything I need for my meeting with the accountants tomorrow. I don't want to give them any excuse to brush me off.'

Thankfully Jonathan is free and, after I've explained the situation, he explains that he's hoping to submit the paperwork to transfer the directorship of the café later today, so he should be able to provide suitable documentation for me to take to the accountants either late this afternoon or tomorrow morning.

'Daisy?' Katie ventures, as I put the phone down.

'Yes?'

'Aren't you supposed to be going down to the coast tomorrow, to spend the rest of the week with Paul?'

9

Damn. I have to confess that I haven't given Paul a single thought since receiving the letter. Hurriedly, I pull out my mobile and compose a quick WhatsApp to him.

Hi, really sorry but something big has come up that I need to deal with. Are you OK if I don't come down this week? Xx

I'm not expecting a reply, as he likes to lie in when he's on holiday, but he's obviously awake, as the two ticks turn blue almost immediately and I can see that he's typing. Sure enough, a few seconds later, his reply arrives.

R U OK?

Yes, fine. I'll explain everything when I see you next. Sorry about this. Hope you're having a nice time.

NP. CUL8R

Paul's never been exactly verbose, either in speech or text, but his responses are even shorter than usual. Normally, I'd start worrying about why this might be and whether I've upset him in some way, but I don't have mental space for that today. I put my mug and plate in the dishwasher and head off to the bathroom. I wash and condition my hair in the shower, before meticulously blow-drying it and brushing it until it falls in soft waves down my back. I pay similar attention to my make-up, before giving myself a spritz of scent and putting on my smartest work suit.

Katie is still sitting at the kitchen table in her pyjamas chatting to Nan when I walk in.

'Is that what you're wearing?' she asks.

'Yes, why?'

'Nothing, it's just a bit...'

'A bit what?'

'Well, we're only going to a café. You look like you're dressed for a convention.'

'Too much, you mean?'

'It's up to you, but we're supposed to be going in there undercover to begin with, aren't we? I think you might stand out a little in that.'

'Fair point. I was power dressing to give myself a bit of confidence, but you're right. It's way over the top for a greasy spoon café. I'll be back.'

Katie follows me to my bedroom, where I spend nearly half an hour rummaging through my wardrobe trying to find a combination that says 'don't mess with me', but which also looks casual enough that it won't stand out during our undercover visit. She sits on the bed and offers comments on each one.

'That's the one!' she exclaims, as I'm standing in front of the mirror in a red and white checked shirt and a pair of figure-hugging blue jeans.

'Are you sure?' I reply. 'Don't you think it's a bit *Calamity Jane*?'

'No, it's perfect. You look casual but also confident. I'll help you put your hair up, if you like.'

'But I've just washed and blow-dried it!'

'Okay, it's up to you, but I was just thinking it would look more professional up. I could do you a nice chignon.'

I look in the mirror again, and I have to agree. Despite the fact that my hair is looking as good as I can make it, it probably would look better up. When did my seventeen-year-old sister get so wise, I wonder? Obediently, I sit down and let her get to work.

'There,' she professes a few minutes later. 'What do you think of that?'

I turn my head from side to side; it looks good.

She smiles. 'Stick your FMBs underneath, and the look will be complete.'

'FMBs?' I ask.

'Fuck-me boots. Sorry, another rugby boy term,' she explains when she sees my eyebrows shoot up.

'Are you sure there isn't anything you need to tell me? You seem to be very close to the rugby team, from all these fascinating expressions you've learned.'

'It's nothing like that. I think I'm invisible to them, so they don't bother to moderate their language when I'm around. I don't mind. It just highlights how tragic they are. I pretty much know their opinion of every girl in our year, plus all their slang phrases. It might come in useful one day, you never know.'

'Only if you accidentally get transported back in time and find you need to be able to speak Neanderthal,' I tell her with a smile. 'Don't you need to get yourself ready? We ought to leave soon.'

'I haven't got much to do. I'll have a quick shower, bung on a pair of jeans and a shirt. I'm just the sidekick today, after all.'

* * *

As we step out of Sevenoaks station, I pull out my phone to try to work out how to get to the café, and I'm pleasantly surprised to see that it's just a little way up the road. Sure enough, a couple of minutes later, Katie and I find ourselves standing in front of the parade of shops that I remember from yesterday. The café looks only marginally more inviting with the lights on, and I can see through the window that only a couple of the tables are occupied.

'Whoever did the signwriting needs a spelling lesson,' Katie observes.

I didn't notice the writing on the windows yesterday, but I look at it now and can see her point. Large letters promote the 'All Day Breakfast's' and, slightly more worryingly, 'Traditional Roast Diner's'.

As we push open the door, the first thing I notice is the smell of stale fat. It's not strong, but it's enough to be off-putting. There's nobody behind the counter, so we settle ourselves at a table and peruse the menu, which is also littered with spelling mistakes.

'I think I might have a bacon roll and a cup of tea,' Katie remarks. 'What about you?'

'Sausage roll and a coffee, I think. How do you suppose we order?'

I look up and see a large, late middle-aged woman standing behind the counter with her arms folded and a disdainful expression on her face. I'm certain she's the person I spoke to on the phone earlier. I know she's seen us, but she's making no attempt to come over, so I ease myself out of my chair and approach the counter.

'What can I get you?' she asks, in a bored voice.

I give her our order, which she writes down on a small pad

before ringing everything up on an ancient-looking till. I extract my debit card from my purse to pay.

'Eight pounds twenty. We don't take cards,' she says, as if I've tried to pay with buttons. I put the card back and hand over a £10 note.

'Have you got 20p?' she asks.

'No, sorry.'

She sighs dramatically as she counts out my change, which she places on the counter, before turning and slowly waddling off to the kitchen with the order.

'I *really* don't like her,' I say to Katie, when I get back to the table.

'It'll be interesting to see how her attitude changes when she finds out who we are,' she replies.

'Assuming it does change.'

A few minutes later, the woman appears at our table with a couple of mugs and some cutlery, which she plonks down unceremoniously. Without a word, she turns her back and wanders over to clear one of the other tables.

'Unbelievable,' I mutter, causing Katie to snort with laughter.

It takes us a little while to work out which is the tea and which is the coffee. Neither of them appear to smell of anything, they're both the same colour, and neither of them appear to taste of very much either. Eventually we decide that the one that tastes like dishwater must be the tea, and therefore the other one must be the coffee.

'This is obviously instant, and it's either so cheap that it has no flavour, or they've been incredibly stingy with it. Bit of a cheek to charge one pound seventy for this,' I observe, after a few sips of the scalding liquid. 'How's yours?'

'Yeah, not good. I was expecting a proper strong builder's tea, you know? This is pretty horrible, and the mug feels a bit greasy.'

Our restaurant review is cut short by the reappearance of the woman, this time holding two plates.

'Bacon roll?' she sniffs.

'That's me,' Katie replies, and the woman dumps the plate in front of her.

'Yours must be the sausage, then,' she remarks, placing the other plate in front of me. 'Sauces are on the table. Help yourself.'

Katie reaches for the brown sauce and lifts up the top of the roll to squirt it on the bacon.

'Oh, bloody hell!' she exclaims. 'There's hardly any bacon here at all!'

I look, and she's right. Two tiny rashers look completely lost in the large bread roll. I lift up the lid of mine and find that I've definitely got the better deal, as it does at least look much better filled. I squirt in some ketchup and take a bite.

'How is it?' Katie asks, as she lifts her roll to her mouth.

I wait until I've finished chewing before I reply. 'I'm not sure any vegans would be troubled by the sausages, as I'm pretty sure there's no meat in them. If there is, I can't taste it. This ketchup is horrible too; it's weirdly sweet to begin with, and then you just taste vinegar.'

In the end, neither of us finish our drinks or rolls. Katie picks the bacon out of hers and eats it on its own, and I take a couple more mouthfuls of the sausage bap before I give up.

'Sod this,' I tell her. 'Let's go and get a decent cup of something and a piece of cake. I think we're going to need all our strength later, and this is just depressing me.'

'Good idea,' she replies, and we beat a hasty retreat, leaving the half-finished food and drink behind us.

We end up back at the coffee shop I went to yesterday, and we both groan with pleasure as we sip our drinks and bite into the cakes. The contrast couldn't be starker, and I find myself feeling increasingly angry with Nora's Diner. I'm no longer surprised that the takings are so pitiful, I'm amazed that there are any takings at all.

'I'm seriously wondering whether we might be better off closing that bloody café right now,' I say to Katie, after we've finished our slices of cake. 'There's so much wrong with it, I don't know where to start. It might actually be easier to sell it on as an empty unit.'

'It was pretty bad,' she agrees.

'And that woman! I don't think I've ever met anyone so unbelievably rude. She's in for a shock, I can tell you.'

'What are you going to do?'

'Well, if we close the café then I guess she's not my problem. If we decide to keep trading while we look for a buyer, then I'm not sure. I probably can't fire her, as I expect there are procedures you have to go through with verbal and written warnings and so on. Plus, if she's the only person besides the chef who works in there, that will leave us with a staff shortage. She can't carry on the way she is, though, that's for sure. If the food and drink aren't bad enough to put you off, she certainly is.'

I'm surprised by the strength of my feelings. I have no interest in owning this café whatsoever but, even though none of its failings are even remotely my fault, I somehow feel responsible. As I consider this unwelcome turn of events, I realise that I'm going to have to try to fix the worst of the issues before I sell it, because it's going to be almost impossible to find a buyer for it as it is. The quality of the tea and the coffee should be relatively easy to fix, as should the quality of the ingredients they're using. I can't believe it would make a significant dent in the non-existent profit margin to have slightly nicer bacon that didn't shrink to nothing when you cooked it, as well as sausages that actually tasted of something. I have no idea what I'm going to do about the woman behind the counter, though. I'm not sure anything short of a complete personality transplant will work on her.

I sigh and turn my attention back to Katie.

'Right,' I tell her. 'Let's go and see what they've got to say for themselves. Ready?'

'As I'll ever be.'

10

When we reach the café, the 'closed' sign is back in place, but I can see three people sitting at one of the tables as I knock on the door. There's the woman from earlier, a guy who must be Matt the chef, and a girl who looks to be about Katie's age. Matt unlocks the door to let us in and an awkward silence descends as soon as we're over the threshold. I feel a little bit as if I'm in some spaghetti western, where two opposing sides are sizing each other up before a gunfight. The music from *The Good, the Bad and the Ugly* starts playing in my head. It's not even a film I like, but Grandad loves westerns, so we've had to watch a few over the years.

'Hello, you must be Matt,' I say, to break the silence, and my voice sounds artificially bright. 'I'm Daisy, and this is my younger sister, Katie.'

He reaches out his hand and I shake it. He has a nice, firm grip, without it being overpowering. He's younger than I expected him to be. In fact, I reckon he's not much older than me. He has dark hair, kept short in a buzz cut, and his chocolate-brown eyes crinkle at the edges as if he smiles a lot. He's not conventionally handsome – he obviously broke his nose at some point and there is a scar on his left cheek – but he's not unattractive either. He's broad-chested, with strong, muscular arms sticking out of his T-shirt. I'm relieved to see that his expression is quizzical rather than openly hostile. Of course, that will probably change once I've said my piece.

'Welcome to Nora's Diner,' he replies. He turns and indicates the woman I met earlier. 'This is Rita. She's been here for, what, ten years now?'

'Nearly eleven,' Rita replies, with a sniff. She obviously expects me to be either impressed or cowed by her long service. 'I was brought in when Nora became too frail to keep on top of things herself.' She fixes Katie and me with a beady stare, and her voice turns hostile. 'You two were in here earlier. You didn't even eat what you ordered. I had to throw perfectly good food in the bin. What were you doing, spying on us?'

'I'm sure there's an innocent explanation, Rita,' Matt interjects. 'They were probably just trying to get a feel of the place, to help them come up with a plan.'

'Oh, I know their plan,' she continues, disdainfully. 'They're going to sell the café out from underneath us. Why else would they get it valued, eh? I said to my Derek, "They're only interested in getting their hands on the money. We'll all be turfed out and it'll be bought by some awful chain, like everywhere else."'

She really is a piece of work. Every time I think she can't get any ruder, she manages to surprise me. I'm determined to be polite and friendly, but she's making it hard.

'This,' Matt says firmly, indicating the girl and obviously trying to cut Rita off, 'is Bronwyn. She comes in on Saturdays, and also covers for Rita during the week if she can't come in for any reason.'

'My Derek suffers terribly with his gout,' Rita starts again. 'Sometimes he can't even get himself out of bed, and I can't leave him when he's like that.'

This time, I forcibly ignore her and walk over to shake Bronwyn's hand. She is extraordinarily beautiful, with big blue eyes and a scattering of light freckles across her gently turned-up nose. Her mouth is wide, revealing even teeth when she smiles. Her multi-coloured hair is cut short, in a pixie style that really suits her delicate features. She exudes boho, hippie chic, with multiple ear piercings, white T-shirt, dungaree shorts and flowery Dr Martens. A pair of large aviator-style sunglasses is perched on her head.

'Nice to meet you, Bronwyn,' I say. 'How long have you been working here?'

'A couple of years. I started just after my sixteenth birthday. I also work at an art gallery in the centre of town. I'm an artist, and they sometimes sell some of my pictures for me.'

That makes sense. She looks like an artist, I think to myself.

'Would you like to look around?' Matt asks. He's obviously on his best behaviour while he tries to work us out.

'Let's have a chat first, shall we?' I pull out the chair next to Bronwyn and Katie sits next to me. Matt settles himself next to Rita, who stares at the table, pointedly refusing to meet my eyes. Another tense silence descends.

'Okay,' I start. 'I'm going to be perfectly up front with you and tell you that I have no idea about running a café, and I'm still probably as shocked as you are that we're in the position we're in. I scarcely knew my great-uncle, so this inheritance has come as a huge surprise.'

'Doing all right out of it, though, aren't you?' Rita mumbles, just loud enough to ensure that I hear her.

I ignore her and plough on. 'What I do understand are the books. I'm an accountant, so they're bread and butter to me. The stark reality is that this place is barely breaking even. In fact, since Great-Uncle Fred died, it's been making a huge loss, because the firm that the solicitors handling probate appointed to do the books charges a fortune. That's obviously not sustainable.'

'Yeah, yeah,' Rita mumbles again. 'Here comes the flim-flam, to make you feel better about flogging the place out from underneath us so you and your sister can dance off into the sunset with Fred's money and not have to feel guilty about depriving us of our livelihoods.'

I really am on the verge of losing my temper with her, but I know that's what she's trying to goad me into doing, so I bite my tongue and continue.

'You're right, Rita. Selling is one option and, at the moment, it's the most attractive one. I've already told you that I don't know anything about running a café, but I know enough to see that there are some serious flaws with this one.'

I see that I've finally managed to get her attention and rile her, as her head snaps up and her watery blue eyes meet mine. Good.

'What do you mean, flaws?' she asks, and her voice is crackling with hostility.

'I don't want to malign Great-Uncle Fred's memory,' I say, 'but this place is very run down. It needs a lot of money to be spent on it to bring it up to scratch, and that's before we get to the food and drink. I'm sorry to say this, but the tea and coffee we had earlier were revolting, the bacon had cooked away to nothing, and the sausages tasted like cardboard.'

I know my words are harsh, but there's no point in glossing over the problems. I look over at Matt, and I'm surprised to see that he doesn't appear to be offended yet. Rita, on the other hand, looks fit to explode.

'Nobody has ever complained before!' she retorts furiously. 'We can't all afford poncy organic heritage food, or whatever it is that you're used to eating. Some of us have to live in the real world, you know.'

How dare she? She knows absolutely nothing about my life, or what I've been through. I feel hot, angry tears starting to prick behind my eyes, and I swallow hard to keep them at bay. If she thinks she can break me, she is seriously mistaken. I take a moment to regain my composure before I continue.

'I expect they haven't complained because they've voted with their feet and gone somewhere else. This place is literally dying.' I fix her with a stare. I'm so pissed off with her that I don't care how much I upset her any more. 'So here are the options as I see them. We could close the place down now, cut our losses, and run. I could try to fix the worst of the issues in the hope of attracting a buyer who would take it on as it is, or we could plough a hill of Fred's money into it, and probably end up losing it all and having to sell anyway. What would you do, Rita, if you were in our shoes?'

There's a long pause while we stare into each other's eyes. The music from *The Good, the Bad and the Ugly* is playing in my head again. Eventually, she speaks.

'I'd do what Fred would have wanted. I'd save the café, regardless of the cost.'

I realise with horror that she's outplayed me. I have no way to tell if what she's just said is true or not. If it's true, and I don't try to save the café, then I'm probably no better than she thinks I am. I'm wracking my brains to try to come up with a suitable comeback when I realise that Matt is speaking.

'That's not true, though, Rita, is it?' he says, surprisingly firmly. 'Fred didn't give a shit about the café. It was always Nora's dream and, beyond keeping the accounts and periodically telling me to cut costs, he hasn't shown a flicker of interest in it since she died.'

Rita's mouth is opening and closing like a goldfish, but no sound is coming out, and I realise that Matt may be riding to my rescue.

'Tell me more,' I encourage him, partly because I'd like to hear some evidence to disprove Rita's theory, and partly to buy me some time before I have to duel with Rita again.

'Nora loved this place,' Matt explains. 'She poured all her energy into it. When I first started, we had a full menu, including a regular rotation of lunchtime specials, as well as home-made cakes and pastries. She was a stickler for quality, and we had a reputation for the best cooked breakfast you could get in Sevenoaks. It wasn't unusual for there to be a queue outside, waiting for a table to become free. When she died, everything changed. Fred didn't care about quality like she did, he was only interested in the profit margins. He substituted all the ingredients for cheaper alternatives and, of course, people started to drift away. As the revenue fell, he kept cutting the costs, going for cheaper and cheaper stuff. I tried to explain to him that we were driving customers away, but he wouldn't listen. In the end, he just saw it as a burden. It wouldn't have surprised me if he'd put it up for sale himself, if he'd lived much longer.'

'So, what would you do, if you were me?' I ask him.

He thinks for a minute. 'Honestly, I'm not sure. I know there's a lot wrong with this place, and I've come close to handing in my notice a couple of times over the years, but I owe Nora, and I can't do it to the customers. Most of our regulars are elderly, and coming in here for a cup of coffee and a bit of breakfast is the only social contact most of them get. If we close down, some of them will literally have nowhere left to go, and they'll be stuck in their flats, fading away until they die. I'd love to see it restored to how it was in Nora's day. I think she had the right idea, and it was lovely being here when it was busy and thriving. I know it's a risk, but I think I'd try to save it if I had the money. Having said that, I wouldn't blame you if you decided to sell it.'

'Thank you,' I tell him, before turning to Bronwyn. 'And what would you do?'

She laughs. 'Leave me out of this, I'm just the Saturday girl! Listen, I love it here, but I totally get what you're saying. It is a bit of a shithole, but the customers are sweethearts. If you close it down, I'll be okay because Gary, who runs the art gallery, will probably give me more hours.'

'Presumably you'll be off to college at some point anyway, won't you?' I ask her.

'No. I want to build my portfolio and get myself known, rather than wasting three years of my life listening to lectures and writing essays about how other people did it.'

Out of the corner of my eye, I see Katie's jaw drop open. Bronwyn obviously spots it too, as she quickly changes tack.

'Don't get me wrong. I know college is good for lots of people, and loads of jobs are only available if you've been to college or uni. It's just not for me. I've got good GCSEs, so it's always an option for later if my current plan doesn't work out, but I'll never know unless I try it my way first, will I?'

I can't help smiling at Bronwyn's ballsy attitude to life. I hope she succeeds, whatever happens to the café. Silence has descended again, and I'm aware that they're waiting for me to make the next move.

'Okay, thank you all,' I say, getting up. 'We've got a lot to think about, and I need to have a proper conversation with Katie. I promise you that, whatever we decide, we will think hard about everything that's been said today. I'm conscious that I've taken up enough of your time, so I'll let you go.'

Bronwyn smiles widely and wishes us luck, before slipping her sunglasses onto her face and disappearing into the summer sunshine. I feel a massive sense of relief when Rita also gets up and waddles out without any more acerbic remarks. She looks rather deflated by Matt's assessment of the situation, but I feel no pity for her.

I'm no closer to working out what to do about this café, but I'm completely certain about one thing: I really, *really* don't like Rita.

11

'I'm sorry about Rita,' Matt says to me, as soon as it's just the three of us and he's locked the front door again. 'I'm not really sure what got into her this afternoon.'

'Are you going to tell me that she's normally a sweetie with a heart of gold?' I ask, disbelief plain in my voice.

'No. She's always been prickly, but she does normally manage to be a little more tactful than she was just now. She probably just needs to get to know you a bit better.'

'Yeah, but the problem is that she was just as rude when we came in earlier, and she didn't know who Katie and I were then. If she's being rude to customers, then we have a serious issue.'

'I can't help you much there,' he replies. 'I'm always in the kitchen, so I don't see what goes on out the front. Anyway, would you like to have a look round now?'

At that moment, my phone pings with an email from Jonathan Moorhouse. I apologise to Matt and turn away to read it. I skim past the usual pleasantries to the substance, which is that Jonathan has submitted all the paperwork to transfer the directorship of the café to me as promised. His secretary has drafted a letter that I can take to the accountants tomorrow, and I can collect it from reception whenever suits me. He also says that he's sent the forms to the bank, and I just need to call in there to show them ID and sign some documents in front of them to finalise myself as the signatory on the business account. Finally, he informs me that he's transferred a pound to my savings account and will transfer the rest as soon as I confirm receipt. I log into the app on my phone and see that the pound has arrived. I reply quickly to thank him and tell him that I have received it, and that I'll pick up the papers shortly. I glance at the Rolex, which tells me that it's already four o'clock. The bank will close in thirty minutes.

'I would very much like to have a proper look around in here, and also see the flats,' I tell Matt, 'but I've just had an email from the solicitors, and I need to pick some stuff up from them and get to the bank before it shuts. I've got an appointment with the accountants at half past two tomorrow. Would it be okay if I came back after that?'

His brow furrows. 'I normally go to the cash and carry after we close on a Wednesday,' he explains. 'I won't be back until after six, I'm afraid.'

An idea pops into my head and, because I really need to get out of here to avoid missing the bank, I blurt it out without thinking it through properly. 'I tell you what. I can't see the meeting with the accountants taking more than an hour at the most. Why don't I come straight here when I'm done with them, and you and I can go to the cash and carry together, maybe see if we can get some better-quality stuff. Then you can show me around when we get back.'

Matt is silent; I've been too pushy, I realise. 'Sorry,' I backtrack. 'I'm not trying to railroad you, it's just that I'm going back to work on Monday, and I thought it might be an opportunity...'

'I think it's a good idea, actually,' he interrupts. 'You caught me slightly by surprise, but yes. I can show you what I normally buy and what I'd like to buy. Let's do that, if you're sure it works for you.'

'Great. Now, I hate to be rude, but we really have to run. Do you have the keys to Fred's car? I was going to take it with me today.'

'They're up in my flat, but I haven't started Fred's car for a few weeks, as it's out of petrol. I've been meaning to fill the container up and put some more in it, but I haven't got round to it yet. Sorry.'

He can obviously see the frustration on my face, because he continues. 'Look, why don't I run you both up to town in my van? You can get your bits of paper and go to the bank while I fill up the container. Then we can come back, put the fuel in and you can go on your way.'

'Are you sure? I don't want to put you to any trouble.'

I'm lying. I do. He's now my only hope of getting to the bank today. I know it's not the end of the world and I could go in the morning, but I don't want to delay anything more than I have to. If I end up with things being pushed out into next week, they're going to be a lot harder to deal with.

'No problem. Follow me.'

He leads us through the kitchen to the back door, which he holds open for us, and locks carefully once we're all through. We walk down a short corridor to the external door, which opens out into the sunshine. There are two parking spaces behind the café. One is occupied by a very dusty-looking car, presumably Fred's, and the other by a Transit van that has definitely seen better days. I don't know how old it is, but the paintwork is faded and I can see several places where the rust has broken through. The driver's door creaks ominously as Matt tugs it open, and I consider my predicament. I'd rather eat my own fist than travel even a hundred yards in a death trap like Matt's van, but I've stupidly already accepted not just a lift into town today, but a journey to the cash and carry tomorrow. My anxiety levels rise even higher as I open the passenger side door and realise that there are no airbags in front of Katie's and my seats. Matt obviously senses my reticence as he smiles.

'Don't worry. I know it's past its prime, but it's never let me down yet.' To prove his point, he twists the key and the engine bursts into life with a deafening clatter. A small cloud of black smoke billows from the exhaust and blows away in the breeze. Oh, God, I don't think I can do this.

'It's only up the road, it'll be fine,' Katie whispers in my ear. 'Just get in.'

It takes all my courage to scramble into the middle seat of the van, and I'm shaking with nerves as I try to fasten the lap belt. Matt takes pity on me and helps me to get it into the socket. I squeeze my hands together tightly and try to focus on Katie's words. Rationally, I know she's right. The chances of anything happening to us during a five-minute journey in a thirty limit are tiny. That doesn't stop my heart pounding or my palms sweating furiously, though.

Matt reverses the van expertly out of its space and appears thankfully oblivious to my mounting panic as he navigates his way up the hill to the main part of the town. The journey literally takes a couple of minutes, but I feel like I've aged ten years by the time he pulls in opposite Lloyds Bank.

'I'll go and fill the can up and meet you at the solicitors' office,' he says as we clamber out. 'Which one is it?'

'Moorhouse & Edgerley,' I tell him.

'Oh, yes, I know it. See you in a bit.' He roars off, leaving another plume of black smoke behind, and we hurry into the bank. There's no queue at this time of the day, so I go straight up to the counter. Once I've explained why I'm there, the whole process is remarkably efficient. I still have the ID in my bag that I took to show Jonathan, so it only takes a few minutes to fill in the remaining forms. The cashier assures me that everything is now in place.

'One final thing,' I ask her. 'How easy would it be to get a card machine for the café?'

She takes me through the terms and conditions, including the transaction costs, and then helps me fill in the order form. Apparently, the machine should arrive within the week. By the time we've finished, the bank has shut and they have to open the door to let us out. Katie and I half run to the Moorhouse & Edgerley offices, arriving with five minutes to spare.

'Mr Moorhouse has left everything you need here,' the receptionist informs me in her cut-glass accent. 'If you have any issues tomorrow, he asks that you contact him directly, and he will do his best to resolve them for you. He asked me to wish you the best of luck on his behalf.' She smiles.

'That's very kind of him. Please thank him for me.'

Matt is waiting for us as we come out of the solicitors and, once again, I force myself to face my fears as he runs us back down the hill and parks up behind the café. He pulls a dirty-looking green fuel container from the back of the van and sets it down next to Fred's car.

'I'll just grab the keys from the flat. Then we can put this in and you'll be all set. Did you want to come up, or are you happy waiting out here?'

Katie and I agree to wait outside and he disappears back through the door, reappearing a couple of minutes later with the keys. He unlocks Fred's car, removes the filler cap, and pours the contents of the can into the fuel tank.

'There you go,' he says, once he's finished and the filler cap is back in place. 'It's only a gallon, but it will be enough to get you to a petrol station. If you turn left once you hit the main road, there's one a few hundred yards along. One more thing before you go. I've written down my phone number in case you need to get hold of me for any reason. It's probably easier than ringing the café landline and negotiating your way around Rita. Also, if you need to get hold of me out of hours, then this is the best number.'

He hands me a piece of paper with his mobile number on, and I plug it into my phone. I then send him a text to confirm I've done it right, which gives him my number in return. We agree that I'll call him as soon as I'm finished with the accountants tomorrow, and Katie and I climb into Fred's car. Matt tactfully retreats back into his flat, leaving me to try to work out the controls of the Micra without an audience.

'He's really nice, isn't he?' Katie remarks, as I locate reverse gear and carefully back the car out of the space. The windscreen is absolutely filthy, and it takes me a moment or two to locate the button for the washer, so I don't reply immediately. Katie takes my silence as an invitation to continue.

'I mean, Rita's a complete bitch, but I liked both Matt and Bronwyn. Matt, in particular, seems to really care about the place, and he went above and beyond to help us out, didn't he?'

'Mmm,' I reply. I don't disagree with her at all, but I'm concentrating on trying to get the feel of the clutch, brakes and accelerator in the Micra, all of which feel very different from my car. The last thing I want is to stall it or end up bunny-hopping down the road. I wait for a much bigger gap than usual before pulling out and setting off. Matt was right, the needle is registering that there's fuel in there at least, but the warning light is still on, so we pull into the garage and I fill it up. I notice that there's a car wash on site, so I buy a token for that while I'm paying for the fuel. After a bit of delicate manoeuvring to get us from the pump into the car wash, Katie and I sit back as the brushes set about removing all the dirt, bird shit, and dust, revealing smart-looking, dark-blue paintwork.

'So, what did you think of them?' Katie pushes.

'Matt was helpful, I agree, although I have got to find an excuse not to go in that van again. I thought I was going to have a heart attack! There's no way I can travel all the way to the cash and carry and back in it.'

'Where is the cash and carry, do you know?'

'No idea but, wherever it is, it's too far to go in that death trap.'

'Do you think,' she lowers her voice and adopts a soothing tone, 'you might be over-reacting, just a little? I know Mum and Dad's car was a complete banger, but that doesn't mean that every clapped-out car or van is going to end up in a big accident.'

'I know you're right, Katie, but I can't help myself. I just didn't feel safe.'

'Maybe you should go with him tomorrow. De-sensitise yourself a bit, you know?'

'Oh, shut up and work out how to get us home!' I retort, handing her my phone.

While she fiddles with the navigation app, I reflect on the meeting this afternoon. She's right, both Matt and Bronwyn are really nice, and Matt is surprisingly passionate about the café. Our decision just became a whole lot more difficult.

12

Given how much I have on my mind, I'm surprised by how well I sleep, and even more surprised to discover that it's after ten o'clock when I wake up. I suppose it's been pretty intense since we got back from Mallorca. It feels like I've been dealing with the café for weeks, rather than the couple of days it's been in reality.

'I'm telling you, Katie, it would be perfect for you!' Grandad is proclaiming as I pad into the kitchen in search of coffee. I have no idea what he's talking about, but Katie certainly doesn't look very enthusiastic about it. She's avoiding his gaze and concentrating on gathering up the crumbs of toast on her plate with her finger.

'What's up?' I ask.

'Grandad thinks I should have Fred's car. Apparently, he's done all the research, and it has a small engine so should be cheap to insure.'

'It's also practically brand new,' Grandad continues, 'so it has all the latest safety gear, which I know will reassure you, Daisy. It's the perfect little run-around for Katie.'

'He has got a point,' I tell her, after I've taken a couple of seconds to think about it. 'I know you're not that fussed about learning to drive and everything, but it is a life skill, something you should know how to do. If we got it insured and everything for you, and found an instructor, then you could use it for practice between lessons. Grandad could take you out.'

'Oh, could I?' he retorts. 'I thought you might like that privilege.'

'Hardly! I can only just about cope when I'm driving. I'd be useless with a learner.'

Now Grandad is the one looking less than enthusiastic. His brilliant idea has slightly backfired on him, but he knows as well as I do that I'd be hopeless teaching Katie.

'Fine,' Katie sighs, after a long pause. 'I'll have some lessons and we'll see how things go. I'm not making any promises, though.'

* * *

The rest of the morning, once I'm showered and changed, is taken up with sorting out Katie's licence application, filling in the paperwork to transfer Fred's car into her name, and booking her in with a local instructor. This is a major concession from her, as she's always made it clear that she has no interest in learning to drive, so Grandad and I are keen to make sure she's completely boxed in before she has the opportunity to change her mind. The insurance quote is horrific, despite Grandad's assurances, but we press ahead anyway.

I check the app on my phone, and the new balance of my savings account makes me feel slightly queasy. There's no way all that money can stay in there, so I ring the financial adviser that Jonathan recommended and make an appointment to see her on Friday morning. She asks a few questions about what I'm hoping to achieve, which I find difficult to answer because I've never had to think about sums like this before, and promises to put some ideas together for us to look at when we meet.

After a quick sandwich lunch, I'm once again heading to Sevenoaks, this time to meet with the accountants. I've got the paperwork from Jonathan on the passenger seat, and I realise that I'm actually looking forward to this meeting. It turns out that the accountants' offices are quite close to the café so, rather than paying for parking, I swing my car into the little road that leads to the parking spaces at the back. Matt's van is parked in its usual spot, but I'm surprised to find that Fred's space is already occupied by a red hatchback. Thankfully, there is just enough room for me to squeeze my car across the back of the two spaces without it sticking out beyond our car parking area. I bang on the back door of the café a couple of times, but nobody answers, and I realise that Matt probably can't hear me knocking because of the corridor between the back door and the kitchen, so I fish out my mobile and dial his number.

'You're early! I wasn't expecting you to call for another hour and a half,' he says, when he answers.

'I haven't been yet. I'm outside the back door. Can you let me in?'

He hangs up and, a couple of seconds later, the door opens.

'Whose car is that?' I ask, pointing to the red hatchback.

He smiles. 'Guess.'

'Is it Rita's?'

'Got it in one.'

'She's unbelievable! She could at least have asked. Well, I haven't got time to deal with it now. She'll just have to stay there until I'm finished at the accountants. Maybe that will teach her a lesson. Are you okay with me blocking you in?'

'Yes, I'm not going anywhere until you get back. Rita might be a bit put out, though. She likes to leave on the dot of three.'

'She should have thought of that before she helped herself to a space that she has no right to be using then, shouldn't she?'

Matt laughs. 'Do you know, I think she may have met her match in you. This is going to be interesting.'

I glance at my watch. 'It'll have to be interesting later. I've only got five minutes to get there now, so I'd better dash. I'll come straight back down when I'm finished.'

I haven't decided what to do about the journey to the cash and carry yet. I did wonder whether we could take my car, but I have no idea how much stuff Matt normally buys, and whether it would fit in. I really don't fancy another trip in the van. I have toyed with the idea of suggesting that I meet him there, but I realise that won't work now that we're leaving from the same place. He'll think I'm snubbing him, and I don't need any more enemies. Rita is quite enough to be going on with, thank you. I dash through the café and walk the short distance to the accountants. I've dressed for the trip to the cash and carry, so I'm wearing faded jeans, a T-shirt, and a pair of trainers. The receptionist looks me up and down with evident disdain when I arrive.

'Please take a seat. Mr Carter will be with you shortly,' she tells me, once I've explained who I am.

The contrast to the Moorhouse & Edgerley offices couldn't be more pronounced. Not only am I not offered any refreshment, but the chairs are those stackable ones with plastic padding on the seats and the carpet in here is thin and cheap. Whatever they spend their exorbitant fees on, it's not their office environment.

'Miss Jones, how nice to meet you.' Alan Carter is a perfect caricature of how you would imagine an accountant to look if you'd never met one before. He is thin, and his sallow skin looks strangely lifeless. He has washed-out blue eyes behind his gold-rimmed glasses, and he's dressed almost entirely in beige. Even his loafers are beige, I notice. I shake his hand and I'm not at all surprised by the limpness of his grip.

He does at least ask me if I'd like a cup of tea or coffee when we reach the meeting room, but I have no desire to string this out longer than necessary, so I decline and we take our seats.

'Before we start, I have to tell you that I'm only authorised to share any financial records pertaining to Nora's Diner with the appointed director, Mr Moorhouse. What this means is that, while we can have a *theoretical* discussion today about your concerns and the possible way forward, we can't do anything *concrete* without his approval, I'm afraid.' He smiles, obviously happy that he's managed to outmanoeuvre me so swiftly.

'Let me help you with that,' I reply, and hand him the documents from Jonathan. 'As you will see, the directorship of the café has already transferred to me. I'm also the signatory on the bank account. I think that means that we probably can have some fairly *concrete* discussions, don't you?'

I may have landed a blow, but he's not on the ropes yet, that's for sure. He changes tack seamlessly, and his manner is no less patronising than when he started.

'Very well. Mr Moorhouse has obviously been very efficient, as usual. So, on the phone you mentioned that you were unhappy with our fees?'

'I am. Not only do I think they're unnecessarily high for the work that you're doing, but you will know as well as I do that the café was barely breaking even before my great-uncle died. Your fees are threatening to sink it completely.'

'Have you done any research to find out what accountants normally charge for their services?'

'I have, as a matter of fact.' I'm keeping my cards close to my chest. I'm quite enjoying the fact that he obviously thinks I'm a silly young woman; it will make the big reveal all the more satisfying.

'Google is a fickle mistress, Miss Jones. As I explained on the phone, you may be able to find firms who advertise a lower rate than us, but they will either quickly hit you with a raft of hidden charges, so that you actually end up paying more overall, or they will lack our ability to optimise your tax position and you'll end up paying more in duties. If the café is making a loss, then my advice to you would be to address that within the business itself, rather than cutting your ties with us. I hope I've managed to explain why that would certainly be a false economy in the long run.'

'Can I ask a question?'

'Of course, I'm here to help in any way I can.'

'How do you plan to "optimise the tax position" of a small business that's currently making a loss? There isn't exactly any money to hide, is there? Furthermore, the rules governing tax and so on are very clear, so if you're being creative with the numbers in any way, there is substantial risk to me. There's a very fine line indeed between creative accounting and fraud.'

This time I've landed a decent blow. I can see his eyes harden behind his glasses. Bring it on.

'Fraud is not a word we like to use in these offices, Miss Jones,' he replies, and his voice has lost its smugness. There's a bit of an edge to it now. I'm starting to wonder whether their accounting methods are, in fact, on the wrong side of 'creative', but that's not part of the battle I'm here to fight. I decide to close in for the kill instead.

'I've actually found someone who is able to do everything that you can do, at no charge,' I tell him.

The look of surprise that crosses his face is so fleeting that I almost miss it but, to his credit, he's not done yet.

'I assume this person is an acquaintance of yours? Relying on friends is hardly sound business practice, Miss Jones. What if you were to have a falling out, or they found they didn't have time to do your accounts because of other work? I must counsel you against any type of informal relationship. They never end well. At Horn-castle's, we always strive to make sure that every customer knows that they are our top priority.'

That's bullshit, and I know it. I file it away to tell Grace when I get back to work. She'll love it.

'I'm not talking about a friend. I'm going to be doing the books from here.'

'You?' The surprise is unmistakeable now.

'Yes, me. I'm a qualified accountant, so I'm sure you'll agree I have the necessary skills.' This isn't strictly true as I'm an accounting technician rather than an accountant, but I'm given a lot of responsibilities beyond my job role, so I don't feel uncomfortable with the tiny lie.

I've got him. Checkmate. He has nowhere to go, and I can see from his face that he knows it. Time to put him out of his misery.

'If you have no further objections, Mr Carter,' I continue, smiling as sweetly as I can, 'I would like to request that you hand over the books at your earliest convenience, along with your final invoice. I'll take it from here.' I slide a piece of paper with my address on it across the table.

He is a gracious loser, at least, and takes the paper. 'If you're happy to wait until the next banking run is complete, I'll send everything after that. I hope you agree that's a good cut-off point?'

'That sounds perfect. Thank you.'

I almost dance back down the hill to the café. The meeting was so much more fun than it had any right to be. I hope Mr Carter will learn from it, and not dismiss any other young women as readily as he tried to dismiss me. When I walk through the door, I notice that Rita is almost puce with rage. Can this afternoon get any better, I wonder?

'You blocked me in!' she thunders. 'My Derek will be waiting for his tea, but it's going to be late now, because of you.'

Oh no you don't.

'Tell me, Rita,' I ask, keeping my voice light and unconfrontational, 'who gave you permission to park there?'

'Nobody was using it.'

'But you don't have permission to park there,' I repeat, without raising my voice.

'And you do, I suppose!' she counters, aggressively.

'Well, yes. On account of the fact that I own it. You could have done the decent thing and asked me if you could park there, but you didn't. You just helped yourself. I'm sorry about Derek's tea, but you left me no choice. If it happens again, I might have to get someone to clamp you, and that will be much more inconvenient than being delayed by half an hour. Do you understand?'

She's so angry that I'm actually worried she might have some sort of seizure, so I decide to leave it there.

'I'll go and move my car now so you can get home. Don't park there again, okay?'

She's muttering furiously as she follows me out of the back door but, thankfully, I can't make out the words.

13

My exhilaration from the victories against Alan Carter and Rita is short-lived. I now have to face the van again, and I can feel my anxiety levels shooting up as Matt locks up the café and we step back out into the sunshine.

'How far is it to the cash and carry?' I ask him, and I'm embarrassed to hear the quaver in my voice.

'About twenty minutes to half an hour, depending on the traffic. It's just off the A21 in Tunbridge Wells, so it should be a pretty quick sprint down the dual carriageway once we get out of Sevenoaks.'

Fuck. This is much worse than I thought. Just pottering around town in his van was scary enough. Now he wants to take me on the open highway in it? My stress levels are going through the roof, and I'm suddenly aware that my legs have turned completely to jelly and I'm going to collapse if I don't sit down. I plonk myself down at the top of the concrete stairs leading down to the car parking spaces and put my head between my knees. I concentrate hard on keeping my breathing under control; the last thing I need right now is a full-scale panic attack. In the first few years after my parents died, I used to have panic attacks quite regularly, and they terrified both me and those unfortunate enough to be around when I had them. It's something my counsellor and I worked hard on, and I haven't had one for years. I still recognise the warning signs well enough, though.

'Are you okay? Daisy, what's the matter?' Matt's voice sounds far away, even though I'm aware that he's sat down next to me. I can feel his arm against my side, and there's something reassuring about the hardness of the muscle and the warmth of his body. I can feel my anxiety levels starting to creep down but, as they do, I realise that I'm going to have to come up with some sort of explanation for my erratic behaviour. I lift my head slowly and turn to face him.

'Sorry,' I start. 'This is going to sound stupid, but I'm frightened. I don't think I can come in the van with you.'

'I'm not sure I understand. Can you tell me what, specifically, you're frightened of? I know I look rough and ready, but you're quite safe with me, I promise.'

Great. Now he thinks I'm worried that he's going to attack me or something. I need to put him straight on that, at least. I break eye contact and stare straight ahead.

'It's your van,' I whisper.

'My van?' he repeats, incredulously. 'I'm sorry, but I'm going to have to ask you to give me a bit more. I can't think of anything threatening about the old rust bucket.'

'It's because it's an old rust bucket! Look, I know I'm not making much sense here, so let me try to explain. My dad made a point of never paying more than he absolutely had to for a car. If it was under ten years old or had fewer than one hundred thousand miles on the clock, it was too new and shiny for him.'

'He sounds like a sensible guy, if you don't mind me saying so. Cars are a terrible investment.'

'Yes, but it turned out to be the worst kind of false economy. He and my mother were killed in a road accident ten years ago. The car he had at the time was barely roadworthy, and it gave them no protection at all.'

I see the comprehension dawn on him.

'Shit, Daisy, that's awful. I'm so sorry. It makes sense now, though. Because of that, you're worried that my van won't protect you if we have an accident?'

I nod.

'Okay, well, of course I'm not going to force you to come. I'd suggest we take your car, but I've got a lot to get this week, particularly if we're changing some things up, so I need the space. We could take a different route on quieter roads if that helps?'

'Not really, but thanks for trying. At least everyone's going in the same direction on a dual carriageway, aren't they?'

'True. The only other thing I can say is that, although my van looks a bit tatty, it's perfectly sound structurally. However, if you really can't face it, you could follow me in your car if you like? I'm not going to pretend that I wouldn't rather you came with me, because I was hoping to get to know you a bit better on the way, but I don't want to make you uncomfortable. I promise to drive extra carefully if you do come with me, though.'

His kindness is just making everything worse. Of course I'd rather follow behind in my nice, modern Focus with its vast array of safety features and airbags, but I feel like I'd be slapping him in the face. Even though I only met him yesterday, he has really gone out of his way for me, from running us up to the bank to getting fuel for Fred's car. The least I can do in return is try to trust him not to kill me, isn't it? Maybe Katie's right and I need to try to be more rational about this. Statistically, I know we're very unlikely to be involved in an accident between here and Tunbridge Wells, and it's even less likely to be fatal. I can't help how I feel, though, even though I detest how weak it makes me look. A tear of frustration spills out of my eye and runs down my cheek. I take a deep breath and turn to him again.

'I really want to conquer this,' I tell him shakily. 'If you can be patient with a totally neurotic passenger, I would like to try to come with you.'

He beams as he helps me up, and we make our way over to the van together. I'm still very anxious, but the fact that I've been able to explain, and he hasn't ridiculed me, makes me feel a little better. I am still struggling to believe him when he says that it's not the death trap it appears to be, as it looks pretty dangerous to me. I climb into the cab and Matt carefully closes the door behind me, before walking around and opening the driver's door. The creak makes me jump again, but I concentrate on my breathing as he fastens his seatbelt and starts the engine.

As we head out of Sevenoaks, I notice that he's driving much more gingerly than he did yesterday. It's not that he was over-exuberant or anything, I'm simply aware that he's being extra careful today, driving smoothly, braking early and leaving a large gap between us and the car in front. It's working, and I can feel the tightness in my chest start to loosen. When we reach the dual carriageway, the noise levels increase dramatically, but he keeps to the left-hand lane, doing a steady sixty miles an hour.

'Is this okay?' he shouts, trying to make himself heard over the din. 'It will do seventy, just about, but the noise gets much worse and I don't like to stress the engine.'

'Fine!' I shout back, and I realise that I mean it. I don't feel safe, exactly, but his driving style inspires confidence, and I'm no longer terrified in the way that I was back at the café. I'm still hyper-aware of every noise and every other road user around us, but my heart rate is slowing and I'm breathing more easily. I decide to try to strike up a conversation as an extra distraction.

'So, Matt,' I yell. 'What's your story? How long have you worked at Nora's Diner?'

'Twelve years,' he shouts back. 'I was doing a delivery to the photo studio next door when I saw the advert in Nora's window for a chef. I didn't have any qualifications, but I knew a bit about cooking from looking after my mum and working in a pub, so I applied and she took me on. Of course, she realised pretty quickly that I didn't really know what I was doing, but I was keen to learn, and she was incredibly kind, you know? She offered to train me, and quite often we'd be in the kitchen well into the evening, after the café had closed, so she could teach me new recipes and techniques.'

'She sounds like an amazing woman,' I reply.

'She was. In the end, she was more of a mum to me than my own mother has ever been.'

I wait to see if he's going to elaborate and, after a deep breath, he continues.

'I didn't exactly have a privileged upbringing, and I didn't have a lot of prospects when I left school. My mum was an alcoholic, so I had to fend for myself from an early age. The estate in Peterborough where we lived was completely ruled by two gangs and, if you were a boy, you were expected to join one of them as soon as you were old enough. Depending on which gang you belonged to, you were either in the drugs business or the prostitution business. There was a certain amount of trade between the gangs, drugs to keep the girls docile, payment in kind, that kind of thing. It was mad. A couple of the guys from my school were pimping out their own sisters, and one even had his mum on the game. Anyway, I refused to join either of the gangs, which meant they both had it in for me. I'm sure you've noticed the scar on my cheek. That was given to me by a boy who was my best friend in primary school. It soon became pretty obvious that

I couldn't stay at home if I wanted to live, so I ran away to London.

'I didn't have any money, so I was sleeping rough to begin with, but then someone told me about a hostel for homeless people that might take me in. It was pretty basic, but at least I had somewhere I could shower and wash my clothes. I managed to get a job washing up in a pub and, as soon as I had enough money, I bought a van. When I wasn't working, I'd cruise around the streets, looking for skips. You'd be amazed what people throw away. Anyway, I soon had a pretty good bedroom in there. I also started to do a bit of courier work, which is how I found myself in Sevenoaks, reading the ad at Nora's. I didn't tell her that I was living in my van but, a month or so after I started, I forgot to pay for the parking one day and it got towed away. The only way I could get it back was to pay the fine, but all my money was inside the van, so I was in a catch-22 situation. Nora couldn't understand why I was so distraught and, in the end, I had to tell her the truth.'

'What happened next?' I'm so completely wrapped up in his tragic story that I'm no longer focused on my own peril at all.

'She was horrified. She took me to the pound and lent me the money to get the van back, and then demanded that I show her inside. She gave me the keys to the flat the very next day. The deal was that I would pay a tiny rent, but my pay would also be adjusted down to reflect the fact that I was getting very cheap accommodation. That's how it's been ever since. I did think Fred might try to turf me out of the flat when she died. He could have let it to someone else for far more money, but she must have done a number on him, because he never said a word. Ah, here's our turning.'

As he pulls onto the slip road, the noise starts to lessen and I don't have to shout any more. The whole setup with the rent for the flat and his pay is as I thought, and I file that piece of information away.

'I understand your loyalty to the café now, I think. You can't walk away, because you feel indebted to Nora.'

'That's definitely part of it, yes. There are also the customers, and the fact that, despite Fred's penny-pinching, I enjoy my work.'

'One thing still doesn't make sense, though,' I continue. 'I've been completely up front with you from the beginning that I'm probably going to sell Nora's Diner. I'd like to turn it around first if I can, because I think it'll be easier to sell if it's at least making a small profit, but my instinct is very much to offload it. Given that you'll probably lose both your home and your job if I do, why on earth are you being so nice to me?'

14

'Look, I'd obviously prefer it if you didn't sell the café,' Matt tells me, as we cross the car park towards the cash and carry. 'But I know as well as anyone that Fred's cuts have sucked the life out of the place. I still think it can be saved, but it needs someone with Nora's passion, who's willing to take a gamble on it. As you rightly said yesterday, it also needs a lot of money to be spent on it. I honestly don't know what I'd do if I were in your position. It's a risky prospect, I can see that. So, even though it's not what I want, I can't blame you for wanting to sell it.'

'I'd love to wave a magic wand and turn it around, but you're right,' I reply. 'It's just too big a risk for me. Sorry.'

'I get it,' he continues, as he grabs a low trolley that looks like it's escaped from a garden centre. 'All I would say is this. I watched you yesterday when Rita was going for you, and again today when she was arguing about the parking space. You weren't cowed at all by her attempts to bully you. You showed real grit, and that's got to be a key skill for running a business, hasn't it?' He smiles crookedly.

'That woman seems hell-bent on winding me up. Whatever

happens with the café, I don't think she and I are ever going to become friends.'

'Mm. Possibly not.'

Our trip round the cash and carry is a real eye-opener, partly because I've never been anywhere quite like this before, and partly because Matt is showing me the things he normally buys. Everything is from the budget range, irritatingly branded 'SuperValu'. It's not even that much cheaper than the branded stuff. We replace the tea and coffee with branded products straightaway, and I load a couple of trays of bottles of Heinz ketchup and HP sauce onto the trolley as well. We take our time selecting better-quality ingredients to improve the food. Not the most expensive stuff, we both agree the café can't afford that, but a couple of rungs up from the 'SuperValu' crap. I also splash out a bit on cleaning products, as I'm determined to get rid of the horrible sticky feel of the tables, and I suspect the 'SuperValu' products simply aren't up to the job.

'I think we should get some of those air fresheners too,' I say to Matt, 'to make the place smell a bit nicer.'

'I'm not sure that would work,' he replies. 'It might be better to attack the problem at the source.'

'Go on.'

'The reason the smell is there is because Fred never let me change the oil in the fryer as often as I should. Cooking oil breaks down over time, and that's when it starts to smell. If I could change it more often, I reckon the smell would go away. Also, it would definitely improve the flavour of the food.'

'Okay, let's do that then,' I tell him, and he walks away to get more oil. I slip a tray of air fresheners onto the pile anyway, just in case.

The trolley is groaning with stuff as we drag it back to the van. I help Matt load up, and then climb in. Having survived the drive here, I'm feeling a bit calmer about the return journey. In fact, I'd say I'm doing pretty well until Matt has to brake sharply to avoid hitting someone who pulls out in front of him without looking. Instantly, I'm back on full alert and grabbing for anything I can find to hold on to. I'm so rigid that my legs soon begin to shake from the tension.

'Are you okay?' Matt asks. I grit my teeth and nod, and we spend the rest of the journey in silence. Matt is lost in thought, and I'm just trying to keep myself calm, while offering up all sorts of bargaining prayers about how I promise to be a better person if I can just get back to the café alive. When we arrive, I scramble out as fast as I can, but my legs are still a bit shaky, so I have to stand and lean against the van for a few moments. Matt unlocks the back door and starts carrying our haul inside.

'I think you could do with something sweet,' he announces, once we've carried everything in and he's locked up. 'Why don't you come up to the flat and I'll make you a hot chocolate before you head off?'

'That sounds lovely,' I reply, 'but there's no need for me to come up. We just bought hot chocolate for the café. I'm sure a mug of that will do the trick.' In truth, I feel a bit awkward about going into his personal space.

Matt wrinkles his nose in distaste. 'That's instant, though. Mine is the good stuff, trust me.' His crooked smile reappears.

I think for a moment. He's trying to be kind again, I know, and I probably ought to have a look at his flat at some point, given that I now own it. I return his smile.

'Go on, then. Lead the way.'

Matt's flat is not at all what I expected. I can see what Jonathan meant when he said that the flats were in need of modernisation; the kitchen units are ancient, the carpets are threadbare, there appears to be no double glazing, and there is Artex everywhere. I'm amused to spot that even the light switches have little Artex surrounds. What surprises me is how clean it is. It may be shabby, but there isn't a speck of dust to be seen anywhere. Every surface is spotless.

'Make yourself at home, I won't be long,' he instructs as he disappears into the kitchen, so I try to settle myself on the sofa. I think most of the springs must have gone, as I sink so far into it that my bum is practically on the floor, and I suspect I might be stuck. In the end, after a lot of wriggling, I manage to pull myself out and sort of perch on the edge. The only problem is that I've obviously pressed on my bladder during the contortions I went through to free myself, and I now need to wee.

'Can I use your toilet?' I call.

'Sure, help yourself.'

The bathroom is hideous. The bath, sink, and toilet are bright pink, and the tiles are light grey with gold swirls and pink flowers. There's an electric shower over the bath that looks depressingly like the one in Paul's flat, and I find myself wondering if it's similarly ineffective. Matt is very well-built, so it would take him ages to wash himself if his shower was as bad as Paul's. An image of Matt in the shower pops into my head and I force it out again as fast as I can. That's a complication I definitely don't need.

'Here you go.' I'm perched back on the sofa as Matt appears with two steaming mugs and hands one to me. 'This will cure anything.'

I have to admit that it smells good and, when I take a sip, the flavours are intense. It's hot chocolate, but on steroids. I suspect the calorie count is enough to make any dietician faint, but it tastes incredible.

'The good stuff, right?' Matt is watching me and smiling. I meet his eyes over the rim of my mug and nod.

'The secret,' he continues, 'is that I've melted real chocolate into the milk instead of using powder, and I've added a little bit of cream to make it extra luxurious.'

'It's amazing,' I tell him.

'I can't take the credit, I'm afraid. It's Nora's recipe. She used to make vats of it, and it was one of our best sellers.'

'I take it Fred axed it?'

'One of the first things to go. The dark chocolate Nora used was expensive so, even though we made a healthy profit on each cup we sold, he took it off and replaced it with the powdered stuff.'

'Hm. It would be a good thing to reinstate, wouldn't it? I don't think I've ever tasted hot chocolate as delicious as this before.'

'I think so. We used to offer it with marshmallows and squirty cream as well, but I think it's best on its own like this.'

I look at him as the realisation of what he's up to dawns on me.

'Matt, are you doing a number on me?'

His eyes widen and he holds out his hands in mock innocence. 'I'm sure I don't know what you mean!'

'Yes, you do. You're gently trying to push the image of what the café was like in Nora's day, selling me her vision, in the hope that I'll get drawn in and decide not to sell.'

'You can't blame a guy for trying!'

I don't know whether to laugh or be annoyed with him. I take another sip of the hot chocolate. God, it's good, there's no denying it.

'Can I ask you one more favour?' he continues. I look at him warily. Now I know what his agenda is, I'm on my guard.

'Go on.'

'If you're free tomorrow morning, why not come in and meet some of the regulars? Rita's got a doctor's appointment or something, so you won't have to deal with her. It'll be the first time we serve the new stuff we bought, so it'll be interesting to see if anyone notices.'

'I'm not sure that's a good idea,' I reply. 'I think you're trying to get me to look at the café as if it's some one-eyed rescue dog that nobody else wants because it's ugly, and I'll end up feeling sorry for it and adopting it.'

'Okay, no pressure. I just thought it might help to give you a better flavour of the place than you got when you first visited.'

I drain the remains of my hot chocolate and stand up. 'Thank you for this. I ought to be heading off now. I'm just going to take a quick look at Fred's flat before I go.'

'Would you like me to come with you?'

'On one condition. No more tricks!' He laughs, takes my mug from me and follows me back downstairs and outside.

'The entrance to Fred's flat is at the front,' Matt explains, as he leads me through a dark passageway between two of the other units. We emerge at the front of the building, and he shows me which key to use to open the external door. Once we're inside, a staircase leads up to a small landing with a door on either side. He indicates the door on the right and once again shows me which key I need. The flat is dark inside, mainly because all the curtains are closed. It smells musty and stale.

I draw the curtains to let in the light, and the sight that greets me is depressing, to say the least. Unlike Matt's spotless flat, this one looks like it hasn't been cleaned in an age. Every surface has a thick covering of dust, and there is stuff everywhere, on the surfaces and piled on the floor. I pick my way through to the kitchen, which is the same as Matt's, only filthy. The bathroom is worse, with thick black rings around the bath, and I can't even describe the state of the toilet. It's no wonder the café was allowed to deteriorate, if this is how Fred was living.

'Fred was a bit of a hoarder,' Matt explains. 'I think it might have been a grief thing. He wasn't very sociable when Nora was alive, but he pretty much became a hermit once she was gone.

He'd drive to the supermarket once a week, and to the chemist to collect his prescriptions, but apart from that he stayed holed up in here. I think he used to spend a lot of time on eBay, mainly buying stuff that he thought would become a collector's item one day. I used to come up here once a week so he could go through the takings with me, and I think I was his only social contact most weeks. There would be something new in here pretty much every time I came, although it was always junk. The only decent thing I ever remember him owning was a Rolex, which Nora bought him not long before she died. It's probably in here somewhere, but goodness knows where.'

'I've got it,' I tell him, and show him my wrist.

'He got himself in such a flap about that. She bought it online and he was convinced that she'd been done over and it was a fake. In a funny way it was good, because it made him go out. He had to go all the way to Bluewater to get it authenticated, and he was happier than I'd seen him in ages when he found out it was kosher.'

I look around me. There's just so much stuff everywhere I wouldn't know where to start. There might be other things of value in here, but I doubt very much that I'd have a clue what they were.

'Can I make a suggestion?' Matt asks.

'Go on.'

'If I were you, I'd get the house clearance people in here to take everything away, and then get some cleaners in. You could be going through this stuff for years and not find anything useful.'

I sigh and turn to leave. As I do, a large book with a floral cover in one of the bookshelves catches my eye. I pull it out and discover that it's not a book, but a binder. I open it and find pages and pages of recipes inside. Some are handwritten, while others have obviously been cut out of magazines. Many of them are annotated, in a neat cursive script. I hand it to Matt, who whistles as he turns the pages.

'I didn't even know this existed,' he breathes. 'I'd recognise that handwriting anywhere, though. This is the motherlode, Daisy. This is Nora's recipe book! It's almost as if she wanted you to find it.'

Oh, great. On top of Matt's thinly concealed sales pitch earlier, I'm now up against a ghost. Thankfully, I don't believe in any of that woo-woo nonsense. If any of it was real, I'm sure Mum and Dad would have found a way to contact me by now, wouldn't they?

My bigger problem, I realise, is that I am going to have to go through everything in this flat to make sure I don't miss anything else.

15

I'm up ridiculously early for my shift at the café. I wasn't going to do it, but Nan, Grandad, and Katie all thought Matt was right that I should get a feel for the place in order to be able to decide what best to do with it, so in the end I'd texted Matt and said I'd come after all. He'd texted back to say that they opened at 7.30 a.m., but he would be there from just before 7.

'I assume you're coming too? After all, it's half yours,' I'd said to Katie, before sending the confirmation text to Matt.

'Nah,' she'd smiled. 'You can tell me about it. I trust your judgement.'

Sometimes, I wonder how we manage to stay as close as we are. I could happily smother her with a pillow, I think, as I pad down the dark corridor to the shower. I'm supposed to be on holiday, relaxing before going back to work on Monday, not stumbling about before six o'clock in the morning getting ready for an unpaid shift at a shitty café. I'm tempted to wake her up anyway, just so she knows what it's like, but decide to bank the injustice for future use instead. Her time will come.

At least the car parking space behind the café is empty this time, and I park next to Matt's van at a quarter past seven. The back door is open, and I wander into the kitchen to find Matt hard at work already, a chef's bandanna fastened around his head.

'Morning,' I say, sounding surlier than I ought to.

'Hi! I'm just prepping. I've put fresh oil in the fryer, and I've got some of the new sausages under the grill. Can you do me a favour and keep an eye on that thermometer there? When it gets to one hundred and eighty degrees, we need to turn it off unless we're actually cooking.'

He indicates a large thermometer sticking out of the oil in the fryer.

'Doesn't it have a built-in thermostat?' I ask.

'It does, but it's broken. I tried to get a replacement, but the fryer is so old that nobody makes the parts any more, and Fred said we couldn't afford a new fryer. So, I get it up to temperature using the thermometer and then turn it off until I need it. It retains the heat pretty well, so it usually only needs a minute or so before it's ready again.'

'That's a massive fire risk, isn't it?' I remember going to a fair once, where the Fire Brigade were doing demonstrations of kitchen fat fires. The speed at which the oil went from merely smoking to burning, and the intensity of the flames, have haunted me ever since.

'Only if you forget to keep an eye on it. Oh, by the way, if you're going to be in here, you need to cover your hair. I think there are some hair nets in the cupboard, hang on.'

He disappears into the storage cupboard and reappears holding one of those hideous nets that the dinner ladies at my school used to wear. Today is just getting better and better, I think, as I ram it onto my head and tuck my hair up inside it.

'How much is a new fryer?' I ask.

'I'm not sure, a couple of thousand, something like that.'

'Okay. We'll order one today. There's no way the whole place is burning to the ground on my watch. Are there any other dangerous appliances in here that I should know about?'

'I don't think so. It's all pretty old, but Nora bought high-quality stuff, so it's built to last.'

I check the thermometer, which is reading 120 degrees, so I risk diverting my attention for a moment to look around the kitchen. It's exactly like Matt's flat; I can see that the appliances are old, but everything is spotless. I run my finger over one of the worktops and there's not a hint of stickiness. Something doesn't make sense.

'How come it's so much cleaner in here than it is out there?' I ask.

'Ah, yes. Small confession. I've been buying my own cleaning products for the kitchen. The stuff Fred made us use was hopeless. Also, I'm not sure that Rita is the most enthusiastic cleaner, if you know what I mean. Bronwyn does her best, but it's a bit of a losing battle out there. Hopefully, the stuff we bought yesterday will help to turn things around.'

So, Rita doesn't like cleaning either. Does she do anything at all besides annoy customers, I wonder?

I return my attention to the fryer just as Bronwyn clomps through the door. She's wearing a scarf on her head and a red dress with white polka dots. If it wasn't for her multicoloured hair poking out under the scarf, the huge hoop earrings, and the black Doc Martens, she'd look like a fifties housewife. It's an odd ensemble, but she carries it off with aplomb.

'Morning, Matty!' she says brightly, planting a huge smacker of a kiss on his cheek and leaving a bright red lipstick mark, before she notices me. 'Oh, hello! I didn't know you were coming in.'

'Daisy's come in to get a feel of the place and meet a few of the regulars,' Matt tells her. 'You'll show her the ropes and introduce her to some people, won't you?'

Bronwyn beams. 'Of course! It'll be fun to have someone to keep me company. Anyone for tea or coffee?'

'I'll have a tea,' says Matt. 'There's a new box of PG Tips out there and a tub of Kenco granules. I've chucked the old stuff.'

'About bloody time, sorry, Daisy,' Bronwyn replies. 'That SuperValu stuff was disgusting. Even Harold didn't like it, and I'm not sure he has any working taste buds left!'

I can't help smiling. Bronwyn is just as unfiltered as Rita but, where Rita is sour-faced and miserable, Bronwyn exudes life and enthusiasm.

'What about you, Daisy? Tea or coffee?'

'I'll try the new coffee, please,' I reply. The thermometer has reached 170 degrees, so I focus my attention back on the fryer as Bronwyn carries on into the café, switching on the lights as she goes.

As the fryer temperature inches the last few degrees towards 180, I wonder about the relationship between Bronwyn and Matt. They don't seem a very likely couple, but he didn't seem surprised by her kiss, although I notice he's now rubbing the lipstick off with a piece of kitchen towel.

'Don't read anything into that,' he tells me, as he throws the piece of kitchen towel in the bin. 'She's not my type, and I'm definitely not hers. She just does it because she knows it winds me up.'

I try to imagine what Bronwyn's 'type' might be. He's right; she'd probably go for an undernourished, artistic guy, possibly with round wire-framed glasses and a goatee beard.

'Okay. Your fryer is all set, Matty,' I snigger, as I turn it off.

'Don't you bloody start! She does that to wind me up as well. Matt is fine, thank you.'

Bronwyn reappears with three steaming mugs. I notice she's

put an apron on over her dress. It's worn and fraying at the seams, but it is clean at least. It has 'Nora's Diner' embroidered on it and a deep pocket at the front, which I imagine would be useful for carrying an order pad and pen. I don't remember Rita wearing one when we came in before.

The coffee is a huge improvement, but still not quite right.

'Bronwyn, can I ask how much coffee you put in the mug?'

'Half a teaspoon. That's what we've always been told to do.'

'Go mad, will you, and put another half in, please?'

When she brings it back and I have another sip, the difference is palpable. For the first time ever, I'm drinking something that tastes like coffee in this place.

'So, new rule,' I announce. 'From now on, we put a full teaspoon of coffee in the mug, okay?'

We're interrupted by the ding of the bell over the door, indicating the first customer of the day. Bronwyn disappears into the café and soon reappears with an order for two full English breakfasts. Matt sets about the cooking, leaving me feeling a little like a spare part.

'I can't really let you cook anything, unless you have a food hygiene certificate tucked away somewhere that you've never mentioned,' he explains. 'You're welcome to take the hairnet off and go and help Bronwyn, if you like.'

Although there are only two people in the café, a couple of workmen in hi-vis jackets obviously loading up on carbs and protein before starting their day, the atmosphere in here is already different. Bronwyn is busily attacking the tables with the new cleaning products and her energy seems to be permeating the place. I decide to follow her round, helping her to wipe down the tables, removing the old ketchup bottles and replacing them with the branded ones that we bought at the cash and carry.

'Can we have a couple of those on our table, love?' one of the workmen calls.

'Of course you can, here you go.' Normally, I'd tear someone off a strip for calling me 'love' like that, but in here it seems inoffensive, somehow.

'Have you checked there isn't a seal under the cap?' Bronwyn asks. 'The ones we buy at home always have a seal, and they're buggers to get off.'

I check, and she's right so, after sorting the workmen's bottles out, I retrace my steps and remove the seals from all the other bottles. It's a messy job, and my hands are soon sticky with ketchup.

'There's a sink in the corner at the back if you want to wash your hands,' Bronwyn explains, and I scurry over to it just as a bell pings in the kitchen. Bronwyn clomps in and brings out two fully laden plates. After my experience with the bacon roll, I'm surprised by how generous the full English breakfast looks.

'There you go, gents. Is there anything else I can get for you? No? Okay, enjoy.' Rita could really do with taking customer service training from Bronwyn, I think to myself.

It's fair to say that there is no morning rush. A steady trickle of customers comes and goes, and Bronwyn is chirpy and welcoming to them all.

'How come you don't go and take their orders at the table? Why do they have to come up to the counter to order?' I ask her at one point.

'It goes back to before I was here. As I understand it, when Fred first started making cuts, a few people left without paying, as a protest. So, he changed the system to make them come up to the counter to order, and we take their money up front. I don't think people mind, to be honest, as long as they understand the system. It also means they can leave as soon as they're finished, rather than waiting around to pay. Some people like that. We get the most aggro from people who want to pay by card because we only take cash.'

'I've ordered a card machine, it should be here within a week,' I tell her.

'Oh, that's fab! It will make such a difference with walk-in clients. The regulars, they know the system, but the walk-ins don't half make a fuss, and some of them walk straight out again. Mind you, I'm not sure how Rita will react to it. She doesn't like change.'

'She'll just have to adapt, won't she?'

Our conversation is cut short by the arrival of an elderly gentleman. I say elderly, he's probably mid-seventies. He has thick white hair and a copy of the *Metro* newspaper tucked under his arm.

'This is Ron. He's one of our regulars,' Bronwyn explains. 'Ron, this is Daisy. She's the new owner.'

'Hello, Daisy.' His voice is strong, and he smiles. 'You've got your work cut out here, I imagine.'

'There's a fair amount to do, yes,' I reply. 'But I want to try to turn things around if I can.'

'Good girl. Would you do an old man a favour, though?'

'What's that?' I ask.

'Don't go all modern and trendy, like the places in town. I can't bear them, with their unpronounceable coffees and hordes of young women twittering away like budgies while their babies scream the place down.'

Okay, not what I was expecting. As I've just met him, I decide to give him the benefit of the doubt for now. He is a paying customer, after all, no matter how offensive and sexist his views.

'Your usual, Ron?' Bronwyn asks, probably to divert the conversation onto safer ground.

'You're an angel, Bronwyn,' Ron replies, pulling a £5 note out of his wallet and handing it to her, before wandering off and settling himself at a table in the corner.

'He comes in every morning at exactly the same time. Has a bacon roll and a cup of coffee while he reads the paper,' Bronwyn tells me as she counts out his change.

As we move through the morning, various other elderly people come and go. I meet Agnes, who always sits at the table next to Ron's, even though they never actually speak to each other, according to Bronwyn. She has a single poached egg on toast every day. Harold has an egg and bacon roll with a cup of tea. I watch, transfixed, as he adds a hefty dollop of brown sauce.

'That's got to be a weird combination, right?' I say to Bronwyn. 'Egg and brown sauce? Not sure it's for me.'

'I told you,' she replies. 'Taste buds obviously shot to pieces.'

* * *

By the time we close up at three o'clock, I'm exhausted. It's not that it's been busy, but I'm unused to being on my feet for such a long time and my back is aching. We've had a few comments about the changes, all positive, and I'm surprised how much I've enjoyed myself. I did have a conversation with Matt in one of the lulls about whether the new ingredients meant that we'd have to put the prices up, but he informed me that Fred had never lowered them even when he'd substituted cheaper ingredients, so he reckoned there should still be a healthy margin. I'll have to do some analysis at some point to see if he's right. We've also ordered a new fryer, which will apparently be delivered tomorrow. It wasn't cheap, but there's no point cutting corners with these things.

As I drive home, a long hot bath firmly on my mind, I reflect on the day. Bronwyn was a lot of fun to work with, and she and Matt make a good team. It's just a shame about Rita; what on earth am I going to do about her? I've also taken a copy of the menu, so I can work on the spelling mistakes and also give some thought to how we can improve it.

An unwelcome realisation dawns on me as I pull up on the driveway. This bloody café is starting to get under my skin.

16

I resolve to stay away from the café for the rest of the week, partly because I do actually need to try to relax a bit before I go back to work, and partly because I don't want to get any more attached to it than I already am. I deliberately park in the public car park when I return to Sevenoaks for my meeting with the financial adviser, even though I know I could save a fortune by parking behind the café. It's probably for the best. If I went down there and found that Rita had parked there again, there's a good chance I'd slap her.

The meeting with the financial adviser goes well; I can see why Jonathan recommended her. She's done her homework and, in the end, we agree that I'll hang on to £50,000 as 'petty cash', so I can make improvements to the café and flats, and the rest will be invested in various funds, thus ensuring that any risk is nicely spread out.

Nan and Grandad have very kindly offered to help me with clearing out Fred's flat, and I've ordered a skip to be delivered next week. It's going to be hard work, and part of me still thinks getting a house clearance firm in would be a lot less hassle, but I can't risk anything important being thrown away. I've had a flick through Nora's recipe folder, and a lot of the recipes sound absolutely delicious. I can see why the café used to be so popular, if she was churning out food like that. How sad she'd be to see the state it's in now.

It's a fairly normal afternoon at home. Nan is settled in her armchair, working her way through the recipe folder. Every so often, she sucks her teeth and mutters things like 'my, that is a lot of butter', but I notice she's also earmarking a few recipes to try out. Grandad is watching the cricket on TV, and Katie is reading a thriller with her legs tucked up underneath her. Normally, I'd be reading a magazine or something, but instead I'm trying very hard not to think about the café and failing miserably.

Katie raises her eyes from her book and I'm aware of her studying me.

'What's on your mind?' she asks.

'I was just thinking how sad Nora would be to see the state her café is in,' I reply.

'Do you think Fred resented her for it? Let it go downhill deliberately, to punish her?' Nan joins in, lifting her eyes briefly from the recipe folder.

'It's an interesting theory. I wondered whether he felt he had to keep it going in her memory, but lost interest in it, particularly when the profits started to fall. I guess we'll never know for sure.'

'You seem a bit more positive about the place since you did your shift there yesterday,' Katie continues. 'What's your current thinking?'

'I really don't know. It felt so different yesterday, with Bronwyn there instead of Rita. Yes, it was still run down, but at least we were serving half-decent coffee, and bacon rolls with visible bacon in them. We had a really good go at the tables too, and they're not sticky any more. And I get what Matt means, you know? For a lot of the regulars, coming to the café is the only social contact they get all day, even if they're just doing the crossword, like Ron. But, on the other hand, there's no way we're ever going to make a decent profit from people like that. Ron spent less than a fiver, but tied up a whole table for nearly an hour.'

'I still say we sell the place as quickly as we can, if that's any help,' she replies.

'Maybe you should do a shift there before you cast your vote, Katie love. It seems like it's given Daisy quite a lot to think about,' Nan suggests.

'Oh, no, I don't think that's necessary...'

'I think that's an excellent idea!' I say, cutting Katie off. 'What are you doing tomorrow?'

'Well, I don't have any plans, but...'

'Why don't I text Matt and say you'll be in to help out, then?'

'No, leave it. It's too short notice. Maybe I'll go in next week sometime.' She's like a fish caught on a line, wriggling furiously to try to get away. It's payback time, and I'm loving it.

'Why put off until next week what you can do tomorrow?' Grandad pipes up, surprising us all, because we didn't think he was paying any attention to the conversation.

'Okay, fine,' Katie huffs. 'I'll go in tomorrow. There's just one thing. Someone's either going to have to drop me at the station or take me there.'

Well done, Daisy. I patently didn't think that one through. That'll be another early start for me then, and so much for staying away from the place. After a couple of seconds, however, the beginnings of a plan start to form. If I've got to get up to get Katie to the café for 7.30 a.m., I could go on to Whitstable afterwards and surprise Paul. I feel a bit guilty about cancelling on him, and a bit of sex might be fun, even if it is of the lacklustre Paul variety. Sevenoaks is pretty close to the M25, so it shouldn't take me much more than an hour on a Saturday. If I arrive just before nine, he'll probably still be in bed, so I could just wriggle out of my clothes and slip in next to him. Hopefully the smell of damp won't have got any worse, as that's a bit of a mood killer. I'll take some scent with me, give the place a bit of a spray.

'Okay,' I announce, feeling pleased with myself. 'I'll text Matt and tell him to expect you, and I'll drop you off as well. I'm going to go on to Whitstable for the rest of the day, though, so you'll have to get the train back.'

'If you phone me to let me know when you're arriving at Paddock Wood, I'll pick you up,' Grandad volunteers.

Katie looks mutinous, but nods.

* * *

Our journey to Sevenoaks in the morning is largely silent. I'm not sure whether Katie's sulking, or whether the shock of getting up so early has rendered her speechless. I deliver her to the café, and Bronwyn promptly whisks her away to help make the teas and coffees before it opens. I originally intended to leave straightaway, but I end up accepting the offer of a coffee, ramming the unattractive hair net on while I chat with Matt. I notice the new fryer has arrived, and he's already installed it. The old one has been relegated to a corner.

'I've ordered a skip, mainly for clearing out Fred's flat,' I tell him. 'You can bung the old fryer in it, if you like.'

'Thanks. Saves me a trip to the tip. By the way, the card reader arrived yesterday,' he informs me. 'Bronwyn's going to try to set it up this morning.'

'It looks pretty simple,' Bronwyn adds, as she and Katie return with four steaming mugs. 'There are also some stickers that we can put in the window and on the till, to let people know that we take cards now. I'll get those up as well, once I've got the machine connected and working.'

'Great, thanks, Bronwyn,' I tell her, as I take a sip of my coffee. 'Wow, this doesn't taste too bad!'

'Full teaspoon like you ordered, boss,' she replies, and I see Katie smirk. At least she's not sulking any more.

* * *

In the end, it's closer to 9.30 a.m. by the time I arrive at the caravan park, but I'm relieved to see Paul's car parked next to his mobile home. My plan to slip into bed beside him is thwarted by the fact that the door is locked, so I knock instead and, after a short pause, his face appears in the window.

'Daisy, what are you doing here?' he asks, as he opens the door.

'Aren't you pleased to see me?'

'Of course I am. I'm just, well, I wasn't expecting you. It's not very tidy, I'm afraid.'

'Tell me something I don't know,' I reply, pushing past him.

The smell hits me first. The normal whiff of damp is overlaid with an acidic, sweaty aroma of unwashed bodies, and there's something else too. I think it might be the bin. All the curtains are still drawn and, as my eyes adjust to the gloom, I realise that 'not very tidy' is a serious understatement. It's a pigsty. There are open boxes with half-eaten pizzas still inside, empty beer bottles littering every surface and, in the centre of the room, Paul's PlayStation 5, with wires snaking into the TV like some kind of electronic umbilical cord. Any sexual desire I might have felt has completely evaporated; if anything, the smell is starting to make me feel nauseous.

'What the fuck, Paul?' is all I can manage to say, as I start opening curtains and windows to get some fresh air into this foetid man-pit.

'Yo, Paul! Stick the kettle on if you're up, will you?' a voice I recognise calls from the bedroom.

Paul shrugs his shoulders. 'After you told me you couldn't make it, I invited Dan down instead. We've been having a bit of a *Call of Duty* marathon. It's been pretty cool, actually.'

Dan wanders into the room in his boxer shorts and does a double take when he sees me. 'Oh, hi, Daisy. Paul didn't tell me you were coming. I'd have made myself scarce if I'd known.'

'It was supposed to be a surprise,' I tell him. 'However, the real surprise is that you two appear to have been living like animals.' I glance into the kitchenette and see the overflowing bin, which is surrounded by yet more beer bottles. 'You couldn't even take the sodding bin out? Do you have any idea how bad it smells in here?'

'Calm down, Daisy. I'll get it sorted, don't worry. Would you like a coffee?' Paul grabs a couple of stained mugs off the counter and starts rinsing them out. He's hampered somewhat by the fact that the kitchen sink is overflowing with dirty crockery.

'No, thanks. Actually, I think I'm going to go. This was a mistake.' I grab my bag and head for the door.

'Don't leave on my account,' Dan announces. 'Give me ten minutes to get my stuff together, a lift to the station, and I'll be out of your hair. You two lovebirds can have the place to yourselves.'

'That's very kind, Dan,' I reply, 'but all I can see happening here is a shitload of cleaning and getting rid of rubbish, and that's not really what I came down here for. I think I'll leave you guys to it.' I pull open the door and step outside, taking a big lungful of fresh air as I do so.

'I'm really sorry, Daisy.' Paul has followed me out, even though he's only wearing his boxer shorts and a T-shirt. 'If I'd have known you were coming, I would have tidied it up a bit and kicked Dan out.'

'You're right, I should have warned you. Look, I'll see you on Friday, yeah?'

'Yeah.'

What a total bloody waste of time that was, I reflect as I turn out of the caravan park and start heading home. Even though I was probably only inside the mobile home for a few minutes, the stench has attached itself to my clothes, and I have to open the car window to stop myself from gagging. I could really do with a wee, too, but there was no way I was even going to look in the bathroom, so I stop at a service station on the dual carriageway instead.

I'm incredibly pissed off with Paul, but I can't initially put my finger on why. I can't blame him for inviting Dan down when I cancelled on him, nor can I feign surprise that they've had a gaming fest. Paul's always been into computer games, and he was one of the first to get his hands on the PS5 when it was launched. He's never been particularly tidy either, although that did improve a little when he got his own place. There's just something so *immature* about the scene I've just witnessed. If he were still in his teens, it might be funny, but he's not. He's supposed to be an adult, for crying out loud. I want to grab him by the ear, drag him over to Matt's flat and scream, '*This* is how adults are supposed to live, you fucking moron!'

I know I'm being unfair. It's not like this is some new, totally unexpected character trait in Paul. But something has shifted in me, I realise. Matt, Bronwyn, and even horrible Rita are my responsibility for the foreseeable future. I know Bronwyn will be okay whatever happens, and I'm not sure I care whether Rita will or not, but Matt's entire life is tied up in that café. If I get this wrong, he could end up sleeping in his van again. That's a hell of a burden on my shoulders, and I need a partner who can support me, not an immature man-child who can't even tidy up after himself.

17

'You're back early. I thought you said you were going to be away for the day?' Nan remarks as I walk into the kitchen. She's got Nora's folder open on the counter beside her, and a delicious smell is coming from a pot bubbling on the stove.

'Yeah, change of plans. What's that?' I ask, indicating the pot and trying to divert Nan from any Paul-related questions.

'Tomato soup. It's one of Nora's recipes that I thought I'd try for Grandad's and my lunch. I've made plenty, so you can have some if you want. She says it needs to be served with freshly baked crusty bread, but I haven't got time to make that, so I sent your grandad down to the shop to buy a loaf.'

My stomach rumbles loudly. I realise that I haven't eaten anything today and I'm starving.

'That sounds lovely. Yes, please. Have I got time to get changed and stick a load of washing on?'

'Yes, it'll be another twenty minutes before it's ready. I'll call you.'

Once I get into the safety of my room, I rip off the stinky clothes, slip on my dressing gown, and take them straight to the washing machine. I add as much fabric conditioner as I dare and put on a long cycle. Then I head to the shower and wash myself thoroughly, including my hair, to get rid of the last hints of the smell of Paul's caravan. I've just finished drying it and getting dressed when Nan calls lunch.

'Oh, wow, this is something else!' I say, as I take my first taste of the soup.

'It's a bit of a step up from Heinz, isn't it?' Nan agrees. 'Not so much butter, Norman, think of your arteries!' she admonishes Grandad as he spreads a thick layer on his bread. Grandad just looks at me and winks. This is a recurring theme at mealtimes, particularly where butter or cream are involved.

After lunch, I send Katie a text to say that I'm back early and can pick her up at the end of her shift if she likes. A few minutes pass before I get a response.

Don't worry, I'll get the train. Bronwyn and I are going to head up into Sevenoaks later. She's going to show me around and we might do a bit of shopping. Kx

'Seems like Katie has made a new friend,' I say to Nan, showing her the text.

'Who's Bronwyn?' she asks.

'She works at the café. She's the same age as Katie, or maybe a little older. She's an artist, very bubbly. I like her, but I wouldn't have picked her out as a natural friend for Katie. They're completely different.'

'How do you mean?'

'Well, Katie's pretty reserved, isn't she, but Bronwyn is totally in your face. Katie is academic, but Bronwyn has made it clear she has no interest in further education. That kind of different.'

'Sounds like she might be good for Katie, bring her out of herself a bit,' Nan observes.

'Yeah, maybe.'

* * *

Despite my determination to give myself some space from it, I end up spending the afternoon working my way through the café menu, calculating the cost of the ingredients for each dish based on the receipt from the cash and carry, and then working out the margin. I have to text Matt a few times to clarify a couple of pack sizes, and to give me an estimate of how many servings he would expect to get from one of the large tins of beans we bought. By the end, I've worked out that we do still have a pretty healthy margin in the food, even with the more expensive ingredients we've bought. Our issue is volume; we need to be selling an awful lot more of it.

I look at the menu again, but this time I focus on how it looks as a whole, rather than the ingredients and prices. Apart from being littered with spelling mistakes, the layout is pretty sloppy. Whoever did it didn't really seem to care about making it look appealing. Even the fonts look old-fashioned. As I study it, I realise there's something missing. I call Matt again.

'Yes, boss?'

'Ha ha. Quick question. In the window, it says we do traditional roast dinners. I can't see anything about them on the menu, though?'

'We haven't done them for years. We used to do them on a Sunday at lunchtime, but hardly anyone came towards the end. I think people prefer to go to pubs and restaurants, where they can have a glass of wine or a beer to wash it down with. I love a cup of tea, but even I know it doesn't really go with a roast.'

'We probably ought to take it off the window then, oughtn't we?'

'Yeah, I guess so.'

I add 'Find Signwriters' to my rapidly growing to-do list.

Katie texts shortly after six to say that Bronwyn is going to drop her home. I didn't realise that Bronwyn could drive. Given her age, she can't have passed her test that long ago, and I can feel my anxiety levels rising at the thought of Katie being at the mercy of Bronwyn's inexperience. Also, I just know that Bronwyn is going to own some sort of clapped-out old banger, which she'll have given a name to, and which will offer even less protection than Matt's van. By the time Katie leaps out of a perfectly ordinary modern hatchback with Bronwyn behind the wheel, I've managed to conjure up a large number of scenarios in my head, each worse than the last.

'That's not the sort of car I'd associate with Bronwyn,' I observe, as Katie skips through the door, carrying a shopping bag.

'It's her mum's. Bronwyn doesn't own a car. We stopped in at her house for a quick cup of tea before going to the station, and her mum said I shouldn't be on my own on a train and insisted that Bronwyn drive me. Wasn't that nice of her?'

'Very. How was your day?' I ask.

'Yeah, Sevenoaks is an interesting place. At first glance, it's mainly coffee shops and restaurants, but Bronwyn showed me some great clothes shops and we went to the art gallery she works at. Her stuff is really good. I didn't understand all of it, but Gary, the guy who runs it, thinks she's a serious up and coming talent.'

'And how was the café?'

'Hard work. Saturday is their busiest day, apparently. Oh, and you know the art gallery next door?'

'Yes.'

'It's not an art gallery. It's a photo studio. I met the guy that owns it, Toby something or other. He seemed nice. Bronwyn explained about us inheriting the café and he wished us luck, which I thought was kind.'

'Still think we should sell it?'

'I get why you're confused, if that's what you're asking. I wouldn't want to tell Matt and Bronwyn that they didn't have a job. Although Bronwyn said she'd be okay, she really loves the place, you can tell that. And some of the oldies are quite nice; did you meet Ron when you were in?'

'Yes. Charming but sexist.'

'I thought he was really nice. He even gave me a tip! Anyway, to answer your question, I really don't know. If you don't sell it, what are you going to do with it?'

It's a good question, and I'm still pondering it as I get ready for work on Monday morning. I'm looking forward to going back to the office and having a bit of normality. It feels like much longer than two weeks since I was there last, but even our trip to Mallorca feels like a lifetime ago. This has definitely been the longest week of my life. As usual, the emails have stacked up in my absence, and I'm still going through them when Grace appears at my desk, suggesting that we get a coffee from the kitchen.

'Did you have a good break?' she asks, as we pour ourselves two coffees from the jug. Holdsworth & Speke are generous enough to provide a filter coffee machine rather than making us drink instant, but you have to pick your moment. The coffee is lovely when it's freshly brewed, but starts to look and taste more and more like tar the longer the jug sits on the hotplate.

'Yeah, interesting,' I reply. 'Probably easier explained over a drink. Are you free after work?'

'A drink, on a Monday?' she feigns horror. 'Oh, go on then.'

'Morning, ladies. How was your holiday, Daisy?' Rob joins us in the kitchen to top up his mug.

'Good, thanks.'

'What's this?' he asks, grabbing my wrist and turning it to examine the Rolex. 'Get it in a market, did you? I hope you didn't pay more than ten quid, although I have to say it's one of the better knock-offs I've seen.'

I'd forgotten that Rob is a self-styled watch guru. Apparently, he has a large collection of high-end watches, and he keeps banging on about 'haute horlogerie', whatever the hell that is. He certainly seems to have a different watch for each day of the week.

'Actually, it's real,' I tell him. 'I inherited it from my great-uncle.'

'Really? Let's have a better look, then.'

I take the Rolex off and hand it to him. He spends some time turning it over in his hands and examining the bracelet.

'Nice. It'll never be as popular as the dive watches, but it's a classic.' He returns it and I slip it back onto my wrist.

'He's a bit of a knob, isn't he?' Grace observes, as Rob wanders back to his desk.

'He's okay. He means well, I think. He's just a bit clumsy. Anyway, I'd better crack on. I'll see you later.'

'Looking forward to it!'

I try to focus on my work, but thoughts about the café keep pushing in. This isn't helped by a text from Matt, which arrives just before lunch.

Not sure what the problem is, but I just overheard Rita telling a customer that the card machine is broken. Do you want me to see if Bronwyn can stop by and have a look at it?

I'm pretty sure I know exactly what the problem with the card machine is. I slip out of the office into the corridor and dial the café.

'Hello?'

'Rita, it's Daisy.'

'Oh. What do you want?' She really is the rudest person I think I've ever met. I grit my teeth and put on my most saccharine voice.

'Two things. Firstly, I gather there's an issue with the card machine?'

'It's too complicated. I can't work it.'

'It's not complicated, Rita, and I know that Bronwyn left instructions on how to use it. This is the twenty-first century, not the nineteenth, and if I hear that you're refusing to take card payments again, it will be a disciplinary issue. Got it?' I can't believe I've just said that, and evidently neither can she, as there's total silence from her end of the phone.

'The second thing,' I continue, pressing my advantage before she explodes, 'is the way you answer the phone. It's a business line, and you should answer it in a professional manner. Try saying "Nora's Diner, how may I help you?" instead of just "hello". Do you understand?'

'You can't talk to me like that! Who do you think you are? I'm old enough to be your mother, and you should show some respect,' she retorts. She's found her voice, then.

'At the moment, I'm your boss, Rita, and if anyone should be showing a bit more respect, it's you. Do we understand each other?' My voice is still saccharine, but I'm shaking with rage, particularly when I realise she's hung up on me.

I'm more than ready for a drink when 5.30 p.m. comes around, and Grace and I hurry to our usual pub. I fill her in on the café, being careful not to mention the substantial cash inheritance or the amount Katie and I could get if we sold up. Grace's eyes mist over.

'I'd love to run a café in a sleepy town,' she enthuses. 'You know, one of those places where everyone knows everyone, and nobody feels like they have to lock their front door. I'd have gingham tablecloths, water bowls so people could bring their dogs, and I'd serve lovely home-made cakes. People would confide in me, and I'd solve all their problems. I'd have a proper Italian coffee machine manned by a sexy barista that all the women in the town are secretly in love with, only he's gay and has an equally gorgeous boyfriend. I'd do cream teas too, with little sandwiches that I'd cut the crusts off. Egg mayonnaise, cucumber, and smoked salmon. Oh, my glass is empty, fancy another?'

I can't help but smile as she makes her way to the bar. Her description couldn't be further from Nora's Diner if she tried.

18

Friday at last! I have managed to keep on top of my work this week, but it's been a bit more of a struggle than usual as I've been distracted by the café. I've been spending my lunch breaks looking at coffee machines, aprons, and all sorts of other things. If I'm not careful, I could spend a fortune without actually making any tangible improvements to the place. I have decided that I need a laptop, though, with accounting software so I can keep on top of the books and my expenses. I also want to redo the menu, getting rid of the spelling mistakes and generally tidying it up. I've asked Bronwyn if she will draw me a simple logo that I can put at the top, so it looks a bit more professional. Normally, I'd ask Paul to help me choose a computer, but I've been reflecting on my disastrous visit to Whitstable, and I've decided that we need to have a serious conversation about our relationship before I involve him in any of this. Katie's pretty good with computers and things like that, though, so I could probably ask her instead.

I don't know what it is about Nora's Diner, but it's given me a sense of purpose that I've never felt before. I know it's technically half Katie's, but I feel responsible for it, as if it's a sick animal that needs me to look after it and nurse it back to health. I still have no idea what I'm going to do with it in the long term, but I have made up my mind that I will do whatever I can to revive its fortunes before I make any final decisions. I'll worry about the next steps once it's back on its feet. I've never really understood before when people say, 'Such-and-such is the first thing I think about when I wake up, and the last thing I think about before going to sleep,' but I get it now.

I collect the usual takeaway and head for Paul's flat. I don't have a set speech in my head, but I know that something fundamental has changed and, for the first time since Mum and Dad died, I'm thinking about, and planning for the future. I've even found an online food hygiene and safety course, which will allow me to help out in the kitchen once I've completed it. I've decided that I want to start resurrecting some of Nora's dishes as Saturday specials. Matt is going to be busy doing the normal menu, so I need the hygiene certificate to allow me to make them myself. I've also wondered whether we should start to offer cakes and other sweet treats on top of the purely savoury fare that we have on the menu at the moment. The hot chocolate definitely needs to be revived.

I wasn't sure whether I should say anything at work. We all have to do regular conflict of interest training, among other things, but I couldn't see how there could be a conflict of interest between a café and my work at Holdsworth & Speke. In the end, I did tell Mr Holdsworth about it earlier this week and he was surprisingly supportive. He even offered to take a quick look over the books, although we both agreed that I was more than capable of doing the accounts of a small business like that. He did express concern that trying to do my day job and look after the café might prove too much for me, but I assured him I'd be fine, although I'm already beginning to wonder if he might have a point.

I haven't spoken to Rita again, although Matt did text to ask me what I'd said, because she apparently spent the rest of the day in a foul temper, muttering under her breath and banging things around. However, I've checked the bank account and I can see card transactions starting to trickle through, so she's obviously learned how to use the card machine.

'No wine again! I'm starting to think you've gone on the wagon. You haven't, have you?' Paul asks, as I hand over the takeaway bag and walk into his flat. I've lost count of the number of times I've stayed over here, but I feel like I'm seeing it with fresh eyes tonight. It really is a shithole; glancing into the bedroom, I spot the same sheets that were on the bed the last time I was here, which means he probably hasn't changed them for at least three weeks. My skin starts to crawl. Whatever happens tonight, I'm not getting into that bed. I settle myself at the table and wait for him to dish out the food.

'I really am sorry about last weekend,' he says as he hands me my plate and we start eating.

'I was a bit shocked, but I realise I probably should have called ahead rather than just turning up. Don't worry about it.'

'Did you get everything sorted?'

'With what?'

'With whatever it was that meant you couldn't come down as planned.'

It dawns on me that I haven't told him anything about Fred and his will. We don't tend to speak during the week, and there obviously wasn't an opportunity at the caravan last weekend. I fill him in on the basics, leaving out the cash inheritance once again.

'That's why I didn't bring any wine,' I conclude. 'I can't stay, as I have to be in at seven thirty tomorrow.'

His face falls a little. 'But you're not going to be working there every Saturday, are you?'

'I think I am,' I tell him. 'It's my business now. As the owner, I feel I ought to be there at least one day a week.' It feels odd, saying it so bluntly, but it's true.

'That's a shame, I will miss our lazy Saturday mornings,' he says, a little truculently.

For Paul, a lazy Saturday morning usually involves seeing if he can persuade me to have sex without either of us getting out of bed to do anything first. He thinks it's romantic to initiate it as soon as we wake up, and that getting out of bed to brush his teeth spoils the flow. I find it very hard to get in the mood when I'm enveloped in a fog of his morning breath, and I usually need to wee when I first wake up, so it doesn't often work out the way he wants.

When we've finished eating, I steel myself for the conversation I know we have to have.

'Can I ask you a question?' I start. 'Where do you think we're going, you and I?'

He looks blank. 'I don't understand.'

'Where is our relationship going? Is me pitching up here every Friday with a takeaway, followed a bit of sex and a sleepover where you see us being in, say, two years' time?'

'I thought you didn't like to talk about the future,' he replies. 'You've always said to me that you live each day as it comes, so I've never really thought about it. What's brought this on?'

'Well, with the café and everything, I've realised that I have to start thinking about the future now, and it's got me wondering. We're twenty-four, Paul, but it's like nothing has changed since we were seventeen, in a lot of ways. Are we still going to be doing this when we're twenty-six, thirty? Is this enough for you? Because I'm not sure it's enough for me any more.'

There is a long pause before he speaks.

'I think I see what this is,' he says, simply.

'Go on.'

'When we first got together, Mum took me to one side. She's

wise, my mum, as you know. She said, "Paul, I think it's lovely what you and Daisy have, but you have to understand that she's in a lot of pain at the moment. One day, the pain will ease for her and she'll be ready to move on, but then you'll become a constant reminder of the time when she was hurting, and she may not have room for you in her new life. You have to be ready to let her go when that day comes." Is that what this is? All this sudden planning for the future and questioning where we're going, are you moving on, do you think?'

I study him. I can still easily see the quiet, geeky boy who became my friend at the blackest time of my life, and I'll never properly be able to express my gratitude for that, but he's right. I feel like I've suddenly grown up and I can't ignore the fact that, although we're the same age, he's still a teenager in many ways, with his messy flat and video games. I'm scared, though; my relationship with Paul has been part of the security blanket that I've constructed over the last ten years, and if I say the words that are forming in my mind, a big chunk of that security blanket is going to go up in flames. A fat tear escapes and rolls down my cheek.

'I think I might be,' I whisper.

Paul pushes back his chair, comes round to my side of the table, kneels down and puts his arms around me.

'Don't cry, Daisy. You're the bravest person I know, and if you feel you're ready to move on, then it would be wrong of me to hold you back.'

'I'll miss you, though,' I tell him. The single tear has somehow become a deluge, but he doesn't loosen his grip.

'I'm not going anywhere. Any time you need a chat, or even just a new phone, you can call me, okay?'

I gently ease myself out of his arms, partly because I'm aware I'm making his shirt wet, and partly so that I can look him in the eyes.

'Will you be all right?' I ask.

'I'll probably mope around a bit after you've gone,' he replies. 'But I think I'll live. There's very little that a few hours of *Fortnite* can't cure.' He smiles ruefully.

'You might meet someone new – you never know.'

'I might. There's a woman who comes into the shop a lot. She says she's having trouble with her phone, but I reckon she breaks it deliberately because she fancies me.'

'Idiot!' Despite my tears, I can't help but laugh.

After that, there doesn't seem to be much more to say. I gather my stuff together, and we have an awkward hug at the door, neither of us wanting to be the first to say the final goodbye. In the end, he breaks the embrace.

'Good luck with the café and everything,' he says. 'And I meant what I said. If you ever need anything, I'm right here.'

I kiss him one final time, then turn away and start walking towards the car. I think we both know that I won't be calling him. I need a clean break and, painful as it might feel now, I know I've done the right thing.

In a funny way, I'm quite proud of both of us, for the emotionally mature way we handled it. But then, perhaps we were able to break up so peacefully because there wasn't much there to hold us together any more. As I head for the car, I realise there's one more thing I ought to do before I leave. I turn around and head for the Chinese takeaway.

'Are you all right, Miss Daisy? Was everything okay with your meal?' The woman behind the counter looks worried. She obviously thinks my second visit is bad news. I guess it is, in a way, although I doubt very much that our weekly takeaway made much of an impact on their books.

'Everything was fine, as always. I just thought I ought to tell you that I'm moving away, so I won't be coming in again.'

'Ah, that is a great shame for us. We will miss you, Miss Daisy. I hope you are very happy in your new life, though.'

'Thank you. I'm going to try.'

The thunk of the car door as I close it feels final, like the closing of a chapter. I feel vulnerable, like a hermit crab that has outgrown the shell that has been its home for so long, but hasn't yet found a new shell to move into. At least I've got a busy weekend ahead, with my shift in the café tomorrow and starting to clear Fred's flat on Sunday, so I won't have time to mope around, wondering if I've made the wrong decision.

There's only one thing I feel absolutely certain about right now.

'Right then, Nora, let's see what we can do about saving your café,' I say out loud, as I start the engine and turn towards home.

19

Mr Holdsworth was right. I can't keep this up, I'm completely exhausted. Over the last month, my work routine has been the same, but then I've carried on working on my new laptop in the evenings, keeping on top of the accounts for the café, researching and ordering things to help smarten it up without spending a fortune, and also doing my food hygiene training. That was an eye-opener, and I've become obsessed with cross-contamination to the point that Nan is threatening to ban me from the fridge at home, because I keep rearranging it and she says she can't find anything. I still haven't actually cooked anything new at the café, but I've started helping Matt a bit in the kitchen on Saturdays and he's being surprisingly patient with me, considering I'm under his feet a lot of the time. I have had moments of missing Paul, but I've been so flat out that they've been few and far between.

Katie's done a couple of shifts with me, but it's a struggle to get her out of bed, so for the last couple of weeks, she's taken the train over to Sevenoaks and pitched up to help with the second part of the day. She doesn't actually do very much, but it gives her an excuse to disappear into town with Bronwyn after we've closed up.

I think Bronwyn is quite good for her, even though they're so different. Katie's wardrobe has certainly got more colour in it than it used to have, and Bronwyn seems to bring her out of her shell a bit. I even heard Katie exchanging some banter with one of the regular customers the other day, which she would never have done before.

On Sundays, I've been clearing out Fred's flat. Nan and Grandad took pity on me when they saw it, so they have been coming over there with me, leaving home after breakfast and staying until mid-afternoon. So far, we've filled two skips and found very little of any interest. Grandad did get quite excited when one of the piles of booklets turned out to be a set of owners' handbooks for various cars from the 1970s, and Katie is helping him to sell them on eBay. There's been no sign of the box or papers for the Rolex yet, although Fred was obviously such a hoarder that I'm confident I'll find them before long. We're getting close to the end now, thank goodness, and Nan and I have been cleaning as we've gone, so the place is starting to look a bit less grotty. It is still going to need a new kitchen, bathroom, double glazing, and complete redecoration before I can think about doing anything with it, though.

Takings at the café have improved, but we've still got a long way to go. I'm pleased to say that the smell of stale fat is long gone; Matt was right that simply changing the oil more frequently was enough to get rid of it. It's a lot brighter in there now too, as I stole one of Grace's ideas and ordered a load of red gingham PVC tablecloths to cover the cracked Formica tables. Ideally, I'd like to replace the tables completely, but the cost is prohibitive at the moment. I'm already wondering whether the £50,000 I earmarked for the café and the flats is unrealistically low, but I don't want to start dipping into the investments if at all possible. Thankfully, the chairs aren't too bad, although they could do with being sanded down and repainted at some point. I've also got new aprons; they don't have 'Nora's Diner' embroidered on them because the embroidered ones were three times the price of the plain, but they look smart nonetheless. I even made sure to get a couple of extra-large ones for Rita, although Matt informs me that she stubbornly refuses to wear them. I've had the awful signwriting removed from the windows, and the new menus look a lot better. I'd like to extend the menu a bit, but I need to talk to Matt about it first, and I just don't seem to have found the right time yet.

There's still one big hurdle I have to overcome, which is Rita. I despair when I think of the amount of head space she's taken up over the last month. She's like a permanent malign presence in the back of my mind. I really want her gone. She's lazy, surly, and rude, and I'm sure she's putting off customers. I don't even have a staffing issue if she leaves any more, as Bronwyn has told me she can cover for a while if needed. My problem is that I don't have any excuse to fire her and she's not showing any signs of resigning. She's kept her head down since our spat over the card machine, and I haven't seen her because she never works on Saturdays. I have spoken to her a few times; I've invented some spurious reasons to call the café, just to check that she's answering the phone properly. I know it drives her mad, but if I don't do it then she'll just revert to her old ways. Even if she did, I couldn't make answering the phone with 'hello' a dismissible offence. I need to up the ante, and I reckon I've found the perfect way to do it.

A couple of weeks ago, I ordered a coffee machine and all the other paraphernalia we need to make proper barista-style coffee. I also asked Matt to pick up a selection of different teas on his latest visit to the cash and carry. We'll still offer the instant coffee and builder's tea, but we'll have a premium range as well. With any luck, the coffee machine will be enough to tip Rita over the edge. It was installed on Wednesday, and Bronwyn and Rita are supposed to have been trained on it. It's the single most expensive thing I've bought for the café so far, even more expensive than the fryer, but it will be worth it if it persuades her to leave. I'd like it to improve our fortunes too, obviously, but if I never sell a single cup from it and it gets rid of Rita, I reckon it will still have been one of the best investments I've made.

It's Saturday morning and I'm dog-tired as I drag myself out of bed. I was up late last night, reconciling the money that I've put into the café. There are tax implications about how the business pays it back, and I had to check my calculations a couple of times to make sure I'd got them right. As I try to wake myself up under the shower, I contemplate the day ahead. I've experimented a bit with the oven at the café since I passed my food hygiene course and, after a couple of burned sponges, I reckon I've got it sussed. I want to make a coffee and walnut cake today to celebrate the arrival of the coffee machine. I'm planning to offer slices this afternoon to test whether there's a market for it. At least I'm not clearing the flat tomorrow; it's Katie's last weekend of the holidays before the autumn term starts, so the four of us are having a big roast lunch at home.

* * *

Both Matt and Bronwyn are already in the kitchen when I arrive. Bronwyn can't have arrived long ago, as Matt hasn't got round to rubbing the obligatory lipstick mark off his cheek yet.

'I was just going to make the teas and coffees,' Bronwyn tells me, as I place my bag of ingredients on the side. 'Do you want a coffee? I can do you an espresso, a latte, a cappuccino, you name it!'

'Can I have a latte with an extra shot, please? I'm struggling to get going this morning, so maybe the caffeine will help.'

Matt looks up from what he's doing, and I'm aware of him

studying me. 'You do look tired,' he observes. 'Are you sure you're not overdoing it? We can manage without you today if you would rather rest at home.'

'No. I'm here, and I have a cake to make. I want to see if there's any interest in them as a product line.'

I set myself up in a corner of the kitchen and try to keep out of Matt's way while I work. Bronwyn brings in the coffee, which tastes amazing.

'Mm, that's really good,' I murmur.

'Isn't it?' Bronwyn agrees. 'I've been watching YouTube videos on how to make those clever patterns with the milk. I haven't quite got it sussed yet, but I will.'

'She's in love with that machine already,' Matt informs me once she's out of earshot. 'If anyone can sell the coffee from it, it's her.'

'And Rita?'

'What do you think? I think she's doing her best to ignore it, in the hope it will go away.'

'Fat chance! It cost me a fortune, so she's going to have to get used to it.'

'Mm. Good luck with that.'

Ron is the first of the regulars to arrive. I've asked Bronwyn to let me know when they come in so I can intercept them. My cake is in the oven and the timer says I have another twenty minutes before I need to check it, so I remove the hairnet and walk out into the front of the café.

'Good morning, Ron. Nice to see you,' I greet him.

'Good morning to you, Daisy.' He smiles as he fishes out his customary £5 note and hands it to Bronwyn. 'The usual, please, Bronwyn.'

'Ron, would you allow me to give you a free coffee this morning?' I ask.

His eyes narrow. 'What's the catch?'

'No catch, I'd just like you to have the opportunity to try a coffee from our new machine here. I won't give you anything weird, just a normal coffee with milk. I'd be interested in your opinion.'

'I'm not sure. I'm quite happy with the coffee I normally have. You've already changed it once, when you first arrived. Why are you changing it again?'

Bronwyn gives me an 'I told you so' look, but I'm determined. I need Ron, Agnes, and even Harold on board if my plan is going to work.

'All I'm asking is that you let Bronwyn make you a coffee using the machine. If you don't like it, we'll replace it with your usual one and we still won't charge you. Deal?'

'This all smacks of up-selling to me, young Daisy. I'm a pensioner, you know. I'm not made of money.'

'It's not much more expensive, I promise you. I'm going to suggest you try an Americano, which is the closest match to your normal coffee. It's literally thirty pence more per cup, so you'll still get your breakfast for a fiver, you just won't get any change.'

'Okay, I'll try it. But I'm not making any promises, understand?'

'Thank you, Ron. Bronwyn, charge Ron for his bacon roll and give him an Americano on the house, please.'

Bronwyn smiles, takes the £5 note, and hands Ron his change before setting about the coffee machine. Even though it's her first day using it, she looks very confident as she dispenses coffee into the holder, tamps it down, and attaches it to the machine. She slides a cup underneath, presses a button, and watches as the machine delivers a steady stream of strong coffee into it. She tops it up with boiling water from another nozzle, adds milk, and carries it over to Ron's table. Together, we stand and watch, waiting for him to take his first sip.

Annoyingly, he seems absorbed in a story in the newspaper

this morning. Just as I'm starting to worry that I'll have to go back into the kitchen to deal with the cake, he lifts the cup to his lips and drinks. I see him swilling it round his mouth, as if he's tasting a fine wine, before he swallows. He raises his eyes and looks at us.

'Worth 30p extra, Ron?' Bronwyn asks.

'It might be,' he replies, smiling.

We repeat the process with Agnes and Harold when they arrive. Agnes is also sold, but Harold pronounces that he can't tell the difference and he'll stick to the old stuff, thank you very much.

'You can't win them all,' Bronwyn reassures me.

'He was the one I was least sure about,' I agree. 'Anyone who puts brown sauce on egg has to have questionable taste.'

'I told you, didn't I? You could feed him sawdust and I doubt he'd notice.'

'Rita's perfect customer, isn't he?' I reply, and we both snigger.

'I thought I might write all the new coffees up on the specials board, what do you think?' she asks.

'I think that's an excellent idea. It looks so sad empty, and it's a good way to advertise them until I get a chance to update the main menu.'

Once the cake has cooled, I make the icing using a shot of espresso from the new machine and decorate it with walnut halves. I'm just about to start cutting it up when Matt stops me.

'You're not going to cut it up like that, are you?' he asks.

'Why? It's not a meat knife, it's quite safe.'

'It's not the knife. If you cut it up without marking the slices first, your portion sizes will be all over the place. Hang on.'

He disappears into the cupboard and reappears with an object that looks like those gadgets you see in kitchen shops for coring and slicing apples, only much bigger.

'How many slices do you want, twelve or sixteen?'

'It's not that big, let's go with twelve.'

Matt removes the walnut halves and carefully lowers the gadget over the cake, leaving a series of radiating lines in the icing. 'There you go. Twelve equal slices. You just have to make sure you get the centre of the divider in the centre of the cake. Now you can cut and decorate.'

The rest of the day passes well. Katie appears at lunchtime, and Bronwyn takes advantage of a quiet period after lunch to teach us both how to use the machine. I'm a bit confused about the different things you have to do with the milk for the different types of coffee, so Bronwyn writes out an aide-memoir that we can refer to. The cake is a sell-out success, and I'm pleased to see some new faces. There are even a couple of young mothers, who we treat with kid gloves. Ron may not approve of them but, if we impress them, I'm hopeful will tell their friends and our customer base will grow.

* * *

By the time we close up, I can barely keep my eyes open, but it's been our most successful day since I took it on.

'You look dead on your feet,' Matt observes.

'Thanks! You really know how to make a girl feel good about herself,' I reply.

'I'm serious. Look, why don't you come up to my flat and have an hour's kip before you drive home? The spare bedroom is clean, and I'm worried you'll fall asleep at the wheel if you leave now.'

I open my mouth to protest, but I realise he's got a point.

'Are you sure you don't mind? I don't want to put you out.'

'Of course I don't mind! I'd never forgive myself if I let you drive home in that state and something happened to you. Why don't you send your grandparents a text to say you'll be late, and I'll wake you in an hour?'

I don't feel entirely comfortable with his proposal, but the idea of a lie-down is too much to resist. I send the text and follow him up to his flat, where he shows me into the spare room. It's like the rest of the flat, tired and dated but scrupulously clean. I draw the thin curtains and stretch out on the bed. It's not particularly comfortable, but that doesn't make a difference. My head has barely touched the pillow before I'm fast asleep.

20

I feel totally disorientated when I wake up, and it takes me a while to remember where I am. I glance at my watch, which informs me that it's nearly seven o'clock in the evening. So much for Matt waking me. I get up quickly, run my fingers through my hair to get rid of the worst of the tangles, and walk out into his living room.

'I thought you said you were going to wake me after an hour!' I exclaim.

'I tried. I knocked on the door and called your name, but nothing. I didn't feel comfortable coming in, so in the end I gave up and left you to it. Do you feel better?'

'Much, but I really have to go. Nan and Grandad will be wondering where I am.' I check my phone to make sure that they got my text, and I'm surprised to read their answer.

No problem, love. As it's just the two of us, Grandad's going to take me out for dinner, so fix yourself something when you get in. Nan x

'Everything okay?' Matt asks.

'Yes. It seems that they're taking advantage of Katie and me not being there to have a romantic dinner out. It looks like I'm fending for myself.'

'You're welcome to stay and eat with me, if you like. It's nothing very special, I'm afraid, just grilled chicken and some salad.'

I'm torn. It would be very easy to let Matt cook for me, but I can't help thinking I've probably outstayed my welcome already. On the other hand, it might be an opportunity to talk about extending the menu.

'I don't want to be more trouble,' I tell him.

'You won't be. In fact, you're doing me a favour because the chicken came in a pack of two, so I was going to have to freeze one.'

'Well, let me go and get some wine at least. What do you prefer, red or white?'

'I like red, but white might go better with this. You choose.'

It takes me a little while to find an off-licence, and I dither a bit trying to choose the right bottle, so it's around half an hour later when I return to Matt's flat. From the aromas that greet me when he opens the door, I would say his interpretation of 'just grilled chicken and some salad' is rather more advanced than mine. He takes the wine and pours us each a glass, respecting my wish for a small one, because I've still got to drive home after this. I settle myself at his table and he brings over the chicken, salad, and some garlic bread that I'm pretty sure wasn't mentioned before, but smells incredible. We clink our glasses, pile our plates, and I take a big mouthful. It all tastes just as good as it smells, and I tell him so. Although Matt is purely a work colleague, it's hard not to draw comparisons between him and Paul. Paul is, and I put this politely, not a good cook. How he hasn't poisoned himself is a mystery. I wonder how he's getting on. Maybe he's in a blissful relationship with the woman who keeps coming into the shop.

'Sorry?' I realise that Matt has been speaking and I haven't taken in a word he's said.

'I said, I've never known anyone who works as hard as you, but I'm worried that you're overloaded.'

My first instinct is to flare up. How dare he tell me what my limits are? But then I realise I've just spent three hours asleep in his spare bed because I was so tired I wasn't fit to drive, and decide to cut him some slack. Plus, the food is so delicious I really don't want to storm out and leave half of it behind. I take a deep breath and prepare to be candid.

'I didn't expect it to be this difficult,' I begin. 'There are some things, like clearing out Fred's flat, that won't carry on forever, but even once that's done, I think I'm going to find juggling the café and my main job a struggle. There's so much more I want to do with the café, but I need my main job for the income.'

'Do you, though?'

'What do you mean?'

'Well, you own Fred's flat outright. I know it needs a bit of work, but I bet you could get quite a nice monthly rental income from it. That would go quite a long way towards tiding you over, wouldn't it?'

'Yes, maybe. It would mean taking quite a substantial pay cut, but I have done some calculations, and I could probably survive on it.'

Matt smiles.

'What?'

'Well, you've obviously been giving it some thought. That's encouraging. It means you might not be in quite such a hurry to sell up.'

'Nice try! I'm focused on trying to turn the café around at the moment. I'll make a decision about selling it once we see whether I'm successful or not. Can I ask you a question?' Time to change the subject, I think.

'Go on.'

'I was thinking about what you told me when we went to the cash and carry together that time. When you were growing up, why didn't you just pick a gang and join it? Wouldn't life have been a lot easier for you if you had?'

I see his jaw tighten, and I wonder whether I've crossed a line. There's an awkward silence.

'Sorry,' I continue. 'I don't mean to pry, if it's something you'd rather not talk about. I was just curious.'

He sighs. 'No, it's fine. You might as well know it all. I used to have a sister.'

The penny starts to drop. 'When you say you "used to have", I take it that means...'

'She died.'

'God, I'm so sorry.'

'Yeah. She was seven years older than me. I thought we were close, but it turned out I didn't know anything about her at all. She worked in the local newsagent, but used to keep strange hours. She'd come home really late, or sometimes not at all. If I asked about it, she'd say she was with friends, and I had no reason not to believe her. It was only after she died that I found out she was doing sex work. She was my world and I loved her. Mum was useless, so Laura was the one that made sure I had a uniform for school and all that stuff. I had no idea that she was selling her body to pay for it, and I still feel guilty about that to this day.

'She was found inside one of those big bins that shops have out the back. The post-mortem said that the cause of death was an overdose, but she didn't climb in there by herself, did she? Some bastard put her in there. I don't know if she was with a client when it happened, and he got spooked and dumped her in there, or whether it was someone from the gang, but it didn't matter to me. In my mind, the gang was responsible, and the way she was disposed of showed that they didn't even care when she died. They just moved on to their next victim. I was so angry. You know I told you where my scar came from?'

'Your best friend at primary school, if I remember correctly.'

'Yes, well, that's not quite the whole story. He was a member of the gang, and I was sure he was somehow involved in her death, so I went looking for him. When I found him, I messed him up quite badly. Stupidly, I didn't think that there might be consequences. A week or so later, he and some of his mates jumped me. His mates held me while he sliced my face open and told me that I was a marked man. That's when I realised that I had to leave.'

I can see the pain in his eyes and my heart goes out to him. It shifts something in me to hear a story that's just as tragic as mine in many ways. I feel less alone, somehow. I want to hug him, but I'm very aware that, although he's bared his soul to me, our relationship is still fundamentally a professional one, and I don't want to cross any boundaries that could make working with him awkward.

'Thank you for trusting me with it,' I say instead.

'It's not a story I share a lot, but knowing what you went through made it a bit easier, I suppose.' He glances at my empty plate. 'Would you like a coffee?'

'No thanks, I'd really better go. This was absolutely delicious, though. Thank you.'

'My pleasure.'

* * *

Nan, Grandad and Katie are all home before me, sitting in the kitchen with cups of tea.

'Ah, there you are, Daisy. We were starting to worry!' Nan exclaims.

'Sorry, when I got your text saying you were going out, Matt

very kindly offered to cook for me.' Out of the corner of my eye, I
see Katie's eyebrows shoot up. 'Nothing like that,' I tell her firmly. 'I
was just so tired at the end of my shift that he took pity on me. I
slept in his spare room for three hours, then he fed me, and then I
came home.'

'You have been burning the candle at both ends, love,' Grandad
chimes in. 'I'm not sure how long you're going to be able to keep
this up for.'

'I know. Something's got to give, but I just don't know what
to do.'

'What does your head say?' Grandad asks.

'Easy. Stick with the job at Holdsworth & Speke. It's steady, reli-
able income from a job I know how to do. It's safe. I can do up
Fred's flat, let it out, and that will give a boost to my salary, plus
Katie can have half to put towards her uni costs. I back off from the
café, leave Matt to it and just act as book-keeper until it's hopefully
stable enough that we can sell it.'

'And your heart?'

'The total opposite. I'd love to get properly hands-on with the
café, reintroduce the specials that Matt doesn't have time to cook,
extend the menu, see if I could make something of it. It's got so
much potential, I know it, but it's also a massive risk. I still don't
really know what I'm doing; I'm completely reliant on Matt. What
if I make a complete mess of it, or Matt leaves? I don't know if I'm
ready to make such a big leap of faith.'

'I'm not being funny,' Grandad observes, 'but you're sitting on
nearly half a million in cash, plus the value of the building, which
will be there even if the café fails. I'd say you can afford to make
some pretty expensive mistakes. Let's say you stick with your
current job and back away from the café. How will you feel?'

I take a moment to contemplate it and envision it in my head.

'Frustrated, I think. I'll always wonder if I missed an opportunity. I'm no believer in fate, as you know, but what if this is where I'm supposed to be?'

'Okay. Now look at it the other way. You take on the café, and for some reason it doesn't work out. How would you feel then?'

'I'd be sad, because I would have failed. I guess I'd know that I'd done everything I could and, as you say, I do have a pretty good financial buffer behind me. As long as I was careful, I'd have plenty to support myself with while I looked for a new job.'

'Well, it seems clear to me which way you ought to go,' Grandad concludes.

'If you did take on the café, would you move into Fred's flat?' Katie asks.

'Blimey, I haven't got that far! Why?'

'Well, if you moved out, I was thinking that I could maybe get the train over from Paddock Wood after school on Fridays and come and stay for weekends with you. I could carry on helping out in the café on Saturdays and come home on a Sunday.'

'You could bring her home, Daisy, and we could have Sunday lunch together. That would be nice,' Nan adds.

'Hang on a minute, everyone. I haven't even decided whether I'm going to take this café on, and you've already moved me out and planned how it's all going to be? I'm starting to feel quite unwanted!'

'Of course you're not unwanted,' Nan soothes. 'You can stay here for as long as you want, you know that. Grandad and I love having you both around. We're just aware that you're twenty-four now, and you might want more independence. We want you to know that we'll support you, whatever you decide to do, okay?'

I eye them all suspiciously. 'I still think there's an agenda here that you've been working on behind my back.'

Their faces are masks of innocence, but I'm not taken in. The really irritating thing is that it is actually quite a neat solution. I'd have to finish clearing Fred's flat and then get the work done on it, but dealing with the café would be a lot easier if I were on site. Of course, this only matters if I decide to quit my job at Holdsworth & Speke and invest myself fully in it, and I haven't come to any conclusions about that yet.

Oh, who am I kidding? Of course I know what I'm going to do.

21

Now that I've made the decision, I feel strangely nervous as I walk into the office. My resignation letter is in an envelope in my bag. I've checked my contract and I've given a month's notice, as required. I feel like everyone is looking at me and treating me differently, as if they have somehow worked out what I'm about to do. It's completely irrational, I know, but I feel like a traitor whose guilty secret is about to be discovered. I wonder how Mr Holdsworth will react. Will he be angry that I'm taking the opportunity that he's given me and throwing it back in his face? I've never resigned from a job before; I've always been sacked, and they've tended to be fairly angry occasions, so I'm expecting something similar.

'Morning, Daisy. How was your weekend?' Grace perches herself on my desk and I jump slightly, as I didn't hear her approach.

'Gosh, you're twitchy this morning!' she observes. 'Been over-doing the caffeine? Perhaps I won't invite you to come and make a coffee, after all. You look like you'd be better off with water.'

'Sorry, you just surprised me, that's all. I had a good weekend, thanks. We had a big roast with all the trimmings. It was Katie's last weekend before she goes back to school for her final year, and she invited her friend Bronwyn, so it was fun. You?'

'Same old, same old. Laundry, cleaning, homework. I feel like I've come back to work for a rest!' She totters off in the direction of the kitchen and I sigh with relief. The sooner Mr Holdsworth comes into the office and I get this done, the better. I don't know how long I can keep up the pretence that everything is normal.

Typically, there is no sign of Mr Holdsworth. By 10.30 a.m., I'm starting to sweat. What if he's not coming in today, or he's sick? I don't think I can wait until later in the week; I need to do this today. Mr Speke is in his office, and I contemplate asking Rosemary if I can see him, but I'd rather see Mr Holdsworth. I can't concentrate on my work; the numbers are just swimming around in front of me. Out of the corner of my eye, I spot Rob making his way to the kitchen. He's bound to know where Mr Holdsworth is, so I follow him.

'Morning, Rob, good weekend?' I ask, as nonchalantly as I can.

'Yes, thanks. Played golf with the lads yesterday and had a bit of a catch-up afterwards. Always good to see them. You?'

'Yes, thanks. Out of interest, do you know where Mr Holdsworth is today?'

'He's meeting a new client this morning. He should be in at around midday. Is it something I can help you with?'

'Sorry?' I stopped listening after he said 'midday'.

'Whatever you're waiting for Mr Holdsworth for. Is it something I can help with?'

'Oh! No, umm, it's something I really need to discuss with him. Thanks, though.'

'Are you okay?'

'Yes, fine. Why?'

'I don't know. You seem a little on edge. Are you in trouble? Is that why you need to see Mr Holdsworth?'

'No! Nothing like that. Thanks, Rob.' I scuttle back to my desk. That was far too close for comfort. Still, at least I know that he is coming in today. I just have to try to act as if everything is normal for another hour and a half.

'You forgot this,' Rob says, carefully placing the mug of coffee on the coaster on my desk.

So much for acting normally, then.

When Mr Holdsworth finally appears, my heart goes into my mouth. I force myself to wait thirty minutes, so everyone doesn't see me dash into his office the moment he arrives. My hands are trembling as I take the envelope out of my bag, walk across the office, and knock on his door. He's been a kind of father figure to me, work wise, since I've been here, and I hate the idea of disappointing him.

'Come in, Daisy. How are you?' He studies me as I take a seat opposite him, and his voice takes on a note of concern. 'Are you okay? You've looked better, if I may say.'

I decide to build up gradually, which will hopefully soften the blow and reduce the chance of him throwing me out of his office in disgust. To be fair to him, I've never known him raise his voice in all the years I've been here, but nobody's ever resigned in that time either. Holdsworth & Speke is like a family; we stick together.

'Do you remember, when I first inherited the café, you expressed concern that it might all be too much for me?' I ask him.

'I do, and I have to say I'm still concerned. Although Rob tells me your work continues to be excellent, you've been looking exhausted. I was going to try to have a chat with you about it this week, to see if there was anything we could do to make things easier for you. I know we're your employers, but we also have a duty of care towards you. I'm guessing, from the fact that you've pre-empted me, that things have come to a head?'

'I'm afraid they have, Mr Holdsworth. I think I have to make a choice.'

'I see. And would I be right in thinking, from the envelope in your hand, that you've made that choice?'

'I'm so sorry. You know how much I appreciate everything you've done for me, and...'

'I'd like you to stop speaking now, if you don't mind,' he says, cutting me off.

Here we go. Here comes the part where he tears me off a strip for being an ungrateful little bitch who doesn't know not to bite the hand that's fed her for the last six years. I brace myself for the onslaught and focus on trying not to cry. I know I've made the right decision, but right now, I hate myself for letting Mr Holdsworth down.

'I'm going to ask you to trust me, Daisy,' he continues, and I look at him in astonishment. Is he not going to rip into me, after all? 'Tell me, are you up to date with your work?'

'Yes, I think so. I've got a couple of loose ends to tie up on the Watson's accounts before I make a start on KitchenMaster, but that shouldn't take long.'

'How long do you need?'

'A couple of hours, no more.'

'Can you come and see me again when you've finished them, before you start the KitchenMaster ones?'

'Yes, absolutely.'

'I'll see you later then. Oh, and Daisy...'

'Yes, Mr Holdsworth?'

'Shred that letter, would you?'

I find it very hard to concentrate on the Watson's accounts, as I'm trying to watch Mr Holdsworth surreptitiously. I have no idea what he's up to, but he makes a few calls, and then he and our HR person, Rebecca Hitchins, have a long meeting with Mr Speke. In fact, I finish the Watson's accounts before their meeting ends, so I have to spend at least an hour trying to look busy without actually doing anything. He specifically told me not to start work on the next client, so I'm at a bit of a loose end. Eventually, the meeting ends, so I email the Watson's accounts to Rob and cross the office floor once more.

'Ah, Daisy. Have you finished?'

'Yes, Mr Holdsworth.'

'Good. Come in and take a seat. I'm just going to ask Rebecca to join us, if you don't mind?' He places a call, and Rebecca comes into his office a minute or so later, with a sheaf of papers under her arm. She shuts the door behind her.

'Thank you for your patience, Daisy. I'm not going to beat about the bush, if that's okay. The fact is that we have a bit of a problem. You see, you and Grace are both senior accounting technicians, as you're aware.'

'Yes.'

'Mr Speke and I have been looking at the company structure and, on the technicians' side, it's become plain to us that we're top heavy. Realistically, we only have capacity for one senior accounting technician, do you understand?'

Oh, fuck. He's going to fire me. I know I was going to resign anyway, but this is a cruel way to punish me for my disloyalty. I can feel tears pricking and, before I'm able to stop myself, a couple escape and run down my cheeks. Mr Holdsworth notices them. Nothing has ever got past him.

'I'm really sorry, Daisy, but we're going to have to make your position redundant. This is not something we've decided lightly, because our little company feels like a family and we've never had to do anything like this before. As of now, we are going to place you on gardening leave, on full pay, for a month. This is a consultation period, while we try to see if there is another role you can fill within our team. You are also free to make suggestions if you think there is another role that might suit you. At the end of the month, if we haven't been able to think of anything, we will make you redundant, but we will give you what I hope you will agree is a generous package. Do you have any questions while Rebecca is here?'

I don't get it. Why is he making me redundant and effectively giving me money to go away when I was going to resign anyway? Nothing makes sense here. I do need to clarify one thing, though.

'What happens if I find another job while I'm on gardening leave?'

I see Mr Holdsworth struggle to suppress a smile. He knows what I'm up to.

'In that instance,' Rebecca replies, 'we would complete the redundancy process at the end of the consultation period. There is no requirement for you to accept any other role that we might offer you.'

'Thank you. I don't think I have any other questions at the moment.'

'If you do think of anything, you can ring me at any time,' Rebecca tells me.

'Thank you, Rebecca,' Mr Holdsworth says. She gets up, and I stand as well. The meeting is obviously over.

'Daisy, would you stay behind for a minute, please?'

Rebecca leaves the office and closes the door behind her.

'How do you feel about that?' Mr Holdsworth asks.

'To be honest, I'm confused,' I tell him. 'Why are you offering me money to go away, when you could have just waited a month and been rid of me for free?'

'Oh! Was that what you were alluding to earlier? Were you planning to resign?' he asks, in mock incredulity. I just stare at him.

'Let me explain,' he continues. 'In all honesty, you've been a bit of a dilemma for a while. You're incredibly good at your job and we've tried to stretch you as far as we can. In fact, some of the work you've been doing strictly falls under the chartered accountants' remit. The problem is that there's only so far you can go, given your lack of academic qualifications. You've pretty much hit the ceiling, Daisy. Grace has as well, but she's a lot older than you, and I think her current role suits her. But you? You're young. Even without the café, there would have come a time in the not-too-distant future when this wouldn't have been enough for you any more. It seems that your inheritance has forced your hand. I knew exactly what you were planning to do when you came in earlier, but I couldn't let you say the words or give me the envelope, because that would have tied my hands. This way, we get to send you on your way with our blessing and some funds to tide you over for a bit, and you can leave straight away rather than having to wait a month. Do you understand?'

I do, and it's not only genius; it's much more than I deserve.

'Thank you so much, Mr Holdsworth.' I'm overwhelmed by his generosity, and the tears start to flow again.

'I will confess that it's not entirely altruistic,' he smiles. 'By making your job redundant, it gives us the opportunity to recruit another apprentice. The next Daisy, perhaps? Now, be on your way. The waterworks will give your colleagues just the right impression, I think.'

'Can I say goodbye?' I ask.

'Not today, I'm afraid. After you've gone, I'll call the team together and explain what's just happened. When you come back in a month's time for your final send-off, I'm sure we can organise something then. Who knows, we might even have to put together an office trip to visit this famous café of yours!'

'Thank you. For everything.' The tears are flowing freely now. I'm both grateful and sad.

'One last thing before you go.'

'Yes?'

'If you ever need help with the accounts, don't hesitate to get in touch. We'll do you a special deal. I believe it's called "mates' rates" in the trade?'

'Thank you.'

I close his office door, hurry over to my desk and gather my things together before anyone has a chance to ask me anything. I see Grace get up and start to approach, but she's stopped in her tracks by Mr Holdsworth coming out of his office and asking everyone to gather round. I hurry out to the lift, which thankfully arrives quickly at this time of the day. As I step out into the sunshine, I'm suddenly struck by terrible doubt. What if I've just made the biggest mistake of my life?

'It's too late now, Daisy,' I tell myself firmly.

I turn and stride down the pavement towards the bus stop, and the next chapter of my life.

22

I don't even make it as far as the train station before my phone starts pinging with messages from Grace, expressing her shock and asking if I'm okay. I reply that I'm absolutely fine, and we'll hopefully catch up in a month when I come back for my final meeting. I'm amazed how quiet both Charing Cross and the train are outside the commuter hours that I'm used to. I pass the journey looking up how to apply for refunds on both my season ticket and the car park, and wondering about whether I'll stay in touch with Grace in the long term. I like her, but I doubt whether we actually have anything in common apart from our work. I can't tell her that I was planning to quit and Mr Holdsworth effectively did me a massive favour, so she's probably got survivor's guilt. I suspect she'll stop messaging me pretty soon, and our friendship will just fizzle out.

'You're back early, how did you get on?' Nan asks when I get home.

I talk them through my day and explain the redundancy process.

'Well, that's a turn-up for the books, isn't it?' Grandad declares, when I've finished. 'So you're free to start work at the café straight away?'

'Yup.'

'Will you do us one favour, please?' Nan asks.

'Of course, what is it?'

'Give yourself a few days off before you get stuck in. You really need some rest, and there's going to be precious little of that once you start. They don't need you right now, do they? They're used to getting by without you in the week. You could take the rest of the week off, go in on Saturday as normal, and then start in earnest on Monday.'

I consider this. I had planned to go straight in tomorrow, but I realise that Nan has a point. A couple of days' rest might be a good idea. I'm not sure I can take the whole week, though. Now that it's my only source of potential income, I feel like I don't have a day to waste. We debate it for a while and, in the end, we agree that I'll start on Friday.

*　*　*

I do try to follow their advice but, by mid-morning on Tuesday, I'm bored out of my mind. By the end of Wednesday, I've arranged for a house clearance firm to come and take everything that's left in Fred's flat at the start of next week, plus I've made an appointment for Thursday afternoon with a builder friend of Grandad's, to talk about the renovations. I spend Wednesday and Thursday going through the final few cupboards at the flat. The skip has gone, so I load the remaining rubbish into my car and make several trips to the tip. I finally find the box and papers for the Rolex, and I bring them home with me for safekeeping. Matt spotted my car on

Wednesday morning and texted me to ask what was going on, so I called in to explain my new situation, but I have stayed out of the café apart from that. I'm just loading the final bags for the tip into my car at lunchtime on Thursday when my phone beeps to let me know that I've received a text message. It's from Matt.

I know you're not working today, but you might want to pop into the café if you have a moment. Rita says the coffee machine is broken.

I lock up the car and use my keys to let myself in through the back door. Thankfully, Matt is alone in the kitchen.

'What's up?' I ask him.

'I suspect foul play,' he grins. 'Rita's been huffing and puffing even more than usual lately. It seems that Ron and Agnes have teamed up and decided to work their way through the coffee menu, and they've been driving her bananas by ordering all sorts of exotic stuff. I noticed she'd stuck an "out of order" notice on the coffee machine when I popped out there earlier, so I asked her about it. She's adamant that it's broken, but it wouldn't surprise me if it's just a ruse to give her a break.'

'I see. Do you think I should take a look at it?'

'Well, I can call Bronwyn and ask her to drop by when she's free if you like, but as you're here...'

I walk out of the kitchen into the main café, where Rita is at her usual post behind the counter, with her arms folded and her trademark look of disdain. Sure enough, a piece of A4 paper has been taped to the coffee machine with the words 'OUT OF ORDER' scrawled on it in black marker pen.

'Oh, it's you.' Rita greets me with her customary brusqueness. 'Why aren't you at work?'

'I quit, if you must know. From now on, I'm going to be working full-time in here. Anyway, I was just clearing the last bits out of Fred's flat when Matt texted me to say the coffee machine was on the blink. What's the matter with it?'

'I don't know. The bean grinding thing has just stopped working.'

'Okay, let me have a look.'

I place the coffee holder under the bean grinding machine and slide the lever across to fill it with ground coffee. Sure enough, nothing comes out. I check the switch, which is on, and then follow the flex to the plug.

'I think I've found the problem,' I tell her. 'It's turned off at the plug.' I turn it on, and I'm instantly rewarded by the sound of grinding coffee. When it finishes, I'm able to dispense coffee into the holder again.

'I don't know how that could have happened,' Rita says. Her voice has that surly tone that teenagers use when they've been caught red-handed doing something they shouldn't, but don't want to admit it.

'I think you do. It didn't turn itself off, did it?'

'I don't know. Maybe I knocked it by accident.'

'That would be hard to do, given that the plug is quite difficult to reach. Admit it; you couldn't be bothered with it, so you turned it off.'

'It's too hard!' she says angrily. 'All people want is these ridiculous fancy coffees with different types of frothy milk. How am I supposed to know the difference between a cappuccino, a latte, and a flat white? I'm not a bloody ballerina!'

'I think you mean barista, and the instructions are here.' I indicate Bronwyn's carefully written notes. 'All you have to do is follow them. This machine is a major investment in the future of the business, and I have to take the fact that you've deliberately sabotaged it seriously. This is your second warning, Rita. One more incident like this and you'll be out. Do you understand?'

'You've got a bloody cheek,' she rounds on me. 'I've been here eleven years. You can't just come swanning in here and make threats like that.'

'If you continue to sabotage, or refuse to use, the equipment that I've provided, to the detriment of my business, then I can certainly make threats like that. This café is my livelihood now, so I will be watching you like a hawk. One more incident, Rita. I'm warning you.'

'You wouldn't dare fire me,' she hisses, but there's a hint of uncertainty in her voice.

'Try me,' I reply, and retreat through the kitchen to carry on with my flat clearing. I've just got time to get to the tip and back before Mick, the builder, arrives. I know it sounds bad, but I enjoyed having Rita on the ropes far more than I should have done.

* * *

I'm just taking down Fred's tatty curtains and piling them on a chair for the house clearance people when the bell rings to let me know that Mick has arrived. I press the buzzer to let him into the building, and then open the front door and step onto the landing to meet him.

'Hello, Daisy. You're looking well. I haven't seen you in ages.'

'Hi, Mick. Thanks for coming.' I step back to let him into the flat. 'I'd offer you a cup of tea, but I don't have a kettle or anything up here. Would you like something from the café?'

'I'm fine, thanks. So, what are we looking at?' he asks.

'I've got the house clearance people coming next week to empty the place. After that, I think it needs a new kitchen, new bathroom, double glazing, and redecorating all the way through. Have a look and tell me what you think.'

I sit in one of Fred's old armchairs while Mick takes a look around. I know I should get lots of quotes for the work, but I've known Mick since I moved in with Nan and Grandad. I trust him to give me a good price, and Grandad will be furious if I don't use him. I watch him as he wanders around, whistling tunelessly and writing in his notebook as he goes. I have no idea how he and Grandad met, or even how old he is. All I know is that they've been mates forever. He sticks his head in the cupboard where the boiler lives, as well as the loft. I have no idea what he's expecting to find up there.

Eventually, he declares that he's ready to walk round with me. We start in the kitchen.

'I know it looks shabby, but the underlying units are solid,' he tells me. 'If you were planning to keep the same layout, you could save some money there, as we'll just replace the fronts. I think we could do a better layout, though. I've made a couple of drawings.'

He shows me what he has in mind, and it does look like a huge improvement. He's replaced the standalone cooker with space for a hob built into the work surface and reconfigured the cupboards to give space for a double oven, dishwasher, and microwave. He's also added an island in the middle with extra cupboards underneath. I love it. He brings a catalogue out of his bag, and I choose white shaker-style fronts for the cupboards and drawers, and a wood-look countertop. I liked the look of the real wood ones, but Mick advised me that they're much harder to look after, as well as being considerably more expensive. He also talks me out of a tiled floor, on the basis that everything I drop on it will either break, or break a tile. We do manage to agree on LED lighting so I can see what I'm doing.

In the bathroom, I choose fairly standard white units, a glass screen to replace the shower curtain, more LED lighting, and a large illuminated mirror.

'You've got a dilemma here, Daisy,' he explains, indicating the shower. 'These showers are dreadful. They heat the water inside the unit here, so you never get more than a dribble. I'd like to put in a power shower, ideally. If I do that, though, you're going to need a new boiler, because the boiler you've got will never cope with it.'

'I can't live with a pathetic shower,' I reply. 'Let's go with the power shower. The boiler probably needs replacing anyway.'

'Good choice. I can't do the boiler myself, but I've got a mate who will do it. I'll get a sparky on the electrics, too.'

We continue our tour of the flat. Mick agrees to do everything, including replastering to get rid of the awful Artex, upgrading the loft insulation, and organising floor coverings. 'By the time I'm done in here, you'll be able to move straight in.'

'Any idea what all this is going to cost?' I ask him.

'It's not going to be cheap, Daisy. I'll have to work it out exactly, and obviously I'll do the best price I can for you, but I'm not sure you'll have a lot of change from fifteen grand.'

Shit, that's going to make a big hole in my reserves. Still, there's no point in cutting corners.

'How long do you think it'll take?'

'When are the house clearance people coming?'

'Monday.'

'Give me a key, I'll get my guys started as soon as I can. You should be in within a month.'

I don't have a spare, so I agree to get new ones cut and post them through his door. He only lives a few roads away from Nan and Grandad, so it's not far out of my way.

'One final thing. I might need you to do the same again for the other flat. Just in case you can get any discounts.'

He smiles. 'I'll bear that in mind.'

As I drive home, another thought occurs to me. Although Mick's work will take care of the basics, I don't own any furniture, curtains, or anything beyond what's in my bedroom at home. I'm going to have to buy everything from scratch, even kitchen utensils. Suddenly, this all seems like a very bad idea. Maybe I'll let it, like I originally planned, and stay with Nan and Grandad instead.

23

I'm still tired, but I'm loving my new life. For the last month, I've been getting up at 6 a.m., having a quick shower, and throwing on some comfortable clothes, before leaving the house at 6.30 to get to the café for 7. Matt is always there before me, but I make us a coffee and we have what we've come to call our 'morning meeting'. It's basically a quick chat about what cakes I'm going to make for the afternoon customers and what the lunchtime special is. I've managed to prise Nora's recipe folder off Nan, with a bit of difficulty, and it now lives in the café kitchen. It's become my bible as I've tried to breathe new life into the place. The early signs are that my efforts are paying off, as trade is definitely picking up and we're starting to make a small profit.

Rita generally shuffles in just before 7.30 on the days she's working. She barely speaks to me, but I'm fine with that. She's been keeping her head down; I think she's worked out that I want her gone and is determined not to give me any excuse to fire her. What she hasn't worked out is that I probably wouldn't want to fire her if she wasn't such a surly, lazy old cow. Even now, she does the bare minimum. When Rita's working, I find myself counting the days until Bronwyn's next shift, because the place just comes alive when she's around.

Mick tells me he's made good progress upstairs. The new kitchen and bathroom are in, as is the double glazing and the new boiler. He's just finished the decorating and the carpets are being laid today. I've pretty much let him get on with it; he did come down fairly early on to ask me to choose tiles for the kitchen and bathroom, but I was in the middle of making a broccoli and stilton soup, so just told him what colours I thought would look nice and left him to choose the actual tiles. I did tell him that I might be letting the flat out rather than moving in, but he just laughed and said I wouldn't be able to resist it by the time he'd finished. In terms of the general décor, I've asked him to go for fairly neutral colours. I read online that neutral colours are best when it comes to attracting tenants. I'm looking forward to seeing it later, when it's finished.

Although it's a Friday, I have the day off today. I'm going up to London for my final meeting with Mr Holdsworth and Rebecca. We've scheduled it for 11.30, so we can go to the pub for a farewell drink afterwards. He did offer four o'clock, but I wasn't wild about going for a drink with everyone after work on a Friday, as they'd all be up for making a night of it and I have work in the morning. Even though it's only been a month since I was doing this every day, it feels odd to be putting on a suit and getting the train to London. At least I don't have to pay for parking, as I can leave my car behind the café and walk to the station.

My pass has been deactivated, so I approach the receptionist in the lobby and she calls Mr Holdsworth to come and collect me. I realise that I've probably passed her every day for the last six years and I've never spoken to her in all that time. I look around the lobby, remembering the day I came here for my interview. I try to think whether she was in reception on that day, or the day I started work, but nothing comes.

'Ah, Daisy. How lovely to see you! You look well, how are things going?' Mr Holdsworth looks genuinely pleased to see me, which is nice.

'I'm very well thank you, Mr Holdsworth. The café is starting to turn a corner, I believe. How about you?'

'Yes, all good. We've had a few changes since you were last here. Mr Speke has left the business to pursue other opportunities, and Rosemary has gone with him, do you remember her?'

'Yes, she was his PA.'

'That's right. Anyway, Rob has been acting partner since he left, and is doing very well indeed. He may find himself in the role permanently. We've also posted an advertisement for a new junior, and the applications are coming in. I'm hoping that, somewhere in among them, there is an applicant as promising as you were. Shall we go up?'

He lets me through the barrier, and we take the lift together. The office looks unchanged, apart from the fact that everyone turns to look at me as I walk in. I can feel their eyes on me as I follow Mr Holdsworth to his office, where Rebecca is already waiting. I spot Rob, ensconced in Mr Speke's office, and wonder briefly what prompted Mr Speke to leave so suddenly. I thought he'd be there until they dragged his corpse out.

The formalities don't take long. Rebecca takes me through my redundancy package, which is enough to cover my salary for several months. I sign the forms, hand in my pass, and she informs me that the money will be in my bank account early next week.

'I've taken the liberty of booking a table at an Italian restaurant round the corner for your farewell lunch,' Mr Holdsworth says. 'I hope that's okay. I know you and Grace are fans of the Lord Nelson, but there's no way we'd all get in there, and Rob informs me that this restaurant is very good. I wanted to give you a decent send-off.'

As we troop out of the building and head towards the restaurant, Grace falls in step next to me. I haven't heard from her since the day I left, which doesn't altogether surprise me, but she's obviously keen to make up lost time now.

'Are you okay, Daisy? What are you doing now?'

'I'm fine, thanks. I'm working full-time at the café and doing my best to turn it around. It's a long road, but it looks like we're making progress. How about you? I was surprised to hear that Mr Speke had left. I thought he was a lifer.'

'Is that what they told you?' Grace starts to giggle, and I look at her quizzically.

'One of the cleaners had a hospital appointment, so she came in to clean the offices around an hour later than she normally does,' Grace tells me, keeping her voice low so as not to attract attention. 'She was expecting everyone to have gone, but there they were, going at it hammer and tongs in his office!'

'Who?'

'Mr Speke and Rosemary, of course!'

'No!'

'Yes!' says Grace. 'I knew they were up to something, but nobody believed me, even you. Anyway, she was completely traumatised and filed a complaint.'

'Who, Rosemary?'

'No, the cleaner. Do keep up. Anyway, there was no way he could stay after that, so apparently they've moved to Scotland and he's starting a new firm up there.'

'And you didn't text me immediately because...?'

There's a pause, and I notice that she's no longer meeting my eye.

'I'm really sorry I haven't been in touch. You and I were the only senior accounting techs, and I know that means my name must have been in the frame as well. Although I'm obviously pleased that I still have a job, I felt bad that my job cost you yours. I wasn't sure what to say to you, and then the longer I left it, the harder it got.'

She's so contrite that I decide to put her out of her misery, as far as I can.

'Look, the truth is I was struggling with trying to do my job and look after the café. If Mr Holdsworth hadn't made me redundant, I might have ended up resigning anyway, so it's all worked out for the best. You can stop feeling guilty, okay? Now, tell me more about Mr Speke and Rosemary. Was there much fallout beyond them leaving? I don't even know if either of them were married.'

'He's married, but apparently his wife knew all about it and was happy to turn a blind eye as long as they were discreet. It stopped him pestering her for sex, so she silently condoned it. Apparently, it had been going on for years. Rosemary was starting to want more, to come out of the closet, as it were, but he was worried that it would damage his professional reputation if people knew he was in a relationship with his PA. The irony is that, by trying to keep it secret, they completely torpedoed both of their reputations, and his wife is threatening to take him for all he has. She may have been complicit, but she doesn't want to give up her comfortable lifestyle to fund her husband and his bit on the side.'

'How do you know all this stuff?'

'I've been on a charm offensive with Rosemary, making her cups of tea, going with her to get sandwiches at lunchtime and so on. Did you never notice? I hoped that she might let her guard down and reveal something if she thought I was her friend. After it broke, I rang her to check if she was okay, because it was all very sudden and I didn't believe a word of what Mr Holdsworth had said. She sang like a canary. Ah, here we are.'

The restaurant is as good as Rob promised, and the lunch is a jolly affair. I stick to sparkling water, as drinking during the day makes me terribly sleepy, but the others don't hold back and there are a fair number of empty wine bottles on the table by the time we've finished eating. At one point, it looked like Mr Holdsworth was going to make a speech, but thankfully he thought better of it. What would he have said? 'We love you, Daisy, which is why we had to get rid of you' doesn't quite strike the right tone, and he obviously can't reveal what really happened.

Mr Holdsworth generously picks up the bill, and everyone shakes my hand and wishes me luck as we leave the restaurant. Grace pulls me to her and hugs me fiercely.

'Let's stay in touch, yeah? I'll text you,' she tells me.

I hug her back and smile. I'm certain I'll never hear from her again, but I appreciate the sentiment.

* * *

I feel a surprising sense of relief as the train pulls out of Charing Cross. It was nice to see everyone, and I did enjoy the lunch, but I don't belong here any more. I'm itching to get back to Sevenoaks and my new life. I'm also looking forward to the redundancy payout hitting my account next week; I don't have a lot of outgoings, but it will be a while before I can start taking any money from the café, so it will be a useful buffer to keep me going.

Mick is loading up his van when I get back, and he smiles broadly when he sees me. 'All done. Do you want to see?'

I've purposely not been up to the flat while the renovations have been going on, partly because I didn't want to annoy Mick and his team by being under their feet, but also because I find it difficult to visualise how something is going to look when it's a work in progress. Mick hands me the spare keys and we walk round to the front of the building together, let ourselves in the bottom door, and climb the stairs.

'Oh, wow!' I gasp, as I push open the front door and step into the living room. Fred's flat is unrecognisable. What was a dark, dingy, cluttered space when I first saw it is now bright, airy, and feels thoroughly modern. The magnolia paint on the walls combines with the biscuit-coloured carpet to create an impression of space, and I can barely hear the traffic on the road outside through the double-glazed windows. The kitchen is beautiful; Mick has pandered to my desire for a tiled floor by laying a tile-patterned vinyl, and the dark blue tiles on the walls offset the white cupboards and wood-look worktop perfectly. The double oven still has its protective plastic on it, and a sleek induction hob is set into the counter, with a light and extractor fan overhead. Mick opens one of the cupboards to reveal the built-in dishwasher.

'It's all good-quality stuff, but I didn't go mad on the budget,' he tells me. 'The units came from Magnet Express, so we can replace them easily if they get damaged. I got the appliances from a friend of mine who runs an electrical shop, so I got a decent discount on them. Would you like to see the bathroom?'

I'm reluctant to leave the kitchen, but I follow him. The horrible stained units are all gone, and the bathroom now looks inviting. A sleek-looking power shower stands over the pristine white bath, with a glass screen to stop the water from escaping. I'm trying hard not to fall in love with this flat but I'm failing. I need reminding of the bill to keep my feet on the ground.

'It's beautiful, Mick. Absolutely stunning. Better than I could have dreamed. Give me the bad news now, what's the damage?'

He smiles again. 'I think I said you wouldn't get much change from fifteen grand, didn't I?'

'Yes.' I steel myself for the true figure. I've watched enough episodes of *Homes Under the Hammer* and *Grand Designs* in my time to know that the initial budget is always way too little. It's got to be at least £20,000, probably more.'

'Well, with the discounts and everything, plus a couple of guys who owed me favours and did the work I couldn't do for peanuts, the whole lot has come in at eleven and a half grand so you'll get some change after all.'

I wrap my arms around him and hug him tight. 'You're a star, Mick. I mean it. Thank you so much.'

'The question is, are you still going to let it or are you going to move in?'

'I don't know. I'd love to move in, but I don't have any furniture or anything.'

'That's true, but you do have three and a half grand that you didn't think you were going to have. I reckon that would get you started quite nicely if you were careful. You'd be amazed what you can pick up in the YMCA furniture shop and places like that. Quite a few of them will deliver, too. Just a thought.'

Could I live here, I wonder? I walk back into the kitchen and imagine myself cooking an evening meal. Maybe Katie would be sitting out in the living room, with her legs tucked under her as she concentrated on solving a thorny homework problem. The neutral colour palette is exactly what I would have chosen for myself, and I realise that I don't want anyone else living here.

'You're right, Mick,' I tell him. 'I'd be mad not to move in.'

24

I'm starting to worry that I'll never be rid of Rita. She's still barely civil to me, but she's being ultra-careful to make sure that she stays just within the limits of acceptable behaviour, without actually doing any more work or being less surly. I feel like we're doing some kind of dance around each other; we're both failing to conceal our mutual dislike, but neither of us wants to provoke open warfare. I don't really know why she hasn't resigned, as she can't be enjoying working here. Sometimes, I can hear her huffing and puffing as she struggles with the coffee machine, but at least she hasn't tried to sabotage it again. Ron and Agnes have also settled down. Now that they've worked their way through all the coffees, they're tending to stick to one or two that they like. They've started sharing a table, I notice. Bronwyn tells me that they're also arriving and leaving together. I decide to do a little probing to see if I can find out what's going on. Instead of letting Rita carry their breakfasts out to them, I take them out myself.

'Morning, Ron, morning, Agnes. How are you both?'

'Fine, thank you, dear,' Agnes replies, with a smile.

'It's nice to see you two sitting together and chatting,' I venture.

'I did wonder about suggesting you shared a table a while ago, but I wasn't sure how you'd feel about it.'

'I'd have said no,' Agnes tells me, very firmly.

'Why, out of interest?'

'Well, he's a man, isn't he?' she says, indicating Ron. 'For all I knew, he might have been one of those stalkers, or rapists, or whatever you call them.'

I look at Ron. Try as I might, I can't imagine him as any of those things. He raises his eyebrows but says nothing.

'So, what changed?'

'Well, he bought me a coffee, didn't he? I had to sit with him then, otherwise it would have seemed rude. We got chatting, and it turns out he lives just down the road from me, so now he knocks on my front door every morning and we walk down here together. I've told him we're just friends, and that he's not to get any ideas.'

I do like Agnes, but her sex siren days are quite a long way behind her, so I can't help thinking she's being a little optimistic. Still, it's nice that they've become friends, and it frees up a table for someone else, which is good news for me.

'Perhaps you should invite Harold to join you,' I suggest. 'He might enjoy a bit of company too.'

'Not likely,' Agnes retorts. 'He came in behind me once, when I was at the counter putting my order in, and I'm sure he pinched me on the bum. Dirty pervert, that's what he is.'

'Are you sure?' I ask.

'Well, who else could it have been?'

'I don't know, I just don't see Harold as the bum-pinching type.'

'Ah, well. It's the quiet ones you've got to watch. That's what my mother always said.'

Our fascinating and slightly disturbing conversation is cut short by a commotion to my right. I glance over to see what's happening. A young woman is sitting at one of the tables with a child I imagine must be her son. He's knocked over his glass, and a lake of Coca-Cola is spreading over the tablecloth and starting to drip onto the floor. I can see Rita advancing with a cloth, so I decide to let her deal with it.

'For God's sake!' she says angrily to the boy as she aggressively starts wiping up the spill. 'Look at the mess you've made.' She turns to the woman and continues. 'You shouldn't be bringing him out if he doesn't know how to behave. This is a café, not a nursery.' My jaw drops open. I can't believe what I've just heard.

'Rita, let me deal with this,' I tell her, as I swoop on the table and grab the cloth. The boy looks like he's about to cry, and the woman looks absolutely gobsmacked. 'Can you clear some of the other tables, please, and wait for me in the kitchen?'

'I'm so sorry,' I say to the woman as I continue wiping up the mess. 'Let me get you another drink, and we'll refund you for your meal today.' I turn to the little boy. 'Don't worry about her, she's just a bit grumpy. Accidents happen all the time. It's not your fault, okay?'

The boy's lip is still trembling, but I think I've averted the worst of the crisis. I bring him another Coke and concentrate hard on being the hospitable owner, but inside I'm boiling with rage. What the hell did Rita think she was doing? Even with the refund and my apology, I'd be very surprised if we ever see the woman and her son again, and they're exactly the type of demographic I need to attract if I'm going to make a success of this place. Once I'm sure I've minimised the damage as best I can by writing out a card promising her a 10 per cent discount on her next visit on top of the refund, I stalk back into the kitchen. Rita is standing there looking defiant, and I can't hold myself in any more.

'What the fuck is the matter with you? Are you actively trying to put me out of business?' I hiss. My voice is trembling with anger, but I'm determined not to shout. I don't want the customers over-hearing.

Matt stops what he's doing and looks at me in surprise. He has no idea what's just happened, so probably thinks I've lost the plot. Rita looks like I've slapped her. Although we've clashed before, she's never seen me properly angry, and I think she's surprised by the force of it. She recovers quickly, though, and her voice is surprisingly calm as she replies.

'Don't swear at me, young lady. He'd been messing about with his glass for ages. It was inevitable that he was going to spill it, and she wasn't doing anything to stop him. Someone needed to tell him off, otherwise he'll never learn.'

I can't believe what I'm hearing. 'Are you criminally insane?' I demand. 'I am working my fucking arse off trying to turn this café around, and you seem determined to sabotage me at every turn! First it was the bloody card reader, then the shit you pulled with the coffee machine, and now you've decided to get rid of the customers by insulting them! I've had to refund them and give them a voucher, and I still doubt we'll ever see them again, let alone anyone else who was in earshot. Do you have any idea how much fucking damage you've just done?'

'You're over-reacting. All I did was…'

'Get out!' I hiss, pointing at the door.

'You can't be serious. You're firing me for that?'

'You're damned right I'm firing you for that. I should have bloody fired you long ago.'

'Okay, fine. I'm fed up with working here anyway, with the stupid coffees and everything. You don't need to fire me, because I resign. Oh, and good luck finding a replacement because nobody will want to work for you, or even come in here, once I'm done. I know a lot of people in this town, and I'll be sure to tell all of them how appallingly you've treated me,' she says loudly as she grabs her coat and, with a speed I never knew she had in her, marches out of the front door, banging it behind her. My breath is coming in gasps and my legs are shaking, which are sure warnings of an impending panic attack, so I steady myself against the work surface and concentrate on slowing down my breathing.

'Are you okay?' Matt asks. 'What was that all about? I don't think I've ever heard you swear before, and I just counted three fucks in less than a minute!'

'I'll have to tell you later,' I gasp. 'As soon as I've got this under control, I need to get out front. Will you be able to cope in here on your own for the rest of the day? I'll call Bronwyn in a bit and see if she can come in tomorrow.'

'I'll be fine,' he tells me. 'Your soup's pretty much made and the cakes are cooling, so it's all good. Has she really gone?'

'I bloody hope so. I'll physically push her out if she tries to come back. Right, I'd better go and show my face, I suppose.' I take off the hairnet, replace my full-length apron with one of the waist-high ones that I bought for Bronwyn and Rita to wear, and walk slowly out into the front of the café. As I do, the most extraordinary thing happens.

Ron starts clapping.

Agnes joins in.

Slowly, the applause spreads across the tables. Even people I've never seen in here before are joining in. The woman whose son sparked the confrontation is on her feet, giving me a standing ovation. I don't know what to do, so I just stand there, blushing furiously, until it dies down.

'Anybody want a job?' I joke when the applause has subsided, and a ripple of laughter comes back.

I busy myself clearing tables and bringing plates out to help restore my equilibrium. I'm definitely not as comfortable out here as I am in the kitchen, so I pull out my phone and call Bronwyn, who informs me that she'll happily come in tomorrow. I'm just wiping some coffee rings off one of the tablecloths when the woman with the child approaches me.

'Excuse me,' she says. 'Were you serious when you asked if anyone wanted a job?'

'Well, I have a young woman who comes in on Saturdays who can cover in the short term, but I'm not sure whether she'll want to do more than that. Why?'

'I'm new to the area, but I worked in hospitality before I moved down here. I'd certainly be interested if you have a vacancy. I don't have a CV to hand, but I can drop one in later. I'm Penny, by the way.'

I'm not sure what to do. Bronwyn has said she's happy to give me as many days as I need, and I know she'd do whatever hours I asked of her, but I'm not sure that's what she actually wants. I suspect she quite likes the variety of working both here and in the art gallery, but it seems rude to think about taking anyone else on without at least talking to her. I have an idea, and I give Penny a smile.

'Pleased to meet you, Penny. I'm Daisy. How do you feel about doing a trial day? Bring in your CV, but I think we'll learn much more about you from seeing you in action for a day than we will in an interview. I'll pay you for the hours you work, even if you decide it's not for you or we decide you're not quite right for us. What do you think?'

She considers for a moment. 'I could come tomorrow if that's not too soon? I'll bring my CV and references with me.'

'Okay,' I say. 'Your normal hours would be seven thirty in the morning until three but, as tomorrow's a trial day, you can start at nine. You'll be working with Bronwyn. She's young, but she knows this place and the customers like the back of her hand. If she rates you, then we'll look at setting up something more permanent. If she doesn't then, well, I probably don't need to elaborate on that bit.'

'Perfect,' Penny replies. 'I'll see you at nine o'clock tomorrow.'

'One question, if I may?' I ask, as she gets ready to depart.

'Yes?'

'What are you going to do about childcare? I know it's none of my business, but it's better to be up front if it's likely to be an issue, don't you think?'

Penny laughs. 'You don't need to worry about that. Oliver here is my nephew. I'm only looking after him for the day while my sister moves house.'

* * *

I'm still a bit trembly when we close up. I've never had to fire anyone before and, while I'm delighted to finally be rid of Rita, doing the deed has definitely taken it out of me. I can't collapse, though, as my first furniture delivery is due to arrive any minute. I took Mick's advice, and Katie and I had a happy time in the YMCA furniture store. It's amazing what people get rid of; we found a very sturdy double wooden bedframe for Katie's room, a couple of matching sofas that look brand new, as well as a few other bits and pieces. Matt has offered to bring my double bed from home in his van on Sunday, which will be my official 'moving in' day. Nan and I measured my bedroom curtains and they will fit in the bedroom in the flat, but I've had to order new curtains for Katie's room and the sitting room. Mick's friend with the electrical shop has sorted me out with a TV and a dongle that I can plug in to allow me to watch programmes on catch-up using my phone. I've probably spent the most money on pots, pans, knives, and chopping boards for the kitchen. As well as making sure I eat healthily, I want to be able to experiment with things we could offer downstairs in the café.

It will be basic in the flat but comfortable, and I can build up slowly from here. I'm looking forward to it. Nan and Grandad are being very supportive, but I've seen the occasional tear in Nan's eye that indicates she's not finding the prospect of me finally moving out quite as joyful as she's trying to portray.

Grandad is being typically practical about it and keeps making remarks about how they will have a spare room again at last, even though I can't think who they would invite to stay in it. After ten years of living with them, some of them far from easy, I feel I ought to do something to say thank you, but inspiration is failing to strike.

The YMCA van arrives, and the two guys make short work of carrying the stuff Katie and I bought up to the flat. There are already a few boxes around the place, and I decide to spend an hour or two unpacking to calm myself down before I drive home. I'm unloading boxes in the kitchen when the doorbell rings.

'Wow, this is a bit different!' Matt exclaims, as I let him in. 'Mind if I look around?'

'Help yourself. I'd offer you a coffee, but I don't have any yet.'

I continue unloading the box I'm working on as he wanders from room to room.

'Is that a power shower?' he calls from the bathroom.

'Yup.'

'Okay, now I'm envious,' he laughs.

'I'm going to do your flat too, don't worry,' I call to him. 'You must freeze to death in winter.'

'It does get a bit chilly, but I just put on an extra jumper. You don't need to worry about me. I'm happy as I am.'

'Okay, let me come at it a different way. If you were paying full rent for your flat, would you consider it good value for money?'

'Well, no, but I'm not paying full rent, am I?'

'Not quite, but the rent you pay isn't the full picture. You also have to consider the hit you take in your salary. Add those two together and you're paying a decent rent. If I were you, I'd be kicking off to the landlord and demanding that she put in a decent shower and double glazing, at least.'

He laughs. 'Maybe you're right, but I think you're missing something.'

'What's that?'

'This kind of work is pretty invasive. It's one thing renovating an empty flat like this one, but the builders won't want to be working round a sitting tenant. Where would I go while my flat was being done?'

He's got a point. I don't want him living in his van again. I do need to modernise his flat, though. As I consider the problem, foolish inspiration strikes.

'You could move into the spare room here while the work was being done.'

'Umm, what about Katie?'

'It would just be for a few weeks, and she'll only be here at weekends, so she could share my bed. You could have the spare room until your flat is done, and then Katie could have it back once you've gone.'

'Don't you think you'd get sick of the sight of me? We work together all day, I'm sure you wouldn't want me hanging around in the evenings as well.'

'Nonsense!' I say, with a certainty I'm not sure I feel. I'm starting to wonder whether I've been a bit rash, but I can't back out now. 'You never know, it might be fun.'

25

Things at the café have improved no end since Rita went. Penny has turned out to be a huge success. Bronwyn declared her to be 'fab' when I debriefed her at the end of the trial day, mainly (I suspect) because Penny was finally able to show her how to make patterns with the milk in the coffees. As I suspected, Bronwyn also prefers splitting her time between the café and the art gallery, so Penny's arrival didn't put her nose out of joint at all. I followed up with Penny's referees, who both gave glowing accounts, and she started pretty much straight away.

'I'm thinking about trading in my car and getting a van,' I say to Matt, as I add some olives and capers to the puttanesca sauce that we're going to have with our pasta. I've been living above the café for three weeks now, and we've got into the habit of cooking for each other most nights, as it seemed silly for us to prepare two separate meals when we're next-door neighbours with nothing much better to do in the evenings. Although it's a Saturday night, Katie isn't here as she's staying over with Bronwyn. They're going to watch movies into the early hours, apparently, and she's promised me faithfully that she'll be back in time for me to take her back to Nan and Grandad's for lunch.

'What's brought this on?' Matt asks.

'I'm sorry, but your van still gives me the heebie-jeebies,' I tell him. 'I know you love it, but I'd feel a lot happier doing the cash and carry runs in something more modern, with airbags and stuff. I don't need anything as big as yours, but I was looking online and found something called a Transit Connect that looks suitable. I just don't know if I'd be able to reverse it.'

'I can help you with that, if you like. If you get one, we can take it across to the station car park one Sunday and you can reverse it around until you feel confident.'

'Are you sure?'

'Yes, absolutely. I'll bring mine along and you can practise parking around it. It's got a fair few scrapes and scratches already, so a few more from you won't do it any harm. Probably better than letting you loose around someone else's pride and joy.'

'Cheeky bastard!' I throw the tea towel at him, and he laughs.

'You'll be fine, I'm sure. You just have to get used to using the wing mirrors to work out where you're going.'

'Maybe I'll give the dealer a call next week to arrange a test drive. Have you finished packing everything up?'

'Nearly. I've kept tomorrow morning free so that we can go and do a shop together before you go off for your lunch, and then I'll do the last bits in the afternoon.'

'A shop together? That sounds awfully domestic,' I say. 'Will you be requiring your pipe and slippers when we get back?'

'Very funny. I just want to make sure I'm paying my way. I can't be accepting charity from the boss, you know.'

Mick is starting work on Matt's flat on Monday, so he's moving into Katie's room for the duration, and tonight is the first night he's staying over. I'm still not 100 per cent sure that it's a good idea, even though it was my suggestion. We get on really well, despite the fact that we're rarely outside one another's company, but he's going to be living with me for a whole month, and that feels like a big commitment.

'How do you feel about being stuck with me for the next month?' I ask him.

'I don't know. I'm looking forward to testing out the power shower in the morning,' he smiles.

'It is nice,' I agree. 'Just don't go using all the hot water.' I wind a piece of pasta onto a fork and bite into it. It's perfect, so I drain it and start plating up.

'Nice try. I noticed that your new boiler is a combi, which means that there's no hot water limit. I might spend a couple of hours in there.'

'I'm regretting this already!'

'Hey, it wasn't my idea to renovate my flat. I was quite happy, but you insisted that I needed this luxury upgrade.'

'You're assuming I'm doing it for you,' I joke. 'I might just be looking after my inheritance. Here you go.' I place the plates on the table and bring out the garlic bread and salad. As it's a Saturday night and we're not working tomorrow, I've opened a bottle of wine and I pour two generous glasses.

'Cheers! Here's to not killing each other over the next month,' Matt says, clinking his glass against mine.

* * *

I wake the next morning desperate to wee. Wine does that to me, probably not helped by the water I drank before going to bed to make sure I didn't get a hangover. Without thinking, I leap out of bed and pad across the living room to the bathroom in my T-shirt and knickers. I turn the handle and throw open the bathroom door, only to be confronted by Matt, who is completely naked apart from a small towel wrapped around his midriff.

'Sorry!' I say, hurriedly closing the door. I now have three problems:

I still really need to wee, and it looked like Matt was in the middle of shaving. I'm not sure I can hold on until he's finished.

It's only his first morning here, and I've already flashed my knickers at him. This is not a great start.

The image of him with just a towel on is burned into my brain, and a lot of surprisingly filthy thoughts are accompanying it. That is a body I would very much like to get to know better. This is a complication I really don't need, especially as I'm stuck with him for a month.

'No, I'm sorry,' Matt's voice calls from the other side of the door. 'I couldn't find the lock, so I gave up in the end.'

'There isn't one. It hasn't been a problem to date, but I'll ask Mick to look at it while he's working on your place. Umm, Matt?'

'Yes?'

'I'm bursting for a wee. How long are you going to be?'

'Probably about five minutes. Do you need me to come out?'

'Please.'

The door opens, and I'm confronted by his body again. I notice that he has the word 'Laura' tattooed over his heart, and there are a few drops of water still on his chest and arms. I have a sudden urge to grab the towel from his midriff and wipe him down, before...

My brief pornographic train of thought is rudely interrupted by my bladder, and I dash into the bathroom and plonk myself down on the toilet, sighing with relief as I let go. I wipe myself, pull up my knickers and wash my hands. As I look in the mirror, I realise I have more problems to add to my list:

If I was going to flash my knickers at Matt, why couldn't I at least have been wearing a decent pair? These ones were white originally, but they're so old that they're now a sort of light grey, the material is so thin that you can easily see my pubic hair through it, and it's starting to fray and come away from the waistband. Not the look I'd be going for if I knew I was going to be showing them off.

He's outside the bathroom, waiting to come back in, which means that I have no option but to flash him again, plus I've got to navigate past *that* body, and I don't have anything to distract me from the fantasies piling into my head any more. Some of them are so outrageous, I'm not even sure they're physically possible. What on earth is wrong with me?

This is a disaster. I like Matt as a person very much, but this has caught me completely by surprise. How on earth am I going to keep my hands off him for the next month? I've always had what I consider to be a healthy sex drive, but it's like someone has flipped a switch and I can't think of anything else all of a sudden.

'For God's sake, get a grip, Daisy!' I tell my reflection, firmly.

'Are you okay in there?' Matt calls, from the other side of the door.

'Yes, fine. Just coming out.' I force my hands to stay at my sides as I open the bathroom door and come face to face with him once more. Stupidly, I let my eyes drop. That towel really is very short, and I can clearly see the outline of his penis pressing against it. That's more than I can cope with, and I flee to my bedroom, closing the door firmly behind me.

'The bathroom's free,' Matt calls, a few minutes later.

I wait until I hear his bedroom door close before wrapping myself in my towelling dressing gown and crossing to the bathroom again. I strip off and step into the shower, letting the water cascade over me as I consider this highly unwelcome development. Apart from anything else, we're work colleagues, and I've read enough agony aunt columns to know that getting involved with people at work is a really bad idea, because you're guaranteed a toxic environment if the relationship doesn't work out. That would be even worse for Matt and me, because it's just us in the kitchen most of the time.

'Fuck, fuck, fuck, fuck, fuck,' I mutter, as I wash my hair and condition it. What the hell am I going to do?

By the time I've finished in the shower, dried my hair, and got dressed, things are in a slightly better place. Matt is dressed, for one thing, although I'm still far too easily able to envision his body under his rugby shirt and jeans. Katie has also returned, looking tired but happy, and I've never been more grateful for a distraction. Matt is obviously a little embarrassed too, as I notice he's not meeting my eyes.

'Did you have a good time?' I ask Katie.

'Brilliant, thanks. We're going to do it again next week, if that's okay with you?'

'No problem from my side, as long as Bronwyn's mum doesn't object to you getting under her feet. What did you watch?'

'We took it in turns to choose. I'm not sure Bronwyn chooses films for the story; she seems to be more interested in the lighting. We watched some French film with subtitles because she was obsessed by the way the director lit one of the characters' eyes. It won a load of awards, apparently.'

'And what did you choose?'

'*French Kiss*, obviously!'

Katie and I first saw *French Kiss* a couple of years ago, and we've probably watched it at least ten times since then. We can quote large sections of the script by heart, and it's our go-to film if we want a bit of cheering up, so I'm not at all surprised.

'What did Bronwyn make of that?'

'She liked it, actually. Or at least she said she did. How's my bedroom, Matt?'

'Very comfortable, thank you, Katie,' he replies.

'Right, shall we go?' I ask. 'Matt and I are going to do a quick supermarket shop before you and I go to Nan and Grandad's. Do you want to come with us?'

'Sure, I've got nothing else to do.'

I'm glad Katie is with us, as the conversation between Matt and me is a little stilted while we make our way around Sainsbury's. We're perfectly civil, but we're tiptoeing around each other like we've only just met for the first time and we're trying to create a good impression. I hate the sudden awkwardness, and I find myself trying to work out if there's anywhere else Matt can stay for the month. I wonder if he's doing the same.

* * *

'So. Weird atmosphere this morning,' Katie observes when we've unpacked the shopping and set off for Nan and Grandad's. 'What did I miss?'

'There was an incident involving the bathroom door,' I explain.

'Oh, yes? I think you need to tell me everything, don't you? Unburden yourself.'

I fill her in on what happened, playing it down as much as I can. I do confess to liking what I saw, but I don't elaborate.

'I was crazy inviting him to stay for a month. We're not even twenty-four hours in and he's already causing chaos!' I exclaim, when I've finished the story.

'It might be good for both of you,' she observes.

'How on earth can it be good for me?' I demand. 'I've got to maintain a professional relationship with him. I don't need to be distracted by him parading around in a towel that barely covers his modesty!'

'Why do you have to make this so complicated? You obviously

fancy him, and it's clear he fancies you. Why not just get on with it?'

'Because having a relationship with a work colleague is a really bad idea, that's why. Hang on, what do you mean "it's clear that he fancies me"?'

'Have you seen the way he looks at you?'

'No. How does he look at me?'

'Totally doe-eyed. Are you really saying you've never noticed? Why do you think he was so helpful when we first met him?'

'I just thought he was being kind because he was a nice guy.'

'Oh, he's a genuinely nice guy, no doubt about that. But he's also potty about you, there's no doubt about that either.'

Oh, God. If she's right, I'm in so much trouble.

26

Matt is watching something on the TV when I let myself back into the flat. He glances up and smiles, before returning his gaze to the screen.

'How was your lunch?' he asks.

'Good, thanks. What did you have?'

'I treated myself and went to the pub. They had a carvery on and it was surprisingly good, although I'm not a fan of generic gravy.'

'What do you mean?'

'Well, if I'm making gravy, I like to flavour it to complement the meat it's going with. If it's beef, I'll put in some red wine, if it's pork, I'll add cider, and so on. I have no idea how they make one single gravy to go with beef, turkey, and pork.'

'It's probably Bisto.'

'Mm. You may be right. Anyway, they had all the trimmings as well. People were loading their plates so high you'd have thought they hadn't eaten all week.'

'The thing I don't get with carveries,' I tell him, 'is when people mix things up. The whole point of a roast is that it should be cohesive, with the right sides and sauces for the meat.'

'So no mint sauce with your turkey then?'

'God, no! And I'd only let you have Yorkshire puddings with beef.'

'I think that's a bit fierce. Everyone loves a Yorkshire pudding. What about pigs in blankets?'

'Chicken or turkey only. Same with Brussels sprouts and bread sauce.'

'Wow, okay. And I thought I was bad with the generic gravy!'

'I'd love to do a Sunday roast in the café. We could do it properly. No generic gravy, and only the sides you're supposed to have.'

'I know,' he sighs. 'I love cooking a Sunday roast. It's pure comfort food, especially when you follow it up with something like apple crumble and custard. You don't need to eat for the rest of the day after that.'

'Only if it's winter.'

'What?'

'You can't have apple crumble and custard in the summer. It's just wrong. You need something with cream or ice cream in the summer. Eton Mess, something like that.'

He considers for a moment. 'I guess I understand that. You wouldn't want a hot, stodgy pudding on a warm summer's day, I suppose. I do miss doing the Sunday roasts, but I just can't see how we could make it viable. Apart from the fact that neither of us could work seven days a week, we just wouldn't be able to drag people away from the pubs. They've cornered the market, so I reckon good luck to them.'

'I guess you're right. I'm going to make a cup of tea. Do you want one?'

'Yes, please.'

As I fill the kettle, I reflect on our conversation. On the surface, it would seem that everything is back to normal, but it's clear to me that we're still skirting around the issue of our encounter this morning. Matt is concentrating on the screen again, but he's not relaxed and sprawled in the way that he usually is. He's sitting forwards and looks tense. Either whatever he's watching is so riveting that it's got him on the edge of his seat, or he feels it too. I really don't want an atmosphere between us, but I'm not sure I'm feeling brave enough to confront the elephant in the room either.

I consider the options as I pour boiling water onto the teabags and let them brew. If I don't say anything, this undercurrent is going to linger, and I definitely don't want that. But what if I say the wrong thing and one of us gets upset? That would make things infinitely worse. Matt and I have had a very harmonious relationship to date, which is nice but means I have no idea how he deals with conflict. What if he's a sulker? I couldn't bear that.

In the end, I make a decision. I carefully place the mugs of tea on the coffee table and settle myself on the sofa next to him, tucking one leg under the other like Katie does, so I can face him. I try very hard not to look at his thighs, but it's proving difficult. I'd love to run my hands up and down them, and...

'Matt,' I begin. 'I think we need to talk about this morning. Can you turn the TV off for a minute?'

He obliges but says nothing. His face is completely inscrutable as he turns to face me, and I'm suddenly plagued with doubt. What if Katie is wrong, or I've misread the signals? What if he's just had some bad news, and that's why he's acting slightly odd? There's only one way to find out.

'When I invited you to stay with me, I guess I didn't really think about the practicalities of sharing a bathroom, particularly one with no lock on the door,' I begin.

'It was a surprise when you burst in,' he agrees, without meeting my eyes. So far, so awkward.

'The thing is, not to put too fine a point on it, we've both seen things that can't be unseen, as it were, and I'm worried that it's made things difficult between us. There's been a strange atmosphere ever since.'

He sighs. 'I know. I'm sorry. Maybe this was a bad idea. Would you like me to start looking for somewhere else? Or I could have a word with Mick, see if there's some way I can move back next door and he can work around me.'

'That's a nice thought, but no. Even if you did that, we've still got to work together. I don't want this atmosphere in the kitchen in the café. It's such a happy place now that's Rita's gone, and I don't want anything to drag it back down. I love working with you, and I like to think we've become good friends. But at the moment, every time I look at you, all I can see is you wearing nothing but that towel.'

He grins. 'Did you like it?'

'Of course I liked it!' I cry exasperatedly. 'Have you seen yourself in the mirror? You are one fine specimen of manhood, Matt.'

'You're not too bad yourself, if you don't mind me saying.'

I blush furiously. 'Thank you, but that's not the point.'

'What is the point?'

'The point is that it would be a mistake for us to do anything with this. If we had a relationship and it didn't work out, consider how toxic things would be in the kitchen.'

'Well, if that happened, then I guess I'd have to leave.'

'But I don't want you to leave! We're building something good here, and I want you to carry on being a part of it. It was partly your passion that persuaded me to take this on in the first place. I can't do it without you.'

'I'm just a chef. There are plenty of other chefs out there who could do just as good a job as me.'

'You know that's not true. You have a real connection to the café. You feel just as strongly about it as me, I know you do. Admit it, we make a good team in the kitchen, and that's what I don't want to risk.'

'I understand. So, we make sure we're fully covered up at all times and keep our eyes firmly above the shoulder. If you like, we could draw up a bathroom rota, so we don't surprise each other again before the lock is fitted.'

'Now you're talking sense. That sounds like a good idea. I'll get a piece of paper, hang on.'

'Daisy?' Matt asks, as I'm rummaging in a kitchen drawer, trying to find the little notepad that I write shopping lists on.

'Yes?'

'There is another way we could deal with this.'

'Go on.'

'Well, even if we draw up the rota, stay covered up, and all the other stuff I just said, I think there's still going to be an issue. We both liked what we saw, and now there's this big "what if" question mark hanging over us. I don't think the current plan is going to get rid of that.'

'What are you proposing, then?'

'What if we answered the question? What if we made love, just once, and got it out of our system? Mystery solved, and we can go back to normal. Plus, if you burst in on me when I'm shaving again, there won't be anything you haven't seen before, and it won't be a problem.'

'Kind of like ripping the plaster off? Get it over with and move on?'

'Exactly. I reckon it's got to be better than us tiptoeing around each other like we have been today.'

I consider his proposal. It's difficult to be objective, though, because every fibre of my being is screaming, 'Yes, yes, yes! What are you waiting for, you stupid cow?'

'One time only?' I ask.

'One time only. Then we go back to normal.'

'Okay.' I walk over to him, take his hand and lead him into my bedroom, leaving the tea to get cold on the living room table.

* * *

'Matt, this isn't working, is it?'

'Hm?'

Predictably, it didn't turn out to be a one-time only thing. So far, we've had to 'get it of our system' every day this week, sometimes more than once. I never knew sex could be this visceral. It's like we can't get enough of each other; we've even had to introduce a 'no touching at work' rule, because getting frisky in a commercial kitchen is a sure-fire way to end up in A&E with an embarrassing story to tell. At least the awkwardness of last Sunday is gone, I suppose. Matt came with me to test drive the van on Wednesday, and because there are only two seats in it, the sales guy had to let us take it out on our own. We were so pent up that it was all we could do not to park up in a lay-by and climb into the back. When we got home, we sprinted up the stairs to the flat and didn't even make it to the bedroom. I did manage to linger at the dealership long enough to place an order and, luckily, they had a van in stock with the spec I wanted, so I'm picking it up next Saturday after work.

'This "one time and we'll go back to normal" thing. It's not working.'

'Ah, well. Maybe we'll just have to live with this as the new normal,' he replies, wrapping me up in his huge arms. God, I love the feel of his skin against mine. I breathe deeply, inhaling the smell of him. It's a heady mixture of deodorant, soap, and fresh sweat from our lovemaking.

'Yes, but what if it goes wrong?'

'What if it doesn't? What if you and I are meant to be? Have you ever thought about that?'

'I'm not good at optimism. I prefer to look at the worst possible outcome of a situation or action and, if I reckon I can deal with that, I'll do it. I'm not sure I could cope with the worst possible outcome of this situation.'

'I guess I'll have to do the optimism for both of us, then. Do you know when I first fell for you?' he asks.

'No, tell me.'

'The very first time I saw you. I can remember exactly what you were wearing. I opened the door, and I was blown away. You're so beautiful, and you looked so damned sexy in your tight jeans and your boots. It was a struggle to contain myself, I can tell you.'

I laugh. 'My FMBs.'

He looks nonplussed.

'Katie refers to those boots as my "fuck-me boots". Looks like she wasn't wrong!'

Matt laughs. 'The point is, I knew I wanted to be with you from the start. When did you first fall for me?'

'Well, I liked you from the moment I met you. You're a good man, and you were kind to me even when you had no reason to be. As I've got to know you better, I've liked you more and more. The sex side of it didn't kick in until I saw you in that towel, though. Seeing you like that did things to me that no man has done before, I can tell you.'

'Shall I go and get the towel now?'

I glance down at our naked bodies. 'I rather think that horse has bolted, don't you?'

He opens his arms and moves slightly away from me. I'm acutely aware of his gaze and, even after everything we've done together over the last week, I feel a little self-conscious.

'I don't think I could ever tire of looking at you,' he says huskily.

'You're not so bad yourself, you know. Now, stop talking and kiss me.'

Any attempt Matt and I might have made to keep our relationship under wraps quickly proves futile. Katie, Bronwyn, and Penny all rumble us pretty much straight away. Katie's delighted, and I have to put up with her saying 'I told you so' on several occasions. At least it simplifies the sleeping arrangements at the flat; Matt has moved into my bedroom and Katie has her room back, not that she sleeps in it that often. She arrives after school every Friday and stays the night. On Saturdays, she works on her homework until around lunchtime, at which point she wanders down to the café to help Bronwyn. They both disappear as soon as we close up, and I don't see her again until mid-morning on the Sunday, when we trek over to Nan and Grandad's for lunch.

It seems there's something in the water, as Penny gleefully informed me a few days ago that Ron and Agnes were 'stepping out', according to Agnes. Apparently, they've been to the cinema a couple of times for the senior screenings, where they show a variety of old films. 'They even give you a cup of tea and a biscuit before the show,' Agnes told Penny in awed tones. He's bought her flowers, and they've even had a bit of a kiss, although Agnes has been firm that she's not the sort of woman who will put up with any hanky-panky outside marriage.

I don't know what it is about Penny, but the customers just seem to open up to her. She's even managed to make some progress in solving the infamous bum-pinching mystery. I've never been convinced by Agnes's story that Harold pinched her bum and Penny has managed to confirm it, as it turns out that Harold is gay. He and his partner, George, were together for fifty years, and were one of the first gay couples in the area to get married when it became legal. Sadly, George was diagnosed with cancer and died just over two years ago. Given all of that, we think it's extremely unlikely that he'd have been making sexual advances on Agnes. Penny has explained all of this to Agnes as tactfully as she can and, apparently, Agnes has now downgraded Harold from 'dirty pervert' to 'a bit suspicious'.

I hesitate to say it in case I jinx something, but the café is really starting to thrive again and we're making a healthy profit. I came across a quick recipe for Hollandaise sauce in Nora's binder, so our breakfast menu now includes eggs Benedict and eggs Florentine, as well as a selection of omelettes for people who fancy something a bit lighter than our traditional fare. Penny somehow got Ron and Agnes to try the eggs Benedict one morning instead of their usual breakfasts, and I think Ron would have it every day if he were left to his own devices. Unfortunately for him, Agnes looked up the sauce and was horrified by the amount of butter in it, so he's only allowed it once a week. We are getting younger people in too and, even though they sometimes bring pushchairs with screaming babies and toddlers, Ron seems far too wrapped up in Agnes to notice.

'I've had two ideas,' Katie announces, as she, Matt and I settle down to our dinner one Friday night. 'Do you want to hear them?'

'If we must,' I tell her, with a wink.

'The first one is about Nan and Grandad. You know you said you were trying to think of a way to say thank you to them for looking after us for all of these years?'

'Yes.'

'What about a cruise? Nan's always wanted to go on a cruise.'

'Ooh. Good idea. Where did you have in mind?'

'I don't know. I was hoping you'd help with that bit if you liked the idea. The Med is nice, but the weather can be a bit iffy. The Caribbean is more exotic, but I'm not sure whether they'd enjoy a long-haul flight.'

'The Caribbean is definitely more special,' I agree.

'It'll be a lot more expensive, though,' Matt counters. 'The Med might be more affordable.'

Although we've been a couple for a few weeks, I don't feel ready to tell him about the money I inherited from Fred – not the full details, anyway – so I decide to move the conversation on.

'Why don't we pop up to the travel agents tomorrow after we close up?' I say to Katie. 'Unless you and Bronwyn already have something planned?'

'Nothing that can't be delayed for an hour or two,' she replies with a smile. 'Do you want to hear the second idea?'

'Go for it. Is it as good as the first?'

'That's up to you to decide. So, I was looking around the café the last time I was in. There's no doubt it looks so much better now than it did when we first saw it, but something is still missing.'

'What?'

'Pictures. There's not a single picture on any of the walls. So, what I thought was, why not ask Bronwyn to put some of her pictures up? You could even let her offer them for sale and take a commission.'

I'm less keen on this idea. Not because I don't think it's good, but because I suspect Katie and Bronwyn are trying to do a number on me.

'Have you already spoken to Bronwyn about this?' I ask.

'God, no! I mean, it may not be something she wants to do anyway. The stuff that she has in the gallery wouldn't be suitable for here at all, but she's so talented and versatile that I reckon she could come up with pictures that would look really good in the café, and they'd certainly be more interesting than the usual generic posters. What do you think?'

'I guess we could ask her and see what she says,' I offer cautiously.

'Great, I'll text her now,' Katie replies enthusiastically, pulling her phone out of her jeans pocket.

I don't know whether to believe her or not when she says Bronwyn doesn't know anything about it, but I definitely feel slightly manipulated. I can't deny that it's a good idea, though, and some pictures on the walls would be nice, so I put my irritation to one side. Katie and Bronwyn are best friends, after all, so it's only natural that Katie would push her forwards.

Bronwyn's reply pings back moments after Katie sends the text.

'She says thank you. She's going to give it some thought and maybe do a couple of rough sketches this evening. If she comes up with anything, she'll bring it in to show you tomorrow, so you can decide if it's suitable.'

'That seems awfully quick,' I say. 'Are you sure this is definitely the first time you've ever spoken to her about it?'

'Yes. Scout's honour!'

'I don't think that works if you weren't a scout.'

'Oh, shut up. I promise you this isn't something we've cooked up behind your back, okay? It was my idea, but there's no way I'd talk to her about it without consulting you. What if she'd been really keen, but you'd hated it? Much better for her to be in the dark, and then she would never have needed to know if you didn't like it.'

As usual, she's thought this through properly. I ought to have known.

'She sketches really fast,' Katie continues. 'It's pretty awesome to watch, actually. Once she's happy with the sketch then she sets to work with whatever medium she's decided on, and that takes much longer. So, it wouldn't surprise me at all if she managed two or even three sketches before she goes to bed.'

* * *

Sure enough, Bronwyn bounces in as usual the following morning clutching an enormous sketch book under her arm. Katie's still fast asleep in the flat, so it's just Bronwyn, Matt, and me in the kitchen before we open up. Bronwyn makes the coffees as usual and brings them in.

'I know you're both busy now, but I've drawn out a couple of ideas that we can look at later, either when we get a quiet moment, or when we close up,' she tells me.

'It's Saturday, Bronwyn. You know as well as I do that we won't get a quiet moment! Let's have a quick look now, before the hordes descend.'

'Okay. The style I'm thinking of is sort of halfway between Jack Vettriano and Beryl Cook. Does that make sense?'

'I've heard of Jack Vettriano, but I don't know anything about Beryl Cook,' I tell her.

'Okay. Think of colour schemes similar to Jack Vettriano, but without the dark undercurrents that his work sometimes has. Beryl Cook was famous for painting people enjoying themselves, so I guess that's where I'm going with this, does that make sense?'

She opens the sketch book near the end, and the first sketch depicts a couple sitting outside a café. She's wearing a knee-length dress and sipping from an espresso cup. He's reclining in his chair and smoking a cigarette. Their calves are touching under the table. Even though it's only a sketch, I can already see the colours in my mind. The second is a beach scene, and this time, the couple are eating ice creams. She's drawn it so that they're each holding the other's ice cream cone and effectively feeding each other. They each have a blob of ice cream on their noses, and you're left wondering whether the blobs are accidental or not.

'These are brilliant, Bronwyn!' I exclaim.

'Well, they're just quick mock-ups,' she replies. 'I wanted to know if I was on the right lines or not.'

'I'd say you were bang on. What would you want to sell them for?'

'Well, I'd probably paint them on a canvas twenty-five inches by twenty with a simple mount and frame. Gary would normally sell something that size for five hundred pounds and give me three hundred after his commission, but these will be simpler than my usual stuff, so let's say a ticket price of three hundred with twenty per cent commission to the café. How does that sound?'

'I don't know anything about art, but that sounds expensive for our clientele. What if they don't sell?'

'If they don't sell, then we can either leave them up for longer, or I'll take them back and sell them elsewhere. They won't be the sort of paintings that Gary would be interested in, but I probably wouldn't have any trouble selling them online.'

'Okay. Let's give it a try. Even if they don't sell, they'll certainly brighten the walls. How long do you think you'll need before you have something to put up?'

'I don't think they will take very long. The trick is to keep them simple. A few weeks, maybe? I'll definitely aim to have something up in the next couple of months, how does that sound?'

'Perfect. Thanks, Bronwyn.' Now that I've seen her work, I'm actually quite excited about having it in the café. I think her prices are way beyond our clientele's budget but, if she ends up taking them away to sell elsewhere, I can always revert to framed posters. We agree that she can put her sketch book on top of the fridge, where it will be out of the way, and I get back to sorting out today's lunchtime special and the cakes for this afternoon.

As I work, I keep glancing at Bronwyn's sketch book on top of the fridge. I'd love to look at some of her other work, but I don't know what the protocols are. Is it private, like a diary, or is it okay to look inside? In the end, I stick my head out of the kitchen door and ask her if she'd mind me looking at some of her other sketches.

'Help yourself,' she replies. 'Just make sure your hands are clean, please. You just have to look at that paper with dirty hands and it stains.'

* * *

It's a typical busy Saturday, so I have to wait until the lunchtime orders are finished before I get a moment to wash my hands thoroughly and take Bronwyn's sketch pad down from its perch on top of the fridge. It's a crisp late autumn day, so I open the back door and sit myself down in the doorway with it. I don't know anything at all about art, but even I can see that Bronwyn's work is exquisite. Frankly, I'd be happy to see some of the sketches in frames on the wall, so the actual paintings must be extraordinary. There's a wide variety here, too. There are landscapes, gritty urban scenes, animals, and still lifes. There's even a sketch of a naked man, and I wonder for a moment if this is her boyfriend but, on closer examination, it looks like he's probably much older than her, so I guess he's a life model. The final sketch before the two she did for me takes my breath away.

It's a head and shoulders sketch of Katie. She's not wearing her glasses and her hair is all tousled, as if she's just woken up. It's clear that her shoulders are bare, which adds to the illusion of just waking from sleep. She looks curiously vulnerable without her glasses on, but that allows the sketch to emphasise her eyes. There's a ferocious intensity in her gaze that I can't quite fathom, but which makes the hairs on the back of my neck prickle. I feel like I shouldn't be here, as if I've stumbled into something private. I close the sketch book and hurry back inside, placing it carefully back on top of the fridge.

28

'How can I help you two today?' the travel agent asks, a little wearily. It's obviously been a busy day for her too, and we had to wait for half an hour while she dealt with the couple in front of us. I did feel for her as I watched; they evidently had no idea where they wanted to go, and she kept having to get up and fetch different brochures for them to browse. It looked like they were going to actually book something a couple of times but, in the end, they left with an armful of brochures, promising to return as soon as they'd had a good look through.

I smile at her. 'We'll try to be a little more decisive than your previous clients. We'd like to look at cruises, please.'

She snorts derisively. 'We won't see them again, I can guarantee you that. We get their kind a lot. They come in here to enquire because they know we've got the brochures and can give them good advice, and then they go home and book something on the internet. Anyway, sorry. Cruises, you say?'

I'm slightly taken aback by her indiscretion, but I also find myself admiring her honesty.

'It's not for us,' I explain. 'We're thinking of a present for our grandparents.'

'Ah, that makes sense. You don't really fit the cruise demographic, if you don't mind me saying. Lucky grandparents! What did you have in mind?'

'We're open to ideas. Our nan's always wanted to go on a cruise, so we want it to be special. We've talked about either the Mediterranean or the Caribbean, but if you have other suggestions then we'd be happy to hear them.'

'Okay. A lot depends on the time of year,' she tells us. 'The Mediterranean is lovely in the summer months, but there's not much going on in winter. The Caribbean, on the other hand, is lovely in December and January particularly, but you want to avoid the summer months as that's hurricane season. Caribbean cruises also tend to be quite expensive, especially between December and April, so you'll need to take that into account if you've got a limited budget. There are other cruises that go to places like the Norwegian Fjords or St Petersburg if you think your grandparents might enjoy that. Shall I get some brochures and you can have a look?'

I never realised how many different types of cruise holiday there are. There are huge ships that look like floating luxury hotels, with every conceivable amenity, ships that cater more to the family market with water slides and kids' clubs, and small ships that specialise in getting you into little ports off the main tourist trail. Our adviser, Sheila, is friendly and helpful, but I'm conscious that she's steering us very much towards the cheaper end of the market.

'I like the look of the Caribbean cruises, what do you think?' I ask Katie. 'Nan and Grandad have never been to the Caribbean, and it looks lovely.'

'I agree,' says Katie. 'Are there any with vacancies in early December?' she asks Sheila.

Sheila spends some time tapping on her computer, investigating the options.

'There are a few,' she says eventually, 'but all the standard cabins are fully booked. You'd be looking at a premium cabin, which is obviously more expensive.'

'That's not a problem,' I tell her with a smile. She conceals her surprise well, but I still spot it flash across her face. 'What are our options?'

By the time we walk out, I'm not sure Sheila can believe her luck. We've booked Nan and Grandad into a suite on a two-week Caribbean cruise at the beginning of December, and we also upgraded their flights to business class. The final bill was fairly eye-watering, but my debit card took the hit without any problems, and Katie has promised that she'll pay half of it back as soon as she turns eighteen and gets her hands on her share of the inheritance. I do the maths in my head and, with what I've spent on the café so far and the flats, plus the deposit for the van and this holiday for Nan and Grandad, I'm down to my final £5,000 from the original £50,000 that the financial adviser and I agreed would be my budget to spend on the café and flats. However, I haven't touched my redundancy payout yet, so my finances are still reasonably healthy. I know I can help myself to more from the main pot if I need to but, now that the café is making a healthy profit, I hope that won't be necessary.

Matt is not as good at concealing his surprise as Sheila was when I tell him what we've done.

'Bloody hell, that must have cost a fortune!' he exclaims, and I decide that I probably need to come clean with him.

'Fred left us quite a bit of money as well as the café,' I explain, 'so we can afford it. It appears he was quite the investor.'

'Really? He always gave the impression that he didn't have two pennies to rub together. Are you saying he was actually rich?'

'He certainly wasn't poor. He left Katie and me just under eight hundred thousand pounds.'

'What a bastard!' Of all the reactions I was expecting, anger wasn't one of them. Matt is unable to contain his fury. 'So, you're telling me that he let his wife's pride and joy run itself into the ground, when he could have just waved his cheque book and fixed it? I bought all that bullshit he told me about how we had to cut costs to keep the café open. Do you know, I haven't had a pay rise for five years because he said he couldn't afford it? When he bought me that thermometer for the fryer, he gave me this big sob story about how it was the best he could do, and I actually felt grateful. I've half a mind to go and dig the tight old fucker up and have a word.'

'I'm really sorry, Matt. Maybe I shouldn't have said anything.'

'No, I'm glad that you did, really. I'm just so pissed off that he played me for a mug. If there's one thing that's guaranteed to send me over the edge, it's being duped.'

'Would you like to talk about your pay?'

'Not now. I'm trying to keep work and leisure separate. It's the only way I can cope with you being my girlfriend and my boss. Does that make sense? Can we talk about it at work on Monday, though?'

'I'm your girlfriend, am I? I don't remember us discussing this!' I laugh.

Matt goes from looking furious to totally crestfallen in a fraction of a second. 'Shit, I'm sorry,' he says. 'I suppose I just assumed, well, you know, from the way things are between us...'

'Oh, don't be an idiot!' I exclaim. 'I'm delighted to be your girlfriend. I was just teasing you because I've never heard you use the word before. Does that mean you'll be my boyfriend?'

'If you want me.'

'Oh, I want you, all right. Would you like me to show you how much?'

He nods, and we head for the bedroom.

* * *

Matt and I have got into a bit of a routine on Sunday mornings. We wake late, and he makes us coffee that we drink in bed. Quite often we'll have sex, but only once we've brushed our teeth, thank goodness. I'm therefore a little surprised to wake up and find the other side of the bed empty. I pad out into the living area, where I find him sitting on the sofa with his head in his hands, looking like the world has just ended.

'Are you okay? What's up?' I ask him.

He hands me an ancient-looking mobile phone that I've never seen before.

'The code is one, two, three, four,' he says. 'Imaginative, I know. There's a voicemail message.'

It takes me a little while to work out how to access the voicemail. I've only ever had a smartphone, so dealing with the buttons on this ancient Nokia is a challenge. Finally, I manage it and listen to the message, which was left on Friday.

'Err, yeah. Hi. My name is Terry and I'm a friend of Tracey's. I found this number on the fridge. I don't know who you are or if this will reach you, but she's in the hospital. I found her passed out on the sofa and I couldn't wake her, so I called the ambulance. The paramedic guys said it looked serious. I don't know if you know her, or if she has any family, but this was the only number I could find.'

I hand the phone back and wait for him to speak.

'Tracey is my mum,' he explains. 'Although she acted like she didn't know who I was most of the time, I felt guilty that she was going to be all on her own when I left. I wrote my number on a piece of paper and stuck it to the fridge, with a note to call if there was an emergency. When I started working here, I got a new phone with a new number, but I always kept this one and I've been checking it once a week ever since, just in case.'

'Who's Terry?' I ask.

'No idea. Could be a neighbour, a boyfriend, or anyone. I certainly don't know him.'

'What are you going to do?'

'I'm not sure. I know that sounds awful because she's my mum, but I don't feel any more connection to her than I do to Terry, whoever he is. I suppose I could call him to find out how she is, at least.'

He presses the button to access the calls list and calls the number. I hear it ringing, and a man's voice.

'Voicemail,' he tells me, and hangs up without leaving a message.

'I don't want to be insensitive, Matt, but Terry rang you on Friday. If she was in a serious condition two days ago, she may not have made it. Is it worth calling the hospital to see if she's still alive?'

'Good idea, I didn't think of that.'

'Which hospital is she likely to be in?'

'I don't know. I don't even know where she's living now. I assume she's still in the same place, but she might have moved.'

'Okay, then maybe Terry knows. Why not try him once more?'

He dials the number on the phone and, after a few rings, it's answered this time. A short conversation ensues and, from what I can pick up, Terry hasn't got any more information about Matt's mum, but he is able to tell him that she's still living in the same house in Peterborough. We do some research on the internet and it appears the most likely place for her to have gone is the Peterborough City Hospital, so Matt calls them. Again, I'm not able to make out much from his side of the conversation, but I can sense his mounting frustration. He keeps repeating his mother's name and explaining that he's her son, but I can tell he's getting nowhere. Eventually, he hangs up.

'Well, that was a total waste of bloody time! They're not prepared to tell me anything at all due to patient confidentiality. They'll only give me any information if I go there in person with documentation to prove who I am.'

'What do you want to do?'

'Well, this Terry bloke sounds like he's probably her current boyfriend. Whoever he is, if she makes it, he'll tell her that I called, so I'm kind of involved now. It sounds stupid, but I don't want to be the bad person here. Useless as she is, I suppose the least I can do is make the effort to check if she's still alive. If she isn't, I guess I ought to sort out some sort of a funeral for her.'

'Do you want me to come with you?'

'No. I don't know how long this will take. If she's died... it might take a few days to sort everything out. Shit, sorry, I forgot about the café! I'll go up there now, get the lie of the land, and then come back this evening. If she's died, then maybe I can sort it out remotely or something.'

'Don't worry about the café, that's my job,' I tell him. 'I'm sure I can manage for a few days without you if I need to. Tell me, when was the last time you had any time off?'

'I was ill about six months after I started. I had a high temperature, and I was in bed for a week. I think that was the last time,' he says, after thinking for a bit.

'Right, you're well overdue for a break then. Go and find your mum. Don't worry about us, we'll cope somehow, okay?'

'Are you sure?'

'I'm sure,' I tell him, even though the prospect of being on my own in the kitchen, with his work to do on top of mine, terrifies me.

He pulls me into his arms and kisses me fiercely. 'You're a very special person, Daisy Jones, you know that?'

'You're pretty special yourself. Now go. The sooner you go, the sooner you'll be back.'

29

I know I did the right thing by encouraging Matt to go and find his mother, but it doesn't feel like it. He's been gone for a week now, and not only do I miss him so much that it feels like a permanent dull pain in my chest – a literal heartache – but I'm also dead on my feet. The only way I've found of ensuring everything gets done is to get up at 5 each morning, spend two hours getting the afternoon cakes done before the café opens at 7.30, and then stay on after closing to prepare the next day's lunchtime special. I'm sticking to things that can be made in advance and reheated, so the specials menu isn't as varied as I'd like it to be, but there's no other way around at the moment. The customers don't seem to have noticed, which I suppose is good news; we're as busy as ever.

Nan and Grandad were absolutely delighted with our gift to them, after they'd finished scolding us for wasting our money, as they saw it. We've agreed that Katie will move in with me while they're away; she can commute to Paddock Wood from Sevenoaks by train for the first week, and then she'll be on her Christmas break for the second.

Matt found his mum on the first day; she was in the hospital that he'd telephoned. They were a lot more helpful once he turned up in person and proved who he was. Thankfully, they'd been able to move her out of intensive care into a ward, but she was still very weak. It seems that a particularly dangerous binge, on top of the damage done by her chronic alcoholism, had tipped her over the edge and caused her collapse. The consultant had taken Matt to one side on Monday morning and explained that this really was her last chance. If she didn't kick the bottle now, she'd be dead within months.

We've spoken on the phone every day, but it's not the same as having him here. I've got so used to him being around, firstly in the kitchen in the café, and more recently in my flat, that I notice the lack of him wherever I go. I even missed him when I was trawling round the cash and carry, that's how bad it is. If this is what being in love is like, you can keep it.

I think it would be easier if I had any idea how long he's likely to be gone for. Although she's been through the acute stages of alcohol withdrawal in the hospital, she's still deemed to be at high risk of relapse, and the consultant has told Matt that her best chance of success is if he stays with her to encourage her and look after her when she's discharged. We had a long conversation about it, because he's still conflicted, but deep down, we both know that his only option is to stay with her for the time being. She's being discharged next week, so we'll see what happens then. The consultant advised Matt to get her into a rehab clinic but, unsurprisingly, the waiting lists for NHS-funded rehab are immense. I did offer to pay for her to go privately, but Matt was so horrified by the cost that he flatly refused to entertain that idea any further. He's found a cheaper option where she will attend intensive group therapy every day, which he can fund out of his savings. Again, I offered to help, but I think this is probably a pride issue for him; he feels responsible for her, so he wants to fix it himself.

It's Sunday today, so Katie and I are due at Nan and Grandad's for lunch. It's a sign of how exhausted I am that I was still asleep when she got home just after eleven, so it was a bit of a rush to get ready. Nan really pushed the boat out with today's roast; we had roast beef with all the trimmings, followed by treacle sponge. I was so grateful to be eating something that I hadn't had to cook that I probably had far too much, and now I'm struggling to stay awake on the sofa.

'You look completely done in, Daisy,' Nan observes. 'Why don't you go and have a lie-down on Katie's bed for a bit? She won't mind, will you, Katie?'

'Fine with me. Nan's right, you do look knackered,' Katie agrees.

As I pad down the hall to Katie's room, I glance into my old bedroom. Nan and Grandad have been unable to agree what to do with it since I moved out, so it's still empty. Nan wanted to turn it into a spare room, but Grandad rightly questioned who they would be inviting to stay. Grandad, on the other hand, wanted to turn it into a study, but Nan put her foot down and said she wasn't going to let him create some sort of 'man cave' where he could hide out all day.

I take off my shoes and climb onto Katie's bed. As I lie down, I can't help wondering whether my life would have been a lot easier had Fred not left us anything. I would never have met Matt, which means I wouldn't be aching from missing him now, and I'd be plodding along in my old job at Holdsworth & Speke, or Holdsworth & whatever they are now. If Rob's made partner, then I guess it will be his surname, but I've completely forgotten what that is. I hunt around in my mind, but nothing comes. I close my eyes and I'm asleep within seconds.

I'm woken by the ringing of my phone. It's completely dark outside, but as it's winter, that doesn't really tell me very much. I glance at the screen and see that it's Matt calling. My heart does a little somersault, as it always does when I see his name.

'Hi! How are you?' I ask, brightly. Maybe this time there will be good news and he'll be able to tell me when he's coming home.

'Yeah, I'm okay. Mum's doing a lot better today; I spoke to one of the nurses and she thinks the consultant might discharge her tomorrow.'

'That's great! What does that mean for you?' *Please tell me it means you can come home,* I think but don't say.

'It means this is where the hard work really begins. She can start at the support group as soon as she's discharged, but I'll need to stay with her to begin with, to make sure she doesn't relapse in the evenings.'

I try not to let the disappointment show in my voice. 'Any idea how long that will take?'

'At the moment, I have no idea. I'm sorry. I know all this is making life difficult for you, and I will come back as soon as I can. It's just that this hospital stay seems to have woken Mum up to herself. She says she's determined to kick the booze this time, and reckons she'll do it with my help. I'm going to move in with her for a couple of weeks, if that's okay, until she's a bit stronger and she's settled into the intensive therapy.'

Another two weeks? My heart sinks at the prospect, but an idea comes to me.

'Maybe you could bring her down here?' I suggest. 'A fresh start and all that? It might be just what she needs.'

'That's not a bad idea. 'I'll give it some thought. Oh, I forgot to tell you that I bumped into Liam yesterday.'

'Who?'

'The guy who gave me the scar. He works for one of the local churches now, would you believe? He goes into schools and youth groups and talks to them about the dangers of gang culture, and his experiences. He's completely different from the way he was when I saw him last. Sadly, we couldn't have much of a catch-up because he was on his way to something. Anyway, enough about me. What about you?'

I fill him in on my day, but don't tell him how I really feel. He's got enough on his plate without me making him feel guilty. As we finish the call, I feel desolate. Another two weeks at least. It's like someone's punched me in the gut. All I can do is hope that his mum is receptive to the idea of moving down here. Even if Matt has to spend all his time looking after her, at least he'll be here.

30

Matt's been gone for four weeks now. The good news is that his mum appears to be thriving in the therapy group. According to Matt, she comes home bright-eyed and full of energy every day and keeps telling him how grateful she is that he's there for her. Terry, whoever he was, appears to be long gone, and it's just Matt and his mum in the house.

The bad news is that, every time he mentions coming home, she bursts into tears and says she doesn't think she'll be able to cope on her own. He did talk to her about moving down here with him, but she shot that idea down, pointing out that she'd be all alone in an unfamiliar town while he worked all day, and what would there be for her to do except drink? So the stalemate continues, and Matt still has no idea when he'll be able to come back.

The other piece of bad news is that, after our initial flurry of phone calls, our conversation has started to dry up, so we're now only talking a couple of times a week. I don't really have much to tell him about, except the café, and he's so focused on his mum that I get the impression he's not really listening a lot of the time. He says he's told her all about me, that she can't wait to meet me 'at some point', but he doesn't seem to have any idea when that point might be, and I'm afraid to press him. Every time we talk about when he might be coming back, there's another reason to delay, so I've stopped asking. I can't bear the disappointment. I feel totally helpless, like he's slowly slipping away and there's nothing I can do about it. The only thing I have to hold on to is that all his stuff is still in his flat, which Mick finished ages ago, so he'll have to come back one day, even if only to collect it.

My body has started to adapt to my punishing schedule, but I still spend large parts of every Sunday asleep. At one point, we did talk about the possibility of me driving up to Peterborough one weekend so we could spend a bit of time together, but it's a two-hour journey each way and I'm not in any fit state to do a four-hour round trip at the moment. I'm trying hard not to resent his mum, but it's getting harder.

'She sounds like a classic narcissist to me,' Bronwyn observes over Sunday lunch in the flat. Nan and Grandad left for their cruise yesterday, so Katie's staying with me for the next two weeks, which is nice. I think she's a bit worried about me, so she and Bronwyn stayed here last night for their movie fest, instead of going to Bronwyn's house like they usually do. I wasn't very entertaining company; we sat down to watch Sleepless in Seattle at eight o'clock, and Katie had to wake me up and send me to bed ten minutes later because I was snoring.

I've had a long lie-in this morning, and Katie and Bronwyn have prepared the roast. It tastes delicious, but the kitchen looks like something has exploded in there. Katie obviously saw the look of horror on my face, because she has promised that they'll clear it up before they go out this afternoon. They invited me to go for a walk with them, but I've said no. I suspect I'll probably go back to bed at some point after we've finished eating.

'What do you mean?' I ask her.

'She reminds me of my grandmother, when she was alive,' Bronwyn continues. 'Everything was always about her and, if it wasn't, she'd kick off in some way to draw the attention back to her. It's what narcissists do. They think they're the most important person in the world, and therefore nobody else's life matters. Matt's mum sounds just the same. She's all sweetness and light while she's the centre of his world, but the moment he talks about leaving, or about you, she has some sort of crisis to make sure he's completely focused on her.'

'Well, considering that she was pretty much absent when he was growing up, she's certainly making up for it now,' I reply.

'What's happening with her therapy?' Katie asks.

'Same story. It was supposed to be four weeks intensive, finishing next week, but she's talked him into paying for another four-week course. She says she's finding the group incredibly helpful, but doesn't feel strong enough to strike out on her own yet. She also says she can't cope without him at the moment, surprise sur-bloody-prise.'

'Classic narcissism,' Bronwyn continues. 'Make her recovery dependent on him so, if he walks away, she can say she tried but he abandoned her.'

'You're probably right,' I tell her. 'I get the feeling she doesn't ever want him to come back. Where does that leave me, though?'

'Have you thought about recruiting another chef, even temporarily?' Katie asks. 'You can't keep this schedule up forever, it's not good for you.'

I sigh. 'I know I can't, but I can't bring myself to advertise the position. It's like an admission of defeat, you know? Another nail in the coffin of my relationship with Matt. Also, I'd have to have a conversation with him about stopping his pay, and I know he needs it to support his mum.'

Thankfully, the conversation moves on to other topics as we

finish our lunch. Katie and Bronwyn are as good as their word, cleaning the kitchen until it sparkles, while I relax on the sofa and try to stay awake.

'Right, we're off to Knole Park,' Katie informs me. 'Are you sure you don't want to come?'

'No, I might head back to bed for a bit. I'll see you later, okay?'

I can't help smiling as I watch them pull on their coats, scarves, and woolly hats. Although they're both wearing knitted bobble hats, each one reflects the personality of the wearer perfectly. Katie's is dark blue and fairly plain, whereas Bronwyn's is a riot of colour, with an enormous bobble on top that swings around whenever she moves her head.

As soon as they've left, I head into the bedroom, draw the curtains, and lie down. I close my eyes, expecting to fall asleep immediately like I normally do these days but, for some reason, sleep proves elusive. My mind is whirring, processing what Bronwyn said about Matt's mother being a narcissist. If she's right, and it's a plausible theory, then there's no way she's ever going to let him go, and there's nothing I can do about it. I realise I've lost the only man who I ever truly loved to a woman I have no way of competing with, and bitter tears start to flow.

I don't know how long I lie there, crying silently in the dark. It feels like hours, but it can't be because it's still light outside when I decide that sleep is not going to come and get up. I pace around the flat for a bit, but it feels confined and oppressive for some reason. I need to get out into the fresh air, so I decide that I'll go and join Katie and Bronwyn on their walk after all. I know Knole Park is a big space, so I might not see them, but being outdoors will definitely do me some good. I grab my coat, scarf, hat, and gloves and head out to the van. It's busy on the little road behind the park, but I spot Bronwyn's mum's car and find a space a little further up the road that's just big enough for me.

When I first got the van, I did find reversing a struggle. It's got beepers to tell you how close you are to things, but I couldn't initially make the connection between what I was seeing in the mirrors and what I needed to do. Matt was as good as his word, though, and after a few hours reversing it and practising parking it alongside his van, I got the hang of it. The memory of that afternoon, and our celebratory lovemaking afterwards, starts the tears again as I slot the van neatly into the space.

'For fuck's sake, Daisy,' I tell myself angrily as I wipe them away.

Although the sun is out, it's that weak winter sun that has no warmth in it, and the wind is bitterly cold as I let myself through the gate and into the park. It hasn't rained for a while, so the ground is still reasonably firm underfoot, and there are a lot of people here. My eye is initially drawn to a young family ahead of me as I set off down the main path. They've got a toddler on reins, and I can't help smiling at the slightly comical way he waddles determinedly ahead of them. A jogger gives me a nod as she passes, earbuds firmly in place. I've never understood jogging, partly because I'd need a sports bra made out of industrial scaffolding to keep my boobs under control, but also because it seems to be such a joyless activity. Sometimes you see a couple of people jogging together, or a group, and I can understand that, but the solo pounding in all weathers, with nothing but whatever is on your playlist and the ragged sound of your own breath for company? That doesn't sound like fun to me. Also, I've read that it does terrible things to your knees in the long run. I reckon I'm probably active enough, being on my feet all day six days a week. I've certainly lost weight since I took on the café; although I'm surrounded by food all day, I hardly ever get time to eat anything.

I raise my eyes just in time to see another jogger have a close shave with a Labrador. The dog is on one of those extending leads and has dashed across the path to investigate a smell, right in front of the jogger. There's a brief exchange where it looks like the dog owner is apologising, and the jogger waves to them as he sets off again. One of Grandad's favourite phrases comes into my head. 'I reckon you're born with a certain number of heartbeats in you. No point in running around using them up for no reason.' They should be boarding the ship any minute now. I hope they have an amazing time.

The fresh air is definitely doing me good. I'm walking fairly briskly so I'm actually quite warm in my coat, although my face feels like it's starting to go numb in the biting wind. There's no sign of Katie and Bronwyn, but I don't mind. I'm just enjoying being out of the flat and in the open air. For the first time in ages, I don't actually feel tired, and I savour the sensation. I turn left, following the path on what I hope will be a wide circuit, and smile as I see the same Labrador straining at the leash once more. It's spotted a couple of deer and is obviously desperate to investigate, but the owner is firmly dragging it away while the deer look on warily.

This part of the park is quieter. I'm off the main drag and there are fewer people around. I can see the main road to Sevenoaks through the fence to my right, so I'm happy that I know where I am and I'm heading in the right direction. I decide to follow the fence round; it should eventually lead me back to the gate I came in through. As I get closer to re-joining the main path, I spot a famil-iar-looking figure in an instantly recognisable bobble hat sitting on a bench up ahead. Bronwyn is facing away from me and is there-fore oblivious to my approach. As I get closer, I can see that Katie is with her and I speed up, hoping to join them before they move on. I'm probably no further than six feet away when I'm stopped dead in my tracks.

Katie and Bronwyn are snogging each other's faces off.

For a moment, I'm too stunned to move. My mind is completely unable to process the scene in front of me and is frantically trying to work out if there can be any explanation for what I'm seeing, other than the obvious one. Thankfully, they're so engrossed in each other that they haven't noticed me approach and, once I've recovered from my initial shock, I turn and hurriedly retrace my footsteps.

By the time I get back to the van, a number of things are starting to drop into place and make sense, particularly my discomfort about the picture of Katie that I saw in Bronwyn's sketch pad and the intensity of the look in her eyes. I wonder if I was wrong about Katie just having woken up when the sketch was drawn. Maybe they'd just had sex, or were just about to have sex. I'm no prude and I've got nothing against gay people at all, I just don't want an image of my sister having sex with anyone, male or female, in my head. That's just weird.

31

'You look better, did you have a good sleep?' Katie asks, as she bounces through the door about half an hour after I get home. Her nose is bright red from the cold and her cheeks are flushed. I study her as she hangs up her coat. She's radiant. How did I never notice before? She doesn't wait for an answer but heads straight for the kitchen.

'I'm going to make a cup of tea. Do you want one?' she calls.

'Yes, please.' Since I've got home, I've been trying to think how best to broach the subject of what I saw at the park with her, but I haven't come up with anything yet. As she busies herself in the kitchen, I think about how much she's changed over the last few months. I'd just assumed that she was growing up and becoming more confident in herself and, to be fair, I've been so wrapped up in my own life with the café and then Matt that maybe I haven't been as observant as I might have been before.

'Here you go.' Katie puts the mugs on the table and settles herself next to me, tucking one leg underneath her as she always does.

'I couldn't sleep,' I tell her. 'So I came up to Knole Park to see if I could find you.'

'Oh, you should have called! We could have arranged a place to meet. What a shame. It was beautiful up there today, though, wasn't it? Where did you go?'

'I just did a bit of a circuit. I did see you and Bronwyn, actually.' I swallow and decide to go for it. 'You were sitting on a bench together. From what I saw, you've definitely lost your aversion to French kissing. When were you going to tell me about the two of you?'

Katie's face falls. 'I'm so sorry. I've been wanting to tell you, but it never seemed like the right time. You were flat out dealing with the café when Bronwyn and I first got together, then you were wrapped up in Matt, and you've been so unhappy since he went that it didn't seem fair for me to flaunt my happiness in front of you. You're not angry, are you?'

'Of course not! I was surprised, definitely. I know you've never shown much interest in boys, but it never occurred to me that it was because girls were your thing. I'm happy for you, though, really.'

'To be honest, I didn't know that girls were my thing either,' Katie replies. 'I'm not the classic gay cliché where I've known since I was small and have been waiting for the right moment to come out of the closet. I'm pretty certain I've never been attracted to a woman before. I just fell in love with Bronwyn, and the fact that she's a woman is just body parts. Does that make sense?'

'Honestly? No. But I'm pretty far up the heterosexual end of the sexuality spectrum, and maybe you're closer to the middle.'

She considers for a moment. 'You're probably right, although I can't see myself fancying a boy now. There's something special about being with someone who truly understands how a woman's body works, and how to make it come alive.'

'Okay. Too much information already!' I cry. 'I don't want to hear about your sex life. Let me just be happy that you've found someone you enjoy kissing. You weren't exactly effusive about the poor boy at school or the guy in Mallorca, were you? I was beginning to think you might turn out to be a nun.'

'God, no!' Katie laughs. 'I totally get it now. I was just looking in the wrong place before.'

'I really am pleased for you,' I tell her. 'And I'm sorry I've been so unavailable.'

'It's not your fault, and I wouldn't say you've been unavailable. I'm so proud of what you've achieved here, although I worry that it's killing you at the moment. Nan and Grandad are proud too, even if they don't say so to your face. But I know how much hard work you've had to put in, and that you've had to give it your undivided attention. I haven't minded, I promise. I've really enjoyed coming over here and being with you, seeing the café come back to life and all of that.'

'And you've also enjoyed spending time with Bronwyn.' I smile at her.

She blushes slightly. 'Yes, that too.'

'So how did it start? As someone said to me a while ago: unburden yourself.'

'It was the first time I went over to watch films with her. You know I told you we watched some French film with subtitles?'

'Yes.'

'Have you heard of the film *Blue is the Warmest Colour*?'

'Vaguely. Didn't it win a load of awards? Some sort of lesbian love story. There was a big scandal afterwards, because the actresses said the director had coerced them, or something.'

'That's the one. It won the Palme D'Or at the Cannes Film Festival. It is beautifully filmed, I can see that, but I was surprised how graphic the sex was. That didn't do a lot for me, but I was completely taken aback by how erotic I found it when they were kissing. We were talking about it afterwards, and I said that I'd never wanted to kiss another woman before, but I'd enjoyed watching Adèle and Emma kissing so much that I wondered if I had missed out on something. Bronwyn told me she'd known she was a lesbian from an early age, and she'd had a brief relationship with another girl when she was at school. It ended badly when the other girl's mum found out and threatened Bronwyn with all sorts of stuff if she didn't stay away. Anyway, we had a bit of a kiss, and things went from there. It's not just about the physical stuff, though. I love everything about her, and being with her makes me feel alive, you know?'

'You really have got it bad,' I laugh. 'Are you going to tell Nan and Grandad?'

'I guess I ought to. How do you think they'll react?'

'They'll be fine. I think they'll just be pleased that you're so happy.'

'I hope so. I know they like Bronwyn, but they think she's just a friend. I want them to carry on liking her as my girlfriend.'

'They will, I'm sure. Bronwyn's almost impossible not to like. You've got yourself a keeper there.'

'I just wish Matt would come back so you could be happy again. Do you think he will?'

I sigh. 'I don't know. I still miss him so much that it hurts, but I can feel him slipping away from me. The reason I couldn't sleep this afternoon was because I was thinking about what Bronwyn said, and that his mother will never let him go now that she's got her claws into him. I'm trying to be generous, but I kind of hate her a little bit. Does that make me a bad person?'

'Of course not! She may be his mother, but she was a pretty shit one when he was growing up, and so it's doubly unfair that she gets to steal your happiness. If I pass my test next month, I'll happily drive up to Peterborough and slap her for you.'

'Bloody hell, is your test next month? Where has the time gone?'

'Don't worry about it. As I said, you've had other things to deal with. Yes, my instructor thinks I'm ready, and Grandad says he's not frightened being in the car with me any more, so I'm hopeful.'

I reach out and pull her into a hug. 'I'm really sorry that I've been such a shit sister lately. I promise to try to do better.'

She squeezes me back. 'Nobody could ever call you a shit sister. You're a bloody star and I love you.'

'I love you too. One final question, though?'

'Go on.'

'I'm sure you said to me that you watched *French Kiss* after *Blue is the Warmest Colour*.'

Katie blushes. 'It's not a total lie! Okay, so we didn't watch it that night, but we have watched it since, I promise.'

'Hm. Too busy French kissing to watch *French Kiss*. There's something almost poetic about it.'

* * *

Now that Katie's term has finished and they're out in the open, with me at least, we are seeing a lot more of Bronwyn. She and Katie have decided to take care of me, cooking me evening meals and clearing up afterwards. I assume she stays over in Katie's room most nights, but as I go to bed long before they do and I'm up long before Katie surfaces, I confess I don't actually have any idea. Now that I know about them, I'm amazed that I never noticed anything before. They're patently crazy about each other and, although their happiness does make me more acutely aware of my own increasingly uncertain relationship status, a little bit of their joy does rub off on me. Enough to keep me going, at least.

Matt is totally unsurprised when I tell him on our now weekly calls. 'It was obvious fairly early on that Bronwyn had taken a shine to Katie,' he tells me. 'I just didn't know whether Katie would feel the same way.'

'So you knew Bronwyn was a lesbian?'

'Yes, she's never hidden it. She had some sort of big bust-up with a previous girlfriend not long after she started and, being Bronwyn, she talked about it a lot.'

'Why didn't you tell me?'

'I did! I distinctly remember telling you that I wasn't her type the first time you came in to do a shift.'

'That's a bit bloody cryptic, Matt. I thought you meant that she went for a different type of man, not that she wasn't into men at all.'

'Sorry. I was trying to be tactful, but obviously I was too tactful. Hang on, are you pissed off with me because I didn't tell you straight?'

'No, of course not!' In truth, I'm delighted. At least we've found something to talk about this week.

We've decided to invite Nan and Grandad over for Sunday lunch at the flat the day after they get back, so Katie can tell them. They'll probably be jetlagged and won't have had a chance to restock the fridge, so it seems a nice thing to do to cook for them for a change. I phone them the day before to invite them and offer to drive over and pick them up. I won't be able to get them both in the van, but I can leave it at their house and bring them over in Katie's car, collecting the van when I take them home again. Katie and Bronwyn are going to cook and clear up.

They've obviously had a fantastic time on the cruise and, by the time they've finished telling us about everything they did, handing round photos and finishing each other's sentences, we've long finished eating. Katie and Bronwyn have done a brilliant job, with beautiful roast lamb that they'd stuffed with rosemary and garlic, crispy roast potatoes, an array of vegetables all topped with the most delicious gravy that reminds me of Matt's comments about the gravy matching the meat.

'The secret,' Bronwyn informs me when I ask, 'is that I put white wine and Worcester sauce in it. Worcester sauce is a match made in heaven for lamb, because it cuts through the fattiness.'

'If Matt doesn't come back, maybe I should employ you as a chef,' I tell her, trying to keep the sadness out of my voice. I obviously don't quite manage it, though, because Nan gives me a sympathetic look and briefly covers my hand with hers.

'So, what's been going on here while we've been gone? I see from Daisy's expression that we still don't know when Matt's coming back?'

'I don't even know if he's coming back, Nan,' I tell her, sadly. 'It seems his mum has got him under her thumb and, every time he mentions coming home, she has a new crisis to make him stay. It's hard, but I think I might have to start trying to move on. We don't even speak that often any more.'

Nan pulls my head onto her shoulder and wraps her arm around me. 'I'm sorry, Daisy love. I thought he was the one, I really did.'

'So did I,' I reply, as I start to cry again. Nan, bless her, does what she's always done. She just sits and holds me, stroking my hair and murmuring words of comfort, while I soak the shoulder of her dress with my tears. It's a routine we've had plenty of opportunity to practise over the years.

'We do have some other news,' I tell her, once I've pulled myself together a bit. 'Katie?'

'Umm.' Katie blushes furiously. 'Bronwyn and I are together. She's my girlfriend.'

Nan beams. 'Of course she is!' she says. 'We may not be in the prime of youth, your grandad and I, but we can spot a couple in love from a mile away. We picked up on you two the first time Bronwyn came for Sunday lunch, didn't we?'

'That we did,' Grandad agrees.

'We didn't say anything, because we figured you'd tell us when you were ready,' Nan continues.

'Was I the only one who didn't see it?' I ask.

'I think you've probably had other things on your mind. Grandad and I have suspected Katie was a lesbian for a long time – are you all right with that term, Katie?'

'I'm getting used to it,' Katie replies. 'How come you worked it out when I didn't have a clue?'

'You never showed any interest in boys at all, ever. You never mentioned anyone at school, you didn't even have any posters on your wall. Daisy was boy mad, especially before the accident. Who was that young man you were so keen on, Daisy?'

'Stefan,' I reply. I haven't thought about him in years; he might be married with children now for all I know.

'I remember your mum fretting about it. You were only fourteen, but you were very precocious, and she was convinced you were having sex with him. She was worried that you'd get pregnant but didn't know what to say to you about it. You were pretty feisty even then, and she didn't want to say the wrong thing and risk a hissy fit.'

'I never actually had sex with him,' I tell her.

'Good, but that's not the point. The point is that you were very keen on boys from the moment you hit puberty. Even when you were at your most unhappy after the accident, you still managed to pick up a boyfriend. Katie, on the other hand, has never shown a flicker of interest, even though she certainly would have had plenty of boys interested in her. You could put part of that down to the fact that she's a very different character, but we did have our suspicions, especially after we watched this TV programme that said homosexuality was much more common in younger siblings. Anyway, I'm delighted for you both. Welcome to the family, Bronwyn dear.'

'Thank you.' Bronwyn smiles and blushes a little.

As the afternoon drags on, Nan and Grandad start to flag, so I offer to drive them home. Bronwyn and Katie disappear into the kitchen to clear up while I'm gone. As I'm driving back after dropping them off, I reflect on the conversation. I knew Nan and Grandad would be fine about Katie and Bronwyn, but I'm still bothered that I seem to have stopped noticing what's going on with my sister. I definitely need to do better.

32

'Daisy, can I borrow you?' Penny has stuck her head round the kitchen door. 'Ron and Agnes want a quick word.'

'Give me five minutes to get these omelettes out, and I'll be with you,' I tell her. I'm still worked off my feet, but Katie has decided to stay on with me until she goes back to school after Christmas, and she and Bronwyn are continuing to cook for me in the evenings and clear up, so I'm managing to get more sleep.

I finish off the omelettes, send them out, and check that there's nothing that can't be left for five minutes before I go out into the café. I'm extra vigilant, because I know I'm tired and more likely to make mistakes; the last thing I need right now is to burn the place to the ground because I forgot to turn something off. The leek and potato soup for today's lunchtime special is ready for me to reheat, but I've got another fifteen minutes before I need to light the burner under it, and I'm currently up to date with the breakfast orders. I wash my hands, carefully remove the hairnet, and head out to see what Ron and Agnes want.

'We're getting married,' Agnes tells me, waving her left hand at me to show off her engagement ring. It's small but tasteful, with what looks like a sapphire in the middle and small diamonds either side.

'Congratulations!' I tell her. 'That was fast work, Ron. It only seems like last week that you started going out together.'

'Well, we can't afford to hang around at our age, Daisy,' Ron explains. 'Who knows how much longer we'll be spared? The sun won't shine forever, so we need to get on and make some hay while we can.'

'Or, as my granddaughter puts it, if he wants it, he's got to put a ring on it. I believe the words come from a pop song,' Agnes adds. I'm starting to wonder if they're drunk, because they're making precious little sense. I think I've understood the gist of what they're saying, even if all the references to hay and pop songs are passing me by at the moment.

'I'm delighted for both of you. Are your families pleased?' I ask.

'It's been a bit difficult,' Agnes admits. 'We've both been surprised and a little disappointed by how greedy our children have been, haven't we, Ron?'

'Yes, all they seem interested in is protecting what they see as their inheritance. In the end, to keep the peace, we've agreed that Agnes won't sell her house when she moves in with me. We're going to let it out so that, if I die before her, she can move back into it and my children can get on and sell my house without having to worry about her. Similarly, if she dies first, her children can turf the tenants out and get their hands on her house.'

'Makes me want to leave the whole bloody lot to charity,' Agnes says glumly.

I'd love to sit and chat with them, but I'm conscious that I need to get back in the kitchen before a backlog starts to build up.

'I'm sorry about that, but I really am delighted for you both. I hope you'll be very happy for a long time. Thank you for telling me.' I stand up to head back into the kitchen, but Ron stops me.

'Hang on, Daisy. We haven't got to the important bit yet.'

'Sorry.' I sit back down.

'We wanted to ask you if we could have a little gathering in here, after the ceremony. We're not inviting lots of people, just close family. It doesn't have to be anything special, just cups of tea, sandwiches, and maybe some cake. We'll pay, obviously.'

'I'd love to do that for you!' I exclaim. 'When were you thinking?'

'We're getting married a week on Friday at two o'clock,' Ron continues. 'They had a cancellation at the registry office, so we grabbed it. I know you close at three, but would you consider opening a bit later for us?'

'Of course I will. Let me go and put it in the diary now. We'll firm everything up closer to the time, okay?'

'Perfect. Thank you, Daisy.'

'My pleasure.'

I make sure to write it in the diary as soon as I get back to the kitchen, otherwise I'm likely to forget, which would be a disaster. As I set about an order for two full English breakfasts, I try to work out how I'm going to manage a normal day at the café, plus make rounds of sandwiches and extra cakes for Ron and Agnes's reception in the afternoon. It seems an impossible task, but I'll just have to deal with it somehow. Katie and Bronwyn have shown themselves to be pretty capable cooks; perhaps I can get them through the food hygiene course and persuade them to help. I'm aware of my mobile phone ringing, but I can't deal with any more interruptions right now. Whoever it is will have to wait.

Penny and I are rushed off our feet for the rest of the day. Bronwyn's working at the art gallery, so Katie is promptly press-ganged into an apron when she appears at lunchtime. Normally, she's not a lot of help and seems to spend most of her time distracting Bronwyn, but Penny is a different prospect and Katie actually looks like she might be breaking a bit of a sweat. By the time three o'clock comes round, I'm starting to flag. Penny heads off, Katie retreats to the flat to wait for Bronwyn, and I start assembling the ingredients for Monday's lunchtime special.

A beep from my phone reminds me that I have a voicemail. I've been so busy that I'd completely forgotten about the call I missed earlier. I pick it up and see that the missed call is from Matt. He never rings me when the café is open, so it must have been some sort of emergency. Cursing myself for ignoring the call, I dial the voicemail number to retrieve the message. It's very short, but it's a big enough shock that my legs go weak and I have to sit down for a minute.

'Hi. It's me. I'm on my way down to you, hopefully arriving around four this afternoon.'

I check the time. Half past three. He'll be here in thirty minutes, assuming the traffic is okay. I'd call back to find out where he is, but he doesn't have any hands-free system in his van and he won't hear the phone over the engine anyway. Why is he coming back now, all of a sudden? He hasn't mentioned it before, I'm certain of that. My heart sinks as I realise he's probably only coming to collect his stuff. I don't know if I can face him. Maybe I should go out and pretend I never got the message. If I go into Sevenoaks now and stay there until the shops shut, he's bound to have packed up and gone by the time I get back. I'm suddenly desperate to be out of here. Monday will have to do without a lunchtime special, I decide as I start putting the ingredients back in the fridge.

I'm interrupted by the sound of a key in the lock of the back door. There's only one person besides me who has a key to that door. I'm rooted to the spot as Matt walks into the kitchen. He looks dreadful.

'Hi,' he says.

'Hello.'

'I knocked at the flat, but Katie told me you were still in here,' he continues.

'Yeah, I'm getting the lunchtime special ready for Monday.'

He looks confused. 'But it looked to me like you were putting stuff away when I walked in?'

I'm annoyed now. I didn't want to be here when he arrived, and now I feel like I've been caught red-handed trying to avoid him. I decide to brazen it out.

'Look, I was putting stuff away because I only just got your message, and I didn't want to be here when you arrived, okay?'

Now he looks hurt. Good.

'I don't understand. Why didn't you want to be here?'

'For fuck's sake, Matt!' I cry in exasperation. 'It's obvious that you've only come to collect your stuff, before you disappear back to Peterborough and your mum for good. Why would I want to be here to see that? I'm hurting enough, I don't need to be hurt any more, okay?'

'I'm not going back to Peterborough,' he says simply. 'In fact, I was hoping you might need a chef.'

There's a long pause while I digest what he's just said. I was so sure he was only collecting his stuff that I can't get my head around it.

'Are you saying you're back for good?'

'If there's a place for me.'

A bubble of joy forms in my stomach, but I can't give it free rein yet. If he's back then that's the best news ever, but a piece of the jigsaw is missing.

'What about your mother?' I ask.

'Fuck her.'

Okay, whatever I was expecting him to say, it certainly wasn't that.

'I think you need to tell me what's happened,' I say to him.

'I will, I promise. But there are other, more important things I need to tell you first.'

Uh-oh. I don't like the sound of this.

'Go on.' I might as well hear him out. If he's going to tell me that he wants to come back as a chef, but that the relationship between us is over, then I'm not sure what I'm going to do. On the one hand, I really need the help in the kitchen, but I don't know if I can work with him and not touch him. Even though things feel really weird with him standing there, shifting awkwardly from foot to foot, I still want to touch him.

He's obviously having difficulty forming the words he wants to say. He goes to speak several times, but nothing comes out. The silence just makes everything even more strained, and I can't bear it. Eventually, I decide to take the lead and lance the boil.

'Just spit it out!' I tell him. 'If you're trying to build yourself up to tell me that it's over between us, just do it, will you?'

'Is that what you want?' He looks horrified.

'I don't know,' I tell him. 'I missed you so badly when you first went, it was like a physical pain. But then, as time went on and the phone calls started to dry up, I figured you were losing interest in me, and that hurt in a whole new way. You've been gone for such a long time and I've been a mess, Matt. I've never felt as strongly about anyone as I do about you, but I don't know what you want any more, and I'm scared to find out, in case it's not me. So, if you've come to break up with me, do the decent thing and get it over with quickly.'

His eyes fill with tears. I've never seen him cry before, and it sets me off too, but he still doesn't speak. 'Just tell me why you're here, Matt, please,' I beg him.

He takes a deep breath, and finally some words come out. 'I'm here because I'm an idiot,' he begins. 'I'm here because I let myself be fooled by a woman who should have loved me, but didn't. I'm here because I bloody love you, Daisy Jones, and I'll do anything to earn your forgiveness. I'm here to do whatever it takes, for as long as you want me, because I never want to be apart from you again.'

I'm gobsmacked, but the bubble of joy is growing. There's still a niggle of doubt, though.

'I want to believe you,' I say. 'You have no idea how much I want to believe you. I want to come over there and wrap my arms around you and never let you go. But I can't go through something like this again, Matt. It's just been too painful. You and your mum have obviously had some sort of falling out, and I trust you to tell me about that in your own time. But what happens next time there's a crisis?'

'There won't be a next time.'

'You can't be sure of that. Whatever she's done, she's still your mum.'

'I can be sure of that, because she won't be able to get hold of me.' He takes the ancient Nokia out of his pocket and extracts the SIM card. 'Pass me the scissors behind you, would you?'

'Oh, Matt. Are you sure this is a good idea?' I say, handing them over.

'I should have done this years ago,' he growls, as he neatly cuts the SIM card in half and throws it in the bin. 'Can I have a hug now, please?'

There's no more doubt. The bubble explodes in my stomach, and I can't help grinning through my tears. I throw myself into his waiting arms, and we stand there, just holding each other and crying together, for what seems like an eternity.

'You have no idea how much I've missed you,' I murmur into his chest.

'Not as much as I missed you,' he replies. 'The calls didn't dry up because I was losing interest. I just couldn't bear hearing your voice and knowing that I couldn't see you. It was so painful, and every time I spoke to you, Mum would kick off about something. She was terrified of you, I can see that now, because she wanted me to herself. So I had to find times when I knew you wouldn't be working and she was out of earshot, and then I wanted to hear your voice so badly, but I knew it would hurt like hell afterwards. If it's any help, I've been a mess too.'

'Stop talking,' I whisper, 'and just hold me.'

33

'Tell me what happened.' We're still in the café, but we've moved out of the kitchen. I've made us both a cup of tea and we're sitting at Ron and Agnes's usual table. We've hugged, cried, and kissed. We've made all sorts of rash promises to each other that I have no idea whether we'll keep, but I can't fully accept that he's back for good until I know everything.

'So, you know I enrolled her on the intensive therapy course?'

'Yes.'

'It was really expensive, well over a thousand pounds, but the consultant at the hospital said it was her best chance of staying sober short of a rehab clinic. I can't remember the last time I saw Mum sober, and it was like she was a different person. She kept telling me how much she loved me, and how she was definitely going to kick it this time. I really wanted to believe her, so I happily paid the money.'

'Okay, I get that.'

'For the first few days after she was discharged from the hospital, I took her to the clinic and collected her at the end of the day.

At the end of the first week, she said she felt some of the others in the group were looking down on her because of my van, and suggested she could use taxis to get to the clinic and back. I was a bit taken aback, I must admit, but in the end, I gave in and agreed.'

'To be fair, your van is pretty tatty.'

'It is, but it's a bit much being looked down on by a load of addicts, don't you think? Anyway, we found a taxi company prepared to take her for a fixed fee of twenty-five quid a day, which I also paid. She was so happy and she seemed to be doing really well, so when she said she wanted to book another course, I didn't feel like I could refuse her, even though she'd already eaten through a hefty chunk of my savings. She was really enthusiastic, telling me how well she'd bonded with the others in the group, and that they were all staying on too. As long as I was there to keep an eye on her when she was at home, she reckoned she would continue to be fine. She was a bit erratic sometimes, but I figured that was all part of the adjustment to her new, sober life. Tell me something, do I have the word "mug" tattooed on my forehead?'

'Not that I can see.'

'I ought to. So, there I was, pouring cash into her rehabilitation and having a thoroughly miserable time in the process, and what was she doing?'

I'm pretty sure I know where this is going. 'How did you catch her?'

'I first got suspicious when we popped into the newsagent on the estate a couple of days ago. We were out for a walk together but I was peckish, so I decided to pop in to get some chocolate. She came in with me and, as soon as he saw her, the guy behind the counter started reaching for a bottle of vodka. I saw her make a slashing movement across her neck, you know, the type when you want to get someone to stop what they're doing without saying anything out loud. I didn't say anything to her at the time, but all the alarm bells were ringing. I made up my mind to follow her to her next appointment, to make sure she was really going where she said she was going. That was yesterday.'

'And where did she go?'

'If I wasn't so angry, it would be funny. She literally hopped in the taxi, got him to drop her round the corner, and went straight into the newsagent. She reappeared less than a minute later, clutching a litre bottle of vodka. She was being crafty, I'll give her that. Vodka doesn't leave a smell, so I wouldn't ever have known what she was doing if I hadn't followed her.'

'Oh, Matt. I'm so sorry.'

'Not half as sorry as I am.' He laughs bitterly. 'I carried on following her all the way to the park and watched her take the first swig. It was like being kicked in the balls. I went back to the house, packed up my stuff, and waited for her to get home. When she got in, I asked her about her day, and I let her spin me all her usual horseshit about the clinic before I confronted her with the truth.'

'What happened?'

'She went batshit, that's what happened. Have you seen *Gremlins*?'

'No.'

'Okay, well, basically it's about these cute furry animals that turn into ugly green monsters if you feed them after midnight. She was just like that. All the stuff she'd said about how much she loved me, how much she wanted to change, it was all a lie. She was screaming at me, telling me that I meant nothing to her, that she'd just used me for the money, and if I wasn't going to give her any more, I might as well fuck off, because she had no other use for me.'

'So all the money for the taxis, and the second stint at the clinic...'

'Yup, she drank it. Well, not all of it. While she was ranting at me, she let on that she'd gambled quite a lot of the money I'd given her for the clinic. She had this mad plan that she'd have a big win, which would keep her going once she'd milked me dry and thrown me out. Of course, she just ended up chasing her losses, stupid cow.'

'I'm so sorry,' I tell him. 'If I had even the slightest inkling that it would turn out like this, I would never have encouraged you to go and look for her.'

'Don't be. In a funny way, it's been good for me.'

'How?'

'I guess I always secretly hoped that she'd change, that she'd see what a mess she'd made of bringing us up and want to make amends. I hoped she'd be proud of me one day. But now I know that's never going to happen. She's only interested in herself. I was just someone stupid enough to let her con me out of a large chunk of my savings to fund her habit. She's not my mother. I have no idea who she is, and I never want to see her again. That chapter of my life is firmly closed.'

I pick up the empty mugs and take them out to the kitchen. Everything's switched off now, so I wash them up in the sink and put them on the side. Matt is still sitting there when I walk back into the café, so I reach out and take him by the hand.

'Come on,' I tell him. 'You look dead on your feet, and I'm knackered too. Let's get some rest. Where did you sleep last night?'

'I booked myself into a Premier Inn. I did think about sleeping in the van, but it was bloody cold and I think I'm too used to my creature comforts now.'

'Why didn't you drive down? It's only a couple of hours.'

'I know, but I was so angry and ashamed. I needed time to think and calm down. Also, there were some things I needed to do before I left.'

'Like what?'

'I went to find Liam, the guy who gave me the scar. I turned up at his church first thing this morning and he happened to be there. We ended up having a long chat. He hadn't had anything to do with what happened to Laura; he was still on the fringes of the gang then, but he told me her story wasn't unusual. Young women get lured into prostitution by the promise of riches, but they're unprepared for the reality of sex work. So, they start taking something every so often to numb the pain, and then they're taking more, and then they're doing more sex work to fund the drugs, and it all turns into a horrific, vicious circle. He helped me see that none of it was my fault, that there was nothing I could have done to save her. We put a lot of stuff to rest, actually. I apologised for attacking him and he apologised for cutting me. He even offered to pray with me, how bizarre is that?'

'What did you do?'

'I let him. It helped, in a funny way.'

'Are you going to keep in touch?'

'No. He suggested it, but I explained that I needed to close the door completely on that part of my life. I think he was a bit disappointed, actually, but he said he understood. Anyway, after that I went and bought some flowers to put on Laura's grave. I sat there for a long time, just chatting to her. I told her about the café, and you, and Mum. She didn't answer, obviously, but it was peaceful. And then I've spent most of the journey home rehearsing what I was going to say to you when I got here.'

'You could have fooled me!' I laugh.

'Yeah, well. None of the scenarios in my head prepared me for how hurt and angry you looked when I walked into that kitchen.'

* * *

The flat is empty when we get up there. Katie and Bronwyn have obviously decided to make themselves scarce for the evening. I kick off my shoes and lie down on the bed, fully clothed. I have no idea what Matt does, because I'm fast asleep the moment my head hits the pillow.

When I wake up, I'm alone in my room, and I wonder whether the events of this afternoon have all been an illusion. The dent on the other side of the bed indicates otherwise, but Matt is nowhere to be seen. I can't help being reminded of the last time this happened, and I feel a sense of dread as I open the bedroom door and poke my head out.

Matt isn't in the living room either, but I can hear movement in the kitchen, and something smells delicious. Katie and Bronwyn must be back so maybe he's talking to them. I wander towards the kitchen but stop in the doorway. Matt is concentrating on what he's doing, so hasn't noticed me. He's obviously had a shower and changed, because he looks much better than he did when he arrived. I stand and watch for a while, enjoying the sight of his torso moving under the tight T-shirt he's wearing now. When we were sitting in the café earlier, I'd made myself promise not to jump straight back into bed with him, but my resolve is weakening fast as I watch him at work. I clear my throat and he looks up. He may have a broken nose and a scar across his cheek, but he's the most beautiful man I've ever seen.

'What are you cooking?' I ask.

'I hope you don't mind, I found some chicken breasts in the fridge, so I thought I'd stuff them and cook them in the oven. They should be ready in twenty minutes or so, and I'm just knocking up a salad to go with them.'

'Twenty minutes?'

'Yes, why?'

I move across to where he's standing, lift up his T-shirt and start kissing his chest. 'I can think of a much better way to spend twenty minutes than making salad,' I murmur.

'Hang on, let me turn the oven down. Twenty minutes isn't nearly enough time for what I have in mind,' he replies.

34

Matt's been back for two weeks, and something is definitely up with him.

To begin with, I was just so glad to have him back that I didn't notice anything. To be fair, I was also busy working out what to do for Ron and Agnes's wedding reception. The reception itself went well, and they both looked really happy. In the end, we made a selection of sandwiches and cakes, which were well received if the empty trays were anything to go by. Ron's son dropped off a case of Prosecco and some glasses the day before, so Katie and Bronwyn dressed up and passed those round for the speeches. Ron looked very smart in his dark-blue suit, and Agnes looked lovely in a simple, cream dress. Their honeymoon was fairly short, just a few nights away at a hotel near Margate, but they obviously had a nice time because Agnes told Penny afterwards that she'd been surprised and delighted by Ron's 'stamina'. Probably the less said about that, the better.

It was a few days after the reception when I first started to feel that I was being excluded from something. Everything seemed fine on the surface; Katie, Bronwyn, Matt and I have all been staying at the flat and getting on very well with each other. Matt has been a bit distracted, though, and he's been spending a lot of time in the evenings chatting with Katie and Bronwyn and looking at things on Katie's laptop. I asked if anything was wrong, but he just told me that everything was fine and changed the subject.

There's definitely something going on, though, I'm sure of it. I've walked out into the café a few times lately to find boxes stacked behind the counter. When I asked about them, Penny apologised profusely and said that they were hers. I was therefore surprised when I saw Matt carrying some of them up to his flat the other day. Again, I asked about it, and he said he was just storing them for Penny for a few days. I don't think he's up to anything bad, but there are secrets and I'm not good with secrets. I've tried cornering Katie, but she just said that I'm imagining things and that I should trust him.

I'm still suspicious, but I don't want to push too hard in case I jinx things. It's lovely to have Matt in the kitchen with me again. Not only because it's reduced my workload to a manageable level once more, but also because the kitchen is back to being a happy place. In some ways, it's as if he's never been away. We work around each other, our dance as perfectly choreographed as ever.

'Have you given any more thought to what you want to do about your flat?' I ask him.

Apart from storing Penny's boxes, Matt hasn't spent any time in his flat since he got back. We seem to have fallen back into the same routine that we had when he was staying with me before, except it feels more permanent this time. I talked to Katie about it, to make sure she wasn't uncomfortable, but she just said we should stop faffing about and admit that we'd moved in together. She did suggest that we ought to do something about getting a lock on the bathroom door, because four of us sharing a bathroom was bound to lead to an incident sooner or later, and Matt has agreed to go to Homebase on Sunday and sort something out.

'I have,' he says. 'Are you sure this is what you want, though?'

'Matt, I don't mean to be funny, but what on earth are you going to use it for? You've barely spent five minutes in it since you got back. It's just an expensive storage unit for Penny's stuff at the moment. If we're going to live together then I'd like to let it out. It's a waste having it sitting empty.'

'I had a thought about that,' says Katie, who's just wandered into the kitchen with some dirty plates.

'Oh, yes? Go on.'

'Well, there are two flats, aren't there? One for you, which is the one you're living in, and one for me, which would be Matt's flat. So, if we're letting Matt's flat out, shouldn't the rent come to me? It would certainly help with the uni bills when I go.'

'You're a piece of work, you know that?' I laugh. 'Fine. If we let Matt's flat out, the income can come to you. But you have to repay the money I spent doing it up.'

She considers for a moment. 'I tell you what,' she says. 'I spend quite a lot of time in your flat, don't I?'

'You do. Nan and Grandad have started muttering about letting out your room at home, because you're there so infrequently.'

'Very funny. I'll be back there when term starts again. My point is, why don't we split the rent on Matt's flat? You can consider your half of the money from it as rent and a contribution towards the renovations, and I'll put mine towards uni.'

I consider this for a moment. 'Okay, deal.'

My suspicions rise again when I'm unceremoniously ejected from my own café at lunchtime on Friday, ostensibly because Katie has decided we need a girly shopping trip to Bluewater. I'm certain that there's a hidden agenda, though. I've caught Matt, Katie, and Bronwyn poring over a piece of paper that appears to have a list on it a couple of times this week but, when I asked, they said it was nothing, just something they were working on for Penny. I'm a bit on edge as I ease the van onto the main road, but Katie is full of bubbles and we end up having a lot of fun. It's well after dark when we get back, and we open the door to the flat to find Matt and Bronwyn in the middle of preparing dinner. It's a typically convivial evening and, even though it's Saturday tomorrow and we have to be up, Matt opens a bottle of wine and we all have a glass. Whatever has been bothering him seems to be resolved, as he's completely back to his usual self, and I can't help feeling relieved.

* * *

In the morning, Matt and I traipse down and let ourselves in through the back door as normal. Bronwyn skips in just before half past seven as usual, but this time she has Katie in tow.

'What's up? Couldn't you sleep?' I ask her.

'Ha ha. Bronwyn's just asked for my help with something,' she tells me.

If I was surprised to see Katie, I'm completely baffled when Penny turns up. 'You're not supposed to be working today!' I tell her. 'I've already got Katie and Bronwyn out there.'

'Don't worry. I'm not expecting you to pay me. I just wanted to catch up on something.' She disappears out into the café, and I start to follow her.

'Don't,' Matt says, surprisingly firmly.

'What's going on?' I ask him.

'Just give it a bit longer, okay? Do you trust me?'

'More than I ought to, I think.'

'Trust me now. Let them do what they have to do.'

I growl with frustration, but return to my cakes. The café is obviously busy this morning, as I can hear the buzz of conversation and the orders are coming in thick and fast. Matt's quickly overwhelmed, so I abandon my cakes to help him get the breakfasts out. I've never known a surge like this. We're always busy on a Saturday, but the orders usually arrive in a steady stream. This feels like a coachload of people has arrived all at once.

We work flat out and eventually send out the final order: a cheese and ham omelette.

'Bloody hell, that was mental!' I observe.

Penny sticks her head around the kitchen door. 'Daisy, can I borrow you for a minute? There are a couple of people who want to speak to you.'

'Okay, give me a second.' I wash my hands and carefully remove the hairnet. I've been working so hard that I'm a bit sweaty underneath it, and my hair is sticking to my head a bit. Ah, well, I didn't come into this job for the glamour, I think. I step out of the kitchen and gasp.

The first thing I notice are the walls, which are now adorned with a selection of Bronwyn's paintings. I have to confess I'd completely forgotten that she was doing them. I don't get time to take them in, though, as I also realise that every seat in the café is occupied. As well as the regulars, including Ron and Agnes, I spot Mr Holdsworth with a woman whom I assume is his wife. Jonathan Moorhouse is also there, along with Nan and Grandad and a whole load of people I've never seen before. Katie, Bronwyn, and Penny are standing by the counter, grinning like Cheshire cats. I notice that Matt has followed me out of the kitchen and is also grinning like a lunatic.

'What have you done?' I say to Katie.

'It was Matt's idea,' she replies. 'We were chatting one evening, not long after he came back, and we were talking about what a fantastic job you've done with the café. We also agreed that you were never going to sell it now, because you've fallen in love with it, haven't you?'

I blush slightly. 'That might be true.'

'So, we decided that it needed a formal relaunch. We invited everyone we could think of and distributed leaflets around the town. We even invited the local paper.' She indicates a couple of guys sitting at a table by the door.

'I hope you won't mind, but we've also taken the liberty of a slight re-brand,' Matt continues. 'I need to take you outside. Close your eyes.'

He takes my hand and leads me through the front door. I'm aware of Katie, Bronwyn, and Penny following behind.

'Turn around, but keep them closed.' Matt's voice instructs, and I do as I'm told.

'Okay, open them.' At first glance, I don't notice any difference, but then I look up and see it. A bright, modern sign above the café with the words 'Daisy's Diner' on it, and a logo made up of two interlocking letter Ds. It's beautiful.

'So this is what you've been up to all this time?' I ask. 'I was beginning to think I was going mad!' They do at least have the grace to look a little sheepish.

'There's more,' Katie says. 'Look at our aprons.' Sure enough, they all feature the name of the café and the logo as well.

'We've done everything. The menus, the lot. Do you like it?'

'I love it!' I tell them. 'Thank you so much!'

'It's the least you deserve,' Matt tells me. 'You've saved this café, Daisy. Nora would want you to have your name over the door.'

Tears of joy are pouring down my face as I hug them all tightly. Once I've calmed down, the guys from the paper ask me some questions and take my photo with the new sign behind me, before heading off to their next engagement.

When I go back inside, Matt and the others get back to work while I'm inundated with compliments. Nan and Grandad both hug me tightly, Mr Holdsworth tells me how proud he is of what I've achieved, and Jonathan Moorhouse booms about how he can't believe it's the same place. Bronwyn introduces me to Toby Roberts, who owns the studio next door, and his hugely pregnant wife, Madison. She's very nice and promises to be a regular once she's had the baby and can move about a little more easily. In the end, I probably spend nearly an hour talking to everyone and admiring Bronwyn's paintings. I can't help noticing that some of them have red stickers on them already, indicating that they're sold.

Eventually, things quieten down to normal café levels for a Saturday. The invited guests have had their fill and headed back to their weekends, and I take up my usual spot with Matt in the kitchen. During a brief lull in the afternoon, I stick my head out into the café. Katie and Bronwyn are behind the counter, with their hands entwined out of view of the customers, and there's a happy buzz of conversation in the room.

As I stand there, I become aware of an unfamiliar feeling coursing through me. It's so long since I've felt it, I'd almost forgotten it existed. Obviously, it's always been there, though, lying dormant and waiting for the right moment to show itself again.

It's hope.

ACKNOWLEDGMENTS

First of all, I need to thank my editor, Tara, and all the Boldwood team. Your support and encouragement is really appreciated, and I'm proud to be part of the Boldwood family. A lot of other people have also helped with this book, either by answering questions on WhatsApp and Facebook Messenger, or because I've cornered them on a dog walk and asked them questions. I want to say a huge thank you to all of you too.

Becka, thank you for all the information on accountancy. Stephen, Rachel, and Neil were a mine of information on the vagaries of commercial property valuation. I also need to say thank you to the team at the Rendezvous café in Margate, and Julia and the Malabar crew for your input on the café side.

As always, I have to thank my advance readers, Frances and Mandy, as well as Bertie, whose walks have been interrupted by sudden exclamations of 'I know! What I'll do is this...'

MORE FROM PHOEBE MACLEOD

We hope you enjoyed reading *Fred and Breakfast*. If you did, please leave a review.

If you'd like to gift a copy, this book is also available as an ebook, digital audio download and audiobook CD.

Sign up to Phoebe MacLeod's mailing list for news, competitions and updates on future books.

https://bit.ly/PhoebeMacLeodNews

Someone Else's Honeymoon, another brilliant read from Phoebe MacLeod, is available now.

ABOUT THE AUTHOR

Phoebe MacLeod is the author of several popular romantic comedies. She lives in Kent with her partner, grown up children and disobedient dog. Her love for her home county is apparent in her books, which have either been set in Kent or have a Kentish connection. She currently works as an IT consultant and writes in her spare time. She has always had a passion for learning new skills, including cookery courses, learning to drive an HGV and, most recently, qualifying to instruct on a Boeing 737 flight simulator.

Follow Phoebe on social media:

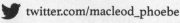 twitter.com/macleod_phoebe
facebook.com/PhoebeMacleodAuthor
 instagram.com/phoebemacleod21

Boldw∞d

Boldwood Books is an award-winning fiction publishing company seeking out the best stories from around the world.

Find out more at www.boldwoodbooks.com

Join our reader community for brilliant books, competitions and offers!

Follow us
@BoldwoodBooks
@BookandTonic

Sign up to our weekly
deals newsletter

https://bit.ly/BoldwoodBNewsletter

Lightning Source UK Ltd.
Milton Keynes UK
UKHW041834181022
410641UK00010B/29